Reputat

An Alan McGill mystery

by

Douglas Mitchell

Copyright © 2015 Douglas Mitchell

All rights reserved, including the right to reproduce this book, or portions thereof in any form. No part of this text may be reproduced, transmitted, downloaded, decompiled, reverse engineered, or stored, in any form or introduced into any information storage and retrieval system, in any form or by any means, whether electronic or mechanical without the express written permission of the author.

ISBN: 978-1-326-19544-1

For Jane

Chapter 1

McGill was feeling the worse for wear. He'd had too many beers last night as he sought to break the cycle of his insomnia. But it had only ended with him getting up several times in the night, and feeling even more depressed.

McGill hated his job. He was a detective at Scotland Yard having been a beat constable, none of whom were ever promoted. He was largely treated like a servant. Of course, strictly speaking, Scotland Yard was just one entrance to the building that housed the detectives in London, but the name had become synonymous with the detection of crime.McGill's simple ways and craggy good looks sat ill with his suave and urbane superiors. He had a good nose for detection, though, and apart from his superior taking the credit, he did derive some satisfaction from breaking a case.

He shaved with a shaky hand and dabbed the nicks between the tufts of hair he hadn't managed to pare. Looking at himself in the mirror, he shook his head. That made him wince, briefly shutting his bloodshot eyes to try to dull the pain. He groaned. The face that looked back at him was handsome in a gentle, manly sort of way, and the usually piercing Celtic blue eyes looked dull and lifeless. The eyes contrasted sharply with his dark hair, supposedly a legacy of the sailors washed ashore in Scotland from the Spanish Armada.

In the third year of the war, London was even more grey and depressing than usual. McGill had been transferred from his East End beat to Scotland Yard in early 1915, as the upper classes and university undergraduates got mown down in France. He had liked the East End. He'd lived there most of his life – still did in fact – and he had friends there amongst the thieves, pimps and whores who he saw as real people in need of help, unlike his masters who saw then as scum to be locked away and brutalised.

McGill's parents had come down from Scotland some years before the turn of the century, in Victoria's reign. There was a distant cousin who had promised his father a job looking after horses, but, as the horse gave way to the motor car over the years, the business had suffered. Finally, the two cousins acknowledged that the way forward was smelly and dirty but offered better pay, and they had turned the old stables into a proper garage, looking after the increasingly numerous cars that were more and more replacing horses. McGill had hated the deference his father gave to the arrogant and haughty. It had paid off over time, though, as the business prospered and McGill's father had bought the little terraced house where he now lived. His mother had been overjoyed and as house proud as any Duchess. Sadly she was only there a short time, dying in the cholera outbreak of 1910. There had been very few deaths in London from cholera that year, but McGill's mother was one. His father never recovered properly and died within the year.

By that time McGill had been in the police for nearly eleven years, patrolling the beat in the East End with his soft accent and gentle eyes, keeping law and order. The cousin had bought out the business from his father's estate (probably to McGill's detriment) but he wanted nothing to do with it. He had the house and a nice little nest egg.

Now, with the war, there almost seemed to be a truce in crime as everyone did their best to help with the war effort. Of course, houses in the West End still got broken in to, and the pimps and prostitutes were doing a roaring trade with the soldiers back on leave. They were largely being left alone by tacit agreement.

McGill really disliked the fact that, because he was 38, everywhere he went he was looked at as if he were a lesser mortal. All because the powers that be wouldn't let him join up. Sometimes he thought he would just run away to the Front, but he knew he would simply be sent back. He'd never even get to France. The controls on the Channel crossings were fierce – in both directions. At least no one had sent him any white feathers yet.

He dressed quickly, pocketing a clean white handkerchief. He shrugged himself into his heavy overcoat and donned his battered brown bowler. It was only November, but there was a distinct wintry feel to the air as he walked to catch the omnibus west.

When he got into his cubbyhole of an office there was yet another pile of folders dumped on his desk. He tried to close the door quietly so that the inspector in the next room wouldn't know he was in. As he stepped around the desk, the floor creaked.

"MCGILL – IN HERE!"

Sighing, McGill stepped back and opened the connecting door.

Inspector Brown looked at him balefully.

"What have you got on?"

" Er well there's a whole lot of paperwork just been put on my desk and…"

"Forget that. Ever been abroad?"

" No Sir"

" Well you're going now." For a moment McGill's heart leapt. Maybe they had decided to let him join up. His face must have betrayed him, for Brown immediately grunted.

" You're going to the front right enough, but not to fight. There's been a murder, and we've been asked to help the Military. Bunch of amateurs."

McGill didn't know what to think. Normally he trailed along after Brown taking notes and running errands. It would just be the same in France.

" Yes, sir."

" So cut off home and pack a bag – we leave from Victoria at 3."

McGill turned to go.

" Oh, and McGill…"

" Yes sir?"

" You've been made up to Sergeant. Now hurry along."

" Thank you sir"

" And don't go thinking it means anything. It just means we've no spare sergeants to send to France."

As he shut the door, McGill grunted to himself. It was only because so many had died that he was even in the detective branch. Neither Brown nor the Superintendent thought he was worth a Sergeant's stripes.

By 2:30 McGill was standing under the clock at Victoria Station, waiting for Brown. He had a battered holdall he had borrowed from a neighbour at his feet. There were hordes of soldiers moving to and fro, as well as smart and not so smart ladies. Quite a few glanced at McGill as he stood waiting, taking stock of his bulk and quiet confidence. A few minutes later, Brown appeared with a porter in tow carrying two large brown leather suitcases. He eyed McGill and his holdall.

" That all you've got? Hmm well I don't suppose they'd let you in to a mess dinner anyway…" So saying he pointed out the relevant platform to the porter, and followed him. McGill picked up his bag, seething inside. What made Brown so special? He was only another policeman like himself, and not that good at his job either. In the nine months McGill had been with him, it was all McGill's work that had led to any arrests. Not that Brown saw it that way of course.

" Don't suppose you've ever been in First Class have you McGill? Just remember to keep your feet off the seats."

" Yes Sir, I'll try," Brown looked at him sideways, but McGill's face was immobile.

"Hmmf"

They settled into their seats, and shortly before the train was due to leave for Folkestone, four young officers got in beside them. One was a Captain, slightly older, and the others, all lieutenants, deferred to him. One of the Lieutenants had a livid scar on his cheek. McGill envied them their uniforms. But when he looked at their faces he saw the fear in their eyes, even as they joked and made light of where they were going.

" I don't suppose you have any details of the crime, sir?" asked McGill.

" Not here," said Brown, glancing sideways at the braying young men. " On the boat"

By the time they got to Folkestone it was already dark, and as they made their way through the huge sheds crammed with soldiers towards the quay, McGill wondered at the numbers. He'd lived in London all his life, but he'd never seen as many people crammed into one place. Military Police were shoving slow movers around and officers were bawling instructions. If this is what it's like with no Hun shells landing, thought McGill, what's it like at the front? He shuddered. Perhaps being a policeman wasn't so bad.

Brown had various passes and letters of introduction, and soon enough they were aboard what seemed to McGill to be an enormous ship. They made their way to an area where they could sit, which was reserved for officers. The troops sat on the floor, or stood about, and a haze of cigarette smoke hung lazily in the air. Brown took a cigarette out of his cigarette case and tapped the unfiltered end on it. He looked speculatively at McGill. He lit the cigarette and blew the first cloud of smoke upwards.

" Did you never smoke, McGill?"

" No sir – never started. My father smoked a pipe but I never had the urge."

" More fool you. Where we're going a bit of comfort won't go amiss." He dragged greedily on the cigarette, making it glow bright red. A bit of ash fell off as he took it out of his mouth.

" No sir, I suppose not." Brown reached down into his attaché case and produced a sheaf of papers. He flung them at McGill, so that some fell to the floor.

" There you are – have a look at that lot."

Patiently McGill picked up the fallen pages. As the ship shuddered to the thrum of its accelerating engines and hooting sirens, McGill put the papers in order again and began to read.

It appeared that a young man had been found dead in a house in Amiens. He had been naked and he had been strangled. The house was occupied by a group of young officers who all claimed they were on duty or on leave and had no idea who the young man was, or where he had appeared from. It was one of their number, Captain Percy Miller, who had found the body when he got back from five days leave on the night of Thursday 25th. October. He'd only noticed it because the body was in his bed and covered up, and when he had gone to wake the usurper, he'd found him dead. He'd sent for the Military Police, who took their time arriving, and in fact didn't appear until the next morning. Miller was mightily annoyed (and probably a little drunk), so had turfed the body onto the floor to get into his bed.

There were no clothes or uniform left anywhere, so there was no clue as to the young man's identity. No one had seen him come into the house. No one had seen anyone leave. There was no sign of a struggle or a break in.

There was more on the other people living in the house, but in essence that was it. McGill looked across at Brown.

" Pretty pickle eh McGill? The military only asked for our help to cover their own backsides, and when we don't get anywhere they will be in the clear. I for one don't intend to take this too seriously. I've already arranged to see some old friends but of course you won't be coming along." He stubbed out his cigarette. "A few days are all we need. You can go round and re-interview all the people mentioned, and once you've got statements from them we can say there are no leads and trot back to the Yard." He yawned." So I'm going to treat this as a paid holiday whilst you carry on with the job. And make sure you do it properly."

"Yes sir, of course sir. Only… "

"Yes?"

" Don't you think we should at least try to find out who the victim was? At worst we could tell his family."

"For God's sake McGill you must have seen the casualty lists? There are thousands dying and being wounded every day. What difference does it make? Anyway, the military haven't been able to find out so what makes you think we can?" McGill looked down at the papers again.

" If I was his family, I'd want to know," he said quietly.

Brown sighed, and waved his hand. " Oh, just do whatever you like. But make sure you don't get us or the military into any bother – and make sure the statements tally with what is already there. Neither we nor the military want any loose ends."

McGill nodded. " I'll do my best sir"

" You'll do better than that – you'll do it!"
■■

Chapter 2

When they arrived in Boulogne it was as it had been in Folkestone – thousands of troops being herded hither and thither, with shouting Sergeants and Military Police shoving and kicking any that were too slow.

The troops were all being driven like cattle towards the rail head, and Brown sought out a small group of more senior officers who were standing aloof from the chaos. McGill trailed after him carrying Brown's suitcases and his own holdall.

" I'm looking for Major Heart of the Provost Marshal's office, " announced Brown. One of the officers looked at him.

"You'll be the detective from Scotland Yard" he said, contempt in his voice.

" I am. And this is my sergeant, Detective McGill." The officer glanced at McGill, dismissing him instantly.

" SERGEANT!" A ram rod straight giant of a man materialised behind Brown.

" Sah!"

" Take these detectives to the Provost Marshall's office." McGill thought he made "detectives" sound like something horrible at the bottom of a cesspit.

The giant saluted, then whirled round and marched off at an angle. Brown and McGill followed as he carved a way through the milling crowds, and out into the cold night.

Outside he turned sharp right and headed for a building which looked like a small railway station. There were red-capped guards on the door, and the sergeant stamped to a halt in front of them.

" Two detectives for Major Heart!" So saying he swung round again with a clatter and scrape of hobnail boots and marched back the way he had come.

One of the redcaps was already holding his hand out for Brown's papers.

"You're the ones from the Yard then?" he said.

Brown nodded.

"I'll tell Major 'eart you're 'ere." He turned towards the door. The other man never moved, though McGill could see his eyes were looking them up and down. The door opened again and an immaculately turned out Major, complete with waxed moustache and swagger stick, stood on the threshold. He proffered his hand.

"I'm Heart, and you'll be Brown. And this is..?"

Brown took the hand and shook it. "This is my sergeant, McGill"

" You better come in. Have you eaten?"

" Not since lunchtime."

"Very good. SERGEANT!"

"Yessir"

" Cut along to the canteen and get a couple of sandwiches, then brew us up one when you get back"

"Yessir"

" And don't dawdle"

" Yessir"

Heart ushered them through an outer office where two extremely large redcaps where sitting either side of a wretch who looked half dead and half drowned as well. McGill looked at him. Heart saw the glance, and smiled crookedly.

" I wouldn't worry about him, sergeant. He tried to desert and my lads had to restrain him." McGill thought a mouse could have done it, but clearly the redcaps had had other ideas.

" What'll happen to him?" asked Brown. Heart smiled again. " Sadly flogging isn't allowed anymore and we can't charge him with cowardice in the face of the enemy as it happened here in Boulogne. He'll get 90 days number one field punishment. And I daresay he'll either attempt to escape again or attack one of my men, so he'll get another beating – or two" McGill grimaced.

" Wellington had it right – they are the scum of the earth, " said Heart as he sat down behind his desk. " Shut the door sergeant." McGill obeyed and sat on the chair farthest from the desk.

" Well now, you've read our reports?"

"We have," said Brown. "Looks as if you've done a very thorough job." Heart smiled again "so I'll just have my sergeant speak to the people mentioned in the report, and that should wrap it up". Heart's smile broadened.

He reached for some headed paper and began to write.

"This is for my opposite number in Etaples, Major Wylie. You have to go through there to be cleared for the front. Strictly speaking Amiens is about 25 miles from where the real fighting is but it's still in the reserve area. Once you've seen Wylie he'll organise the transport to Amiens and hand you over to Colonel Berry and his aide, Major Watkins in Amiens. Anything else you need, they can arrange. I understand the General OC in the sector wants to see you. Wylie will tell you when you are wanted."

" Thank you," said Brown. "I'll be going to Amiens, but I've arranged to see some friends round about. But McGill, here, will be doing whatever is needed."

Heart looked at McGill and raised his eyebrows. Brown caught the glance.

" He's perfectly sound, and he has my instructions. As I said, we shan't be taking too long, we'll just confirm what is already known." Heart seemed mollified, and addressed McGill.

" You know there are no leads of any description? God knows why HQ are going on about this – it's perfectly clear no one is ever going to be caught. We don't even know who he was or what he was doing there. One body more or less isn't going to make a blind bit of difference."

McGill nodded. With that attitude, there was little to say.

There was a knock on the door, and a soldier appeared with a tray of doorstep sandwiches and three steaming mugs of tea.

Heart passed them round, and helped himself to one of the sandwiches.

" In case you're worried, this tea is perfectly ordinary. It doesn't have any of the bromide in it we give to the troops." McGill had no idea what Heart was talking about, but Brown just nodded, and grunted as he bit into the corned beef.

Heart looked at his watch. " You've about 20 minutes until the next train. It shouldn't take more than an hour or so to get to Etaples. But it'll depend on the movements at that end how much longer it'll take to get into the unloading area. Wylie has a couple of billets for you and he'll pass you on as soon as there's space. Here are your movement passes." Brown reached across and took them.

" And don't forget the number one rule of being out here. Keep your head down and sleep whenever you can – you never know when the next chance will be." So saying he stood up and reached his hand across to Brown again.." SERGEANT!"

" Sir!"

" Take these two to the next train and see they are settled, then report back here."

"Yessir"

Brown shook Heart's hand and turned to follow the sergeant. McGill picked up the bags and followed. He noticed Heart never even looked at him. It's as well seeing there are sergeants, thought McGill. Nothing would ever get done otherwise.

By the time the sergeant had pushed and shoved the two detectives onto a train, McGill's senses were swamped with noise and the smell of rank bodies. He felt lots of eyes on them in their civvy clothes as everyone else was in uniform. The train ground slowly along the rails with dozens of trains going in the opposite direction, and at a bend, McGill looked out of the window to see trains following and in front of them. They stopped a couple of times for no apparent reason, then juddered into motion again.

Nearly two hours later they were passing the sea on their right, and a wan ray of moonlight pierced the gloom. McGill was suddenly aware of a murmuring and rumbling about him, which grew louder. With a final, exhausted whistle the train pulled into a siding, and the shouting started. Carriage doors were flung open and obscenities shouted into compartments. Grumbling slack-eyed men gathered up their kit and part fell, part stumbled out into the chill, dank night.

McGill and Brown had been in an officer's carriage, and the door was opened by a redcap Major, who climbed into the compartment.

" Inspector Brown?" Brown nodded.

"I'm Brown"

" Major Wylie. Welcome to Etaples!" Brown and Wylie shook hands.

" Where's your luggage?"

Brown pointed to it on the string luggage racks.

" Corporal Aitket! Take charge of those suitcases!"

A smartly dressed corporal climbed into the compartment. None of the other officers who had shared the journey had moved a muscle. McGill darted glances at them. They were all afraid, not just of the redcaps but of the war. They sat where they were hoping a few extra minutes of safety might be had.

Wylie and Brown dropped out of the carriage, followed by the corporal and McGill.

Wylie turned to him. " And who are you?" Bloody hell thought McGill, those bastards in Boulogne never even mentioned me. And Brown didn't bother to either.

" I'm…"

" He's my sergeant," Brown cut in.

Wylie eyed him. " Ah. I see" He turned on his heels and marched off, swagger stick perfectly positioned under his oxter. The others followed.

As in Folkestone and Boulogne, the noise was overpowering with shouts, the noise of trains and their whistles, and the noise of marching men. McGill, who had been stunned by the seething mass of men before, was even more overwhelmed. The brutality and endless swearing made him ask the corporal as they walked along –" Is it always like this?"

" Twenty four hours a day mate. We takes the new boys in and trains them up. Then we sends them to the front, where they get shot. If they're the lucky ones, they come back 'ere to get patched up"

McGill heard the bitterness in Aitket's voice.

" It can't be as bad as that, is it?" Aitket stopped abruptly and looked McGill full in the face.

" You don't know the 'alf of it. We've only just finished sortin' a bloody mutiny 'ere. 'Ad to shoot some poor sod just a couple of weeks ago. And there's those as prefer going back to the front before they're properly fit, rather than stay 'ere." So saying he marched on, leaving McGill to catch up.

They walked for about ten minutes, gradually leaving most of the noise behind, and finally came to barbed wire and sentries. Wylie simply touched his swagger stick to his cap when challenged and the sentries snapped to attention. Once inside the compound, McGill could make out a guardroom, and leading away behind it a series of what looked like beach huts. More sentries saluted as Wylie walked up the steps. Inside some redcaps were having cups of tea, but leapt to attention as the small group entered.

" Stand easy", said Wylie as he crossed to a shut door, knocked, then entered without waiting for an answer.

Inside, a tall, thin man was sitting with his feet on a desk, a curl of smoke drifting lazily up from the cigarette he held in his right hand. He was staring at the ceiling.

" These are the Scotland Yard detectives, sir" said Wylie, as he threw a dilatory salute. Makes us sound like pig shit thought McGill.

The man behind the desk never moved, and the party stood awkwardly.

Slowly the man's right arm bent, and the cigarette came to his lips. He languidly sucked for a moment then moved his arm slowly back down again. He never took his eyes from the ceiling.

" You deal with it Wylie"

" Yes sir, of course sir." So saying Wylie indicated the others should retreat out into the main area. He shut the door, pointed towards another, and led the way into the room behind. He took off his cap and sat behind the desk.

" Corporal, have you organised sleeping quarters for our guests?"
"Yessir."

" Good. Show them where and what the drill is. We'll meet in the morning say oh-nine-hundred - nine o'clock?" This last was addressed to Brown, who nodded.

Aitket ushered Brown and McGill out of the guard room again and towards the chalets. He stopped at the first one, opened the door, and put the cases inside.

" An orderly will bring you some 'ot water at oh-six-thirty hours, breakfast is in the mess the other side of the guard room, and the latrines is out the back door." So saying he saluted and backed out, indicating Brown should enter. With an inclination of his head, he made McGill follow him further down the line of huts. He repeated the process, and made to leave. McGill put a hand on his arm.

" Stay a minute, chum. Who was the bloke in that room?" Aitket glanced at McGill.

" That's our CO, Colonel Shimpling. Got 'iself bombed behind the lines at the Somme – never been the same since. 'E were only a Major then, so they promoted 'im and gave 'im Wylie to keep things running smooth, like. Wylie keeps putting in for a transfer, 'cos he knows 'e'll never get any further up the ladder where 'e is. They ain't 'avin' it though. Wylie's stuck 'ere and no mistake. Shimpling ent goin' nowhere, neither. Makes 'em both bloody minded"

McGill dropped his hand and Aitket looked at him angrily. Then he lowered his eyes and turned away once more.

" Yea well, likely see yer tomorrow. Don't forget, 'ot water oh-six-thirty." So saying he shut the door behind him, leaving McGill to ponder on how good men could never rise beyond their station.

McGill looked around the dingy room. There was a camp bed, a dressing table with a wash bowl on it, a chair and a bedside table. A skimpy towel hung on the back of the chair. There was no fire or heater. A couple of blankets lay folded on the end of the bed and something he supposed was a pillow.

Sighing, McGill decided to stay in his clothes. He lay down on the bed, took off his boots and pulled the blankets over himself. He started to say a quick prayer but fell asleep before he could finish.

He awoke with a start at a loud rapping on the door and a bellow "Hot water, Sir!" made him realise he'd slept without a break all night through. It was the first decent night's sleep he'd had in a month. He staggered over to the door and yanked it open. A cold blast of air reminded him he had no shoes on.

There stood Aitket holding a steaming urn with a towel and a bar of soap.

Drowsily, McGill took the items and Aitket stamped off.

As he shaved and changed his shirt, McGill reflected on the sudden night's sleep. It couldn't be the change of air, he decided. It must be that he was more settled within himself. Instead of mounds of paperwork and being talked down to by toffee-nosed inspectors who were always swanning off, he was effectively in charge of this investigation. Brown wasn't going to be around, so McGill felt he was going to be able to conduct it the way he wanted to. For the first time in months he was looking forward to his day. He smiled at himself in the mirror, and thought things could be worse.

McGill walked through the cold air back the way he had come in the early hours of the morning. Lights were blazing in the guard room and there were two new smartly turned out redcaps on the door. Their eyes followed him as he sauntered past, slightly exaggerating the casual stroll, something he was able and allowed to do but they were not. He grinned to himself, and thought for the second time that perhaps not being in the army wasn't so bad after all.

Beyond the guardroom he found the mess, and joined the end of the queue, picking up an enamel plate as he shuffled nearer the food. There was no choice – it was a hunk of bread, fried eggs and bacon, with a steaming mug of tea. He looked round for a place to sit and saw Brown waving to him. He was at a table with a dozen soldiers, all redcaps, and was already smoking. He looked as if he had not slept.

McGill sat down opposite him.

" Did you sleep?" asked Brown.

" Yes, sir, very well thank you."

" Hmmpf! Never had a worse night – dreadful camp bed and freezing cold!" He paused. " I'm not sure what we're supposed to do until nine o'clock, so I'm going to take a turn around the camp." So saying he rose and made for the door.

McGill preferred his own company anyway, so that was no hardship. He'd take a turn himself after his breakfast. As he started tucking in, one of the sergeants further down the table spoke to him.

" You're one of them Scotland Yard characters." It was a flat statement, not a question.

" Yes I am."

" Think you'll find out more than us, do you?" McGill paused the fork on it's way to his mouth, then finished the action and started chewing.

He said nothing for a moment or two. There was no point making enemies. " I shouldn't think so, no. From what I've seen so far it looks like somebody did a pretty thorough job". There was a palpable lessening of tension round the table. McGill tore a bit of bread from his chunk, and dipped it into one of his eggs. Thorough job my arse, he thought.

" It certainly seems all very mysterious," he added.

The sergeant glanced across at one of the other redcaps, then back at McGill.

" We think it was some Frenchie who was trying to rob him when he was drunk. Maybe he came to and the Frenchie offed him."

McGill nodded. "Yes that could be it. Mind you, stealing a uniform isn't exactly worth being hanged for."

"Maybe he had money in it."

McGill shook his head. "If that was the motive, he'd have simply taken the money. Why take the uniform ? Anyway, what makes everyone think he HAD a uniform?"

The sergeant blinked. " Stands to reason. Who else could it be but a soldier?"

" Well, it might even be a Frenchman," said McGill innocently, forking a piece of bacon, and carefully using his knife to put a few dabs of egg yolk onto it"… or a journalist."

The sergeant leant back in his chair." Nah, can't see it meself."

McGill shrugged." Doesn't hurt to keep an open mind though. At least until there are some positive facts to go on."

" Ah, now that's a point. There are no facts other than there being a strangled naked man in an empty house."

" My point exactly," said McGill as he finished his plate and took a swig of tea. " We'll have to see if any turn up. But you'd have to ask why no clothes. It can only be to hamper identification." So saying, he downed the last of his tea, pushed back from the table, picked up his now empty plate, and headed for the serving area. He put his plate onto a pile of other dirty dishes, and looked back at the table.

The sergeant was still looking at him. If I didn't know better, McGill thought, I'd say he was a suspect. He made his way out of the mess and started walking back towards the entrance to the redcap's compound.

He spoke with one of the guards and said he was going for a short walk. The guard looked at him suspiciously, as if doing such a thing was tantamount to blasphemy, but nodded and waived him through. The one thing everybody seems to know, thought McGill, is who we are and what we are here for. No one had asked him for any form of identification at any point, yet simply allowed him to wander about. The antipathy was like a solid wall.

He turned left out of the compound. To his right he could see wooden shacks with red crosses on them. To his left the train sidings were already heaving with jostling, pushing troops. On the other side of the tracks were more substantial buildings which he decided must be the HQ block, judging by the cars, guards and the odd red tab.

He came to a cross roads. He could see the river and the bridge which led across to Le Touquet. That was out of bounds to most, apart from officers. To the left, the town of Etaples stretched along the river, exhausted by the continual beating it took from the tens of thousands of troops that used it to try to forget. McGill shuddered slightly. He was definitely going off the idea of being a fighting man. To his right he spied a number of white and blue figures flitting along. Nurses! He turned towards them.

McGill had been sweet on a nurse once. Abigail. After his parents died and he settled in to his family house as master, he had wanted to bring her to be mistress. But McGill's life always seemed to interfere with their plans and eventually Abigail told him she was engaged to another. He hadn't tried hard enough, but he *had* tried with another girl. Abigail stuck in his mind though and he found himself comparing his new girl to her all the time. Now he felt that he was too set in his ways to ever find domestic happiness.

As he walked towards them, their cheery chatter drifted across the open space. McGill stopped and listened. He hadn't heard anything as carefree in years. In London, people walked around with their heads down and grave expressions on their faces. The whores he used to come across on his beat in the East End were cheerful enough, but with an underlying hard, exhausted sadness to them. Not cheery as these girls were. McGill couldn't think why they seemed so happy. He started walking slowly towards them again. As he got closer, one or two glanced towards him, their eyes taking in his size and smooth complexion. As he drew level with the door of the hut, an older more substantial woman emerged.

" Yes? And what do YOU want?"

McGill raised his hat. "Good morning, Matron. I'm only stretching my legs after travelling yesterday."

" Hmpf! Well keep away from my nurses. They've enough on their plates without being bothered by the likes of you!" As she turned to go back inside, McGill ventured " They seem so carefree". The Matron whirled back to him, hands on hips, face blazing.

" And what exactly makes you think that? Just because they are seemingly happy doesn't mean they are!"

" No, I suppose not – sorry Matron. It's just – you know – with all the wounded and so on, how do they manage to be cheery?" The Matron glared at him.

" They have to be or they would cry. These girls have seen things no man ever should. Just you remember that, Mr. Smarmy pants, and leave them alone!" So saying she spun on her heels and went inside.

McGill doffed his hat again to her back, and with a " and a good day to you, too, Matron", he continued his walk.

The sky looked as if it had been punched, leaving heavy bruises. McGill had always thought the weather in France would be better than in London, but looking at the clouds he felt sure there was little to choose between the two places. Well, between London and Northern France anyway. He'd heard the south of France where the toffs went in the winter was like a Shangri-La. Looking up, he sighed. This was more like living in Wales than Shangri- La. He and Brown had been sent there recently on a case. Miserable place and miserable people. No one would even talk to them, until McGill befriended the local trollop, another outsider. It was only through what she knew of the community that they'd been able to make an arrest. The skies had been grey and dark the whole time they were there. The sun hadn't broken through until they had made it back past Bristol.

McGill turned away from the river and nurses' quarters,in towards where the hospitals lay. There were ambulances coming and going, ferrying wounded from the railway sidings. Bandaged soldiers limped about on crutches as cheery nurses chivvied them along. The conversations were all of "mates" who were no longer there, who'd copped it somewhere to the North East, blown up by a shell, chopped in two by a hail of machine gun fire, or hung up on the wire. There's no heroism here, thought McGill, there's only death or survival.

Chapter 3

By nine o'clock he was back in front of the Military Police headquarters. On enquiring he was told Brown was already inside, and the guard waved McGill past. Seeing him enter, a burly sergeant pointed to Wylie's office. McGill tapped on the door, turned the handle and walked in.

" Ah, the sergeant" said Wylie. " I was just saying divisional HQ have asked that you drop in on your way to Amiens. It's almost en route." He lifted some papers from his desk and passed them to Brown. " Here are your movement orders. There's a train leaving here in just under an hour for Querrieu. You'll be met by Major Tupper. He's on the staff at HQ there – nothing to do with us. You're to present your papers personally to General Lee who wants to talk to you before you move on to Amiens."

" I've decided I won't be going to Amiens," said Brown. " I've arranged to leave all that to McGill." Wylie looked at him sharply, then nodded.

" You can speak to the General about that." Brown took out his cigarette case, opened it and passed it across to Wylie. Wylie took a cigarette, and languidly sat back in his chair. He tapped the cigarette on his thumbnail.

" You won't find anything you know – we haven't. The only reason you are here is because Haig wants to be able to tell the politicos back home that he's done everything possible. It would never have got as far as him, except that some bloody busybody on his staff happened to be in Amiens that day and heard about it. Bloody sod tells Haig and the next thing we know is you two are on your way here." McGill could hear the bitterness in Wylie's voice. It increased." We've only just put down a mutiny, and we're being told to help people who have no business being here at all."

Brown was lighting a cigarette as Wylie finished, and blew a stream of smoke towards the ceiling. When he spoke it was more sharply than previously.

" I quite see your point, Major, but we are all required to do our duty and obey our orders." Wylie shrugged as he put the unlit cigarette into his mouth. He pulled open a drawer and took out a box of matches. He slammed the drawer shut, and looked hard at Brown. He took the cigarette out of his mouth.

" Oh yes indeed," he said sarcastically. "Only we did and look where we've landed. Having a pair of London snoops checking up on us."

Brown nodded as he puffed on his cigarette again. "Exactly. So let's get it done and we can all go back to where we started." Wylie grunted. He popped the cigarette back in his mouth. Within moments he'd lit a match and started puffing greedily to get the cigarette drawing properly. Smoke streamed out of his nostrils as he pinched a bit of tobacco off the tip of his tongue.

" Just remember this is our jurisdiction. Anything you do you need our permission." Brown nodded.

" I know. I don't like this any more than you do, but somehow we both need to get the higher-ups off our backs." Brown glanced at McGill." So I'm leaving all the interviews and so on to my sergeant here." Wylie glanced at McGill, and looked hard at Brown again. McGill could have sworn there was a look of comprehension between them. Bastards, he thought. Whatever happens I'm going to get it in the neck.

With that Wylie raised his voice. " Aitket!" Almost instantly there was a knock and Aitket appeared in the room, saluting as he stamped to attention. McGill decided he must have been listening at the door.

Wylie sighed. "At ease, Aitket. All that gives me a headache. Take the detectives to collect their bags, then make sure they catch the train to Querrieu. And Aitket."

" Sir!"

"Make sure they get some rations to take with them."

" Sir." Wylie rose and extended his hand to Brown, who did likewise and shook it.

" Bon chance, as we say here. And make sure you keep your heads down."

Brown nodded and turned away as Aitket held the door open. Wylie never even looked at McGill. As Aitket shut the door behind him, McGill saw Wylie sitting down again and picking up papers with a slight frown. Bastard, thought McGill again.

Aitket spoke to a private, and then hurried them along to their chalets. Luggage collected, they retraced their steps of the night before back to the station. The closer they got the more men crowded about, the louder the noise and the more irritable everyone seemed. By the time they made the actual platform, McGill wondered how anyone could know what they were supposed to be doing. Then, as if by magic, the private Aitket had spoken to appeared before them with two lots of greaseproof paper packets and two water bottles. He handed his bounty across then disappeared amidst the crowds. McGill could hardly believe all the people standing on the platform would get on the train, but when it puffed into sight around the corner, he saw it had more than 20 carriages. He could just make out that there was another engine behind the first. With a despairing hoot the engines passed where they stood and came to a stop fifty yards ahead of them. Suddenly the doors were flung open and a vast tide of brown-clad humanity washed onto the platform, fighting through those waiting to board. As the soldiers pushed past him, McGill saw the childhood in their faces. My God he thought. If this is all we have left to send then the war better finish pretty damn quick or we'll lose it.

At last the carriages were empty, and the waiting tide streamed onto the train. As before there was a compartment reserved for officers, and Brown and McGill were pushed into it. No sooner were they in than three other officers joined them. They were all Majors, and all with wounds. One had a sleeve dangling empty, one a black eye patch, and the third was sporting a crutch. None of them spoke. McGill looked out of the window at the now virtually empty platform. From the corner of his eye he caught sight of a Captain climbing into a carriage further down, last man aboard.

It only seemed like moments before the train was being shunted about and readied to leave on the appropriate track. McGill was glad to be moving away from the great mass of shouting, pushing hordes. With a final jolt and a sharp toot the train began to move away. McGill could see the river with the sea beyond to his left, and the great bulk of the Etaples camp to his right. He marvelled at its size. It was almost like a whole town. There was nothing for him there. There was nothing for anyone there, in fact. McGill could see Brown looking pensively at the camp too.

" Not a pretty sight, is it?" said Brown.

" No, sir, it's not." Brown nodded.

" I think Wylie's advice to keep our heads down is kindly meant. Don't you go stirring up any trouble! We both need to come out of this smelling sweet, so don't you mess it up for me." Not a word about the mess you lot have already dropped me in, thought McGill. God these bloody toffs don't half make sure they're always all right.

When the train pulled in to Querrieu, it was the same performance as the night before in Etaples. Their carriage door was flung open by a pristine Major with a languid air. He saluted lazily and said " Inspector Brown? I'm Major Tupper"

" That's me," said Brown. No bloody introduction again thought McGill. The luggage was collected by a sergeant and the small group headed for the exit. There was nothing like the numbers of men about here. From what McGill could see, Querrieu was a quiet well-ordered town. All the troops were smartly turned out, not the crumpled hordes they had travelled with so far. Must be because it's HQ, thought McGill. Once outside the station there was a beautifully turned out staff car waiting for them. The sergeant put the bags in the rear. He walked to the front and sat in the open with the driver. Tupper climbed into the back followed by Brown and McGill, whose bulk squashed the others.

" It's not far," said Tupper, as he leant forward and tapped the dividing glass with his swagger stick. The car moved off, and McGill looked out of the window at the passing houses. Tupper was speaking to Brown.

" The General just wants to see you and tell you himself how important the Field Marshall thinks this is to get sorted."

" Yes I heard his staff member took it all to heart," said Brown drily." I don't suppose he has any idea about any of this?"

" Couldn't say, old boy. He and I move in different circles!" I doubt that, thought McGill. This whole thing is just pure poison and we're the fall boys – or more precisely, I am.

By now the car had reached the edge of the little town, and turned onto a minor road that wound through open countryside. Within a few minutes a huge wall appeared at the side of the road and the car ran beside it for a few minutes before coming to an entry gate, flanked on both sides by gatehouses. Soldiers snapped to attention as the car made its way onto the gravelled drive, lined with magnificent plane trees. As it approached the end of the drive, a golden-stoned chateau appeared. There were cars drawn up in front of it and soldiers marching to and fro. The car drew up at the bottom of a flight of steps, and no sooner had it stopped than an immaculately dressed sergeant pulled the door open and saluted sharply.

" Thank you sergeant, "murmured Tupper as he stepped onto the gravel. He straightened his cap, and then touched the brim with his stick. " Just leave the luggage in the car – we'll be going back to the train station shortly." The sergeant saluted again. " Very good sir."

Tupper led the way up the marble steps, saluting off-handedly at the guards at the top who snapped to attention. Three soldiers appeared once they were inside the door and in an enormous hall, with double stairs leading up from it. They took Tupper's cap and swagger stick, and Brown and McGill's hats and coats. Indicating a set of double doors to the right, Tupper led the way, and the doors opened as if by magic. In reality there were two soldiers, one on either side, whose job was nothing else but to open the doors. Inside was another huge room, gilded and mirrored, and with two more soldiers on the inside. Their job was clearly to open the doors when someone wanted out. There were three desks with officers behind them, and other doors off to the left. To the right were windows looking out over the area at the front of the chateau and the park beyond.

Tupper moved towards another set of double doors at the far end of the room, which again opened magically. In this room, there was but one desk, with a colonel behind it. Tupper snapped to attention and saluted sharply.

" At ease, Tupper, the General's expecting you." So saying he rose from the desk, and knocked softly on the doors.

" COME!" said a muffled voice from inside, and the colonel swung the doors open, announcing, "Major Tupper and the two detectives from Scotland Yard, sir " as he did so. Stepping to one side he ushered the three men into the room, then discreetly withdrew and closed the doors.

Tupper threw another smart salute and stayed rigidly at attention. The man in the general's uniform and tabs looked up from the map he was studying. He was not tall, but had bright, intelligent eyes. He straightened and came out from behind the table towards the detectives, hand held out.

" I'm General Lee. You must be Inspector Brown."

" Yes sir," said Brown shaking the general's hand. How did he know which of us was Brown, thought McGill. Do I look like an inferior?

" Rum business all this. The Field Marshall is very anxious that no stone is left unturned. Our own detectives - if I may call them that – haven't been able to get anywhere. So Sir Douglas asked for you chaps help as a last resort. He felt very strongly that whoever the murdered chappie is, it's only right his family should know." Well done Sir Douglas, thought McGill. That's someone I can get along with!

Brown was nodding." Yes sir - quite." McGill noted the lack of warmth in Brown's voice. " We can only do our best. From reading the reports, it would appear your people did a thorough job." My arse, thought McGill again.

" Well I leave it to you. Remember you can call on my resources at any time." He strode to his ornate desk and lifted a piece of paper, then walked back to Brown and handed it to him." This is a laissez passer for you and your man signed by me. Show that anywhere in this sector and you will be given every assistance. I am also required to tell you that before you leave for England, you are to see the Field Marshall and give him your report in person. Even if you find nothing further. And you are not to make any report to *anyone* until after you have seen the Field Marshall."

Brown nodded again." I understand sir. I'll do that." I bet you will, thought McGill bitterly. It won't be you who finds anything out, it'll be me – but I don't suppose you'll go so far as to mention that.

"Take the detectives back to the station, Major." So saying General Lee shook hands with Brown, as Tupper saluted once more.

With a solid stamping, Tupper about-turned and made for the doors. McGill was just thinking that he had been ignored again, when the General turned to him.

" You must be Sergeant McGill." McGill was taken aback, but stammered "Yes sir."

" The only McGill I ever knew was in the motor trade in London some years back. Your father, I think?"

" Yes sir – he was."

" Ah. He was a good man and an excellent mechanic. Tragic about your mother." How did he know all this thought McGill. " I remember him telling me you were in the Police, and you couldn't stand the internal combustion engine."

" Well sir, it was just one of those things. He loved engines and I hated them!"

" Ha! Don't blame you. Give me a horse any day – much more reliable!" And then to McGill's intense astonishment, the General extended his hand towards him. " I wish you all the best." McGill took the proffered hand and felt a grip as strong as his own as it was pumped up and down, just the once. Brown was staring but recovered swiftly and headed for the now open doors. McGill was unsure why the General had spoken to him at all. He could just as easily have ignored him – in fact, he could MORE easily have ignored him.

Tupper led the two detectives back out through the ante-rooms then down the stairs to the waiting car. The door was whisked open as they approached and Tupper clambered in first as before. Brown followed and McGill crammed in after them.

They sat in silence as the car retraced its route to the station. "Next stop Amiens for you, then," said Tupper. " Shouldn't take too long." As McGill looked at the passing scene, he felt again the difference between where the soldiers were and where the top brass were. No shouting and shoving here, he thought. As they got out at the station, there were troops hanging about, but all quite smartly turned out. He felt under scrutiny as heads turned, curious, following the group as it made its way onto the platform. McGill thought one particular Captain turned away as they walked past.

A train was waiting in the station and Brown and McGill bundled into a compartment with two officers. Tupper saluted smartly and the door was slammed shut. Almost immediately the train started to move, as if it had been waiting for them to return. Brown pulled his cigarettes out of his pocket and offered the case to the two officers. They each took one. Brown lit a match and offered lights to them both. As he moved to light his own, one of the officers leaned across and stayed his hand.

" Don't do that," he said." It's bad luck. The third person gets shot."

Brown looked at him, then removed the restraining hand. Ostentatiously he lit his own cigarette then shook the match to extinguish it. Blowing a stream of smoke towards the roof of the compartment, he said. " Utter rot! Who's going to shoot me?"

" Well, you are travelling into the war zone, perhaps you should take care." Brown snorted.

" There's no bullets where I'm going." McGill wasn't superstitious but he could understand the two officers being so. Sometimes the only thing that stood between you and complete, stark terror was a superstition. A mascot or a talisman that you knew would keep you safe. Until it didn't matter.

By the time they got to Amiens they had eaten their sandwiches. Little more had been said between the four people in the carriage. McGill didn't think it was his place to say anything, whilst Brown clearly thought little or nothing of the two officers. They had kept up a desultory conversation of sorts as the train chugged through the bleak November countryside. From what McGill could hear of it the two soldiers were rejoining units at the front. I suppose that's making them quiet – and superstitious, thought McGill. The talk was again of comrades lost, of people completely disappearing, blown to smithereens, of identification being impossible. Ha! Thought McGill, and here we have a perfectly preserved body and absolutely no idea who it is. As the officers talked, McGill pondered the riddle of the identity of the murdered man. Why would anyone steal his clothes? It had to be to do with identification. Why was it so important to hide the identity? In the present situation one more dead body would make no difference. Unless… maybe it was some connection that was important, a connection to the murderer. Or maybe it had to do with how he had come to the place. Who could he be?

As they stepped out onto the platform they were assailed again by the hordes of shouting and shoving men that characterised every place they had stopped. They had expected to be met but there didn't appear to be anyone looking for them. McGill and Brown made their way along the platform, pushing against a tide of soldiers who were trying to get into the train. As they emerged onto the main station concourse, McGill spotted two redcaps, a Captain and a corporal, standing waiting. He drew Brown's attention to them. The pair made their way towards the redcaps.

" I say, I'm looking for a Major Watkins."

" He'll be at the Provost Marshall's HQ. Are you Brown?"

" Detective Inspector Brown, actually", said Brown, bristling.

The officer gave a lazy salute. " We were sent to find you. Didn't seem any point being on the platform with all these troops about." The officer pointed at the bags McGill was carrying. " These yours?" Brown nodded and the corporal took the suitcases. The Captain turned sharply on his heel, and the four men trailed out of the station towards a waiting truck.

" Hop in," said the Captain. "You can ride up front with me, Inspector". The corporal was hefting Brown's suitcases into the back and followed them. He turned and offered McGill a hand. McGill clambered up and sat on the hard wooden bench that ran the length of the truck. With a jerk, the Captain set the truck in motion, and it juddered as it moved off.

" Bloody awful driver," McGill said over the noise of the engine.

" Too bloody true. This is my truck by rights and I looks after her. Then along comes toffee nose and insists he drives. Buggers 'er up." McGill sympathised. Brown was like that, messing up what he was working on. Must be a trait of the upper classes, thought McGill. Working people know what gets put into something – so they take care of it. Toffs is careless, he thought as the truck bumped along the road.

They wended their way through the town, which showed some artillery damage. There were a few burned out houses and work parties scurrying about, but McGill couldn't have said that Amiens appeared like a town on the front line of anything. Brown gazed blankly out of the windscreen, lighting yet another cigarette. He was clearly not pleased that Watkins had not come to meet him at the station. He felt his dignity had been besmirched by a mere Captain being sent to collect him.

Soon enough the truck arrived in a wide street where a large building was set back a little from it. Marble steps led from the pavement to a sort of terrace, and guards were stationed both at the bottom and the top. The truck drew up and the corporal jumped down from the back, then reached in and pulled Brown's cases after him. McGill descended rather more gingerly, by which time the corporal was already climbing the steps. Brown and the Captain were close behind, and as they got to the top, there was the noise of gears being engaged. McGill looked back to see the truck being removed from where it had stood. McGill could hear the corporal muttering under his breath about "that sod Mckeever" taking away his truck.

At the top of the steps, the guards presented arms, and the Captain gave a lazy touch of his cap. They entered a large entrance hall and the Captain led them through one door into an anteroom. He knocked on a door, and led the way through. There, a Major was sitting at a desk piled with files, lazily puffing on a cigarette as he concentrated on the words in front of him. He looked up almost absentmindedly, then stubbed out the last millimetres of the cigarette. He rose and extended his hand towards Brown. How did these people always know who to shake hands with, thought McGill. He decided it had to be the black bowler.

" I'm Watkins. You must be the Inspector from the Yard." Brown shook hands.

" Detective Inspector Brown, at your service," he said coldly. " This is my sergeant, McGill." Watkins glanced briefly at McGill, then turned back to Brown.

" I'd better take you in to see Colonel Berry. You won't be having anything to do with him, but he likes to be kept up to date." Watkins stood up, collected his cap from a side table, and set off out the door and on towards the marble stairs that led up from the hall. Brown and McGill followed him as dozens of officers and men paraded back and forth.

Watkins led them up the stairs and through a door. There were various officers at desks, and another door towards the back of the room. Watkins knocked then walked in, followed by Brown and McGill.

Colonel Berry sat at an enormous desk, his arms extended to either side of him, gripping the table. His eyes followed Watkins as he marched towards him. He had a grey and haggard look to him, thought McGill. Watkins arrived at the front of the desk and saluted.

" At ease, Major," rasped Berry. " These are the detectives I suppose."

" Yes sir, Inspector Brown and Sergeant McGill."

Berry glanced at the two men, but stayed seated, hands holding the table.

" Inspector, just so we are clear, my men did a thorough job with nothing to go on. You've been foisted on me by Army HQ. Watkins here will give you every assistance and I expect you to report to him anything you might find. From my point of view it's a waste of time and manpower, and I'd be obliged if you disappear as fast as possible." Not keen on us then, thought McGill.

What Brown did next almost endeared him to McGill.

He walked forward and grasped the table in a mirror image of the Colonel and leaned towards him.

" Thank you for your most welcoming remarks," he said coldly. " We are here to do a job, and that job will be done with or without your help or good wishes. As a matter of courtesy *only*, I will inform Major Watkins of anything we find, but I have no obligation to do so. My report will go to Field Marshall Haig, as I have been instructed and then to my Superintendent, who will decide what the next, if any, steps to be taken are." He turned sharply away from the desk as Berry's face took on a look of fury, and strode out of the room without looking back. McGill almost cheered and followed. Watkins scuttled out after them and shut the door.

The three men stood looking at each other, Brown furiously, Watkins in astonishment and McGill with what might have been seen as a slight twitching of the mouth.

At last Watkins spoke. " Well, that's that then. I suppose we better get on and get started." He led them back down the stairs and in to his office.

Chapter 4

As McGill and Brown sat, Watkins rummaged amongst the files on his desk, then pulled one out.

" So you've read the reports, I take it", he said coldly. " We didn't ask for you, but the brass wanted it. We've no idea about who the murdered man might be. He could be a Frenchie for all we know." Brown nodded.

" I don't think so sir," said McGill. Both Brown and Watkins looked at him.

" And why, pray, do you think that?" asked Watkins.

" I can't be sure of course, but why were all the clothes and any identification removed? If he was French, the whole thing would have been handed over to the French police. But whoever killed him wanted to be sure that there was no connection to anyone. So he made sure there was nothing to link the body to the Army – or anything else - in any way. It's much more likely the dead man is NOT French. It's a British commandeered house with British officers in it. The only reason I can see for removing any identification is because if we knew who the murdered man was, there might be a link to the murderer." Brown was still staring and jumped in as soon as McGill stopped.

" Oh come on McGill you can't just surmise something like that! What proof do you have?"

" None at all sir. But there's nothing to suggest that what I say isn't correct either." Watkins nodded.

" All right – suppose he IS British. We've checked all the units for people who might be AWOL from leave and they are all accounted for one way or another."

" What if he only just arrived and hadn't reported in to his unit yet?" Watkins shook his head.

" We have that covered. Every soldier is checked onto the boats and onto the trains and there's roll call every day."

" What if he was an officer ?" Watkins sat bolt upright. Slowly he said," But he still has to report for duty to the commanding officer of the unit he's been sent to." McGill shrugged.

" Suppose he arrived, reported in to the CO and was told to get up to the lines immediately as there was an attack about to start. Suppose in all the chaos and confusion he didn't and went to the house instead."

" Why would he do that?"

" I don't know – to meet a friend perhaps? "

"The people in the house had never seen him before, so how did he get in?"

" Well", said McGill, "someone must have had a key and let him in."

Watkins looked at McGill." But why?"

McGill shrugged. " I don't know yet, but let in he clearly was – there were no signs of a break-in."

Brown snorted.

" This is all nonsense! It's mere speculation." He looked hard at McGill.

" I don't want any more of your theories, if you don't mind."

"But sir..."

" No buts!"

"Wait a minute", said Watkins." He'd need papers to be able to move around – whatever nationality he was."

" Exactly," said McGill. " The papers had to be removed because they would lead to the murderer."

There was silence for a moment. Watkins stroked his chin, and reached for another cigarette.

" So was he in Amiens all the time, and never went to the front? Or did he go to the front and come back for his fatal rendezvous?"

McGill shook his head." He must have gone to the front. He wouldn't be able to stay in Amiens if his orders said he was supposed to be somewhere else."

The three men sat silently for a moment or two, Brown fuming, McGill thinking and Watkins beginning to see that the person he should be talking to was McGill, rather than Brown.

" I was wondering sir...", began McGill.

" Yes?"

" Inspector Brown and I have had travel papers and laissez passers at every stage of our journey. If the murdered man had gone to the front, he must have had papers to do that."

" Correct. He would have been issued them when he checked in and was sent to the front."

" Right sir. So to get back he must have had papers saying he could come back."

Watkins shook his head. "The papers wouldn't have been issued like that. They are always point to point. So he would have had to get papers at Albert saying he could return."

McGill thought for a moment.

" So he must have stolen them – if they weren't issued to him."

Watkins shook his head again. "Even supposing he did, when the person who lost them turned up saying the papers had disappeared and he needed new ones, the lost ones would be cancelled and at any roll call when the name was picked up, the chap would be arrested."

McGill felt his brain clicking through scenarios.

"If he was an officer there wouldn't be a roll call for him. And what if the person he stole them from was an officer as well - and dead?"

" Dead? It would still be the same."

McGill leaned forward.

" Not if he came across a body badly blown up and disfigured. He could have exchanged his tags and pay book. "

There was a silence, then Brown grunted." You'd have two bodies then."

" Precisely. We've been looking for the wrong thing. We need to find two men who disappeared on the same day in the same place and for whom we have no definite, defining identification."

There was a hush for a few moments. Watkins ran his hand through his hair, and looked speculatively at McGill.

" Hm, I see what you're getting at. We've only checked those on leave and with passes before the murder. It could easily be someone who wasn't due back for some days after the murder. Or someone newly arrived from England." McGill nodded again. Brown snorted.

" Surely there must be lots of pairs of men who have disappeared at the same time and place?"

Watkins shook his head. " Not as many as you might think – at least not where we don't know who they are." He thought a moment. He looked at McGill. " How many days before the murder should we go back?"

" What's the usual pass length?"

" Depends very much, but the most is about three weeks."

" Well we'd have to start three weeks before and work forward, then for three weeks after the death"

" Good God man," said Brown." That's thousands of men! And why three weeks after?"

" He might not have started his leave until the morning he was killed." There was silence again, until Watkins let out his breath.

" What if he never went to the front? Suppose he just stayed in Amiens?"

" I think we've covered that, sir. He'd still have to produce papers if challenged. If they said he should be at the front and he wasn't, he'd get arrested. So he must somehow have had papers allowing him to be in Amiens."

Watkins raised his arms and ran both his hands through his hair.

" Very well. I take it we are only looking for people who are definitely unaccounted for in that period?"

" Precisely," said McGill. " And preferably only those that are in pairs" Watkins steepled his fingers for a moment , then leaned forward .

" I can let you have one man to help. But if you don't have a definite name after three days, I expect that to be the end of it." Brown nodded.

" Oh don't worry! I'll make sure we are gone,"said Brown, shooting a venomous look at McGill, and rose.

" I'm off to visit a friend at a mess nearby. I leave it all to McGill." So saying he picked up his hat and went out.

Watkins looked at McGill once more.

"That was good thinking. But it's a needle in a haystack you know." McGill nodded.

" I know. But I just keep thinking that if it was me dead, my family would want to hear. Not knowing would be a terrible penance."

" He'd be reported missing in action."

"Not very satisfying is it?"

Watkins sighed and went to the door. He opened it and shouted "Sergeant!"

" Sir!"

"Tell Corporal Thorn I want him." Watkins left the door open and returned to his seat behind the desk. There was a knock at the door and a corporal came in.

" You wanted me sir"

" Indeed corporal.This is Detective Sergeant McGill from Scotland Yard (Thorn glanced sideways at him) and you and he have a task to do. Find a room somewhere. The detective will explain. You have three days." Watkins had no further interest in either man, and Thorn quickly grasped that he had all the instructions he was going to get. Jerking his head at McGill to follow him, they left Watkins fumbling for his cigarettes.

Once Thorn had closed the door, he looked McGill up and down.

" Well what are we supposed to do?" McGill explained and Thorn grew ever more amazed as McGill told him what they would need.

" Lummy! Hope you don't mean to get much sleep in the next few days!"

McGill shook his head. " If we don't turn up something pretty quickly, I'll be back on the boat to England faster than you can say "knife" so don't expect me to want any. And I'll be a bloody Detective Constable again!" Thorn shrugged his shoulders, and led off towards the back of the building. He opened a door which led into a small room which was more like a cupboard.

" This'll have to do us. It's Captain Grover's office but he's on leave for a few more days. We can use it just now." McGill looked about. It was definitely a one man office.

" Where will you sit?" he asked Thorn, who shook his head.

" I'll be too busy looking for stuff and bringing you files to start with."

" Right – let's get started then!" McGill peeled his coat off and hung it on the hat-stand. He carefully put his hat on it too, then turned and sat down behind the desk. He took out his notepad and started to make notes. McGill's notebook was a model of precision. Every thought he had or fact uncovered went into it, to be eventually weighed up and analysed.

For the rest of that day the two men worked steadily, Thorn bringing files to McGill who checked lists and cross referenced places, dates and times. Thorn produced cups of tea and thick sandwiches, and they worked on as the sky darkened. By the time McGill felt the need for more food, he had three sets of men who had gone missing at the same time, but he was only up to ten days before the murder.

Thorn came in with another pile of files, and McGill looked up from his reading.

" We'd better get some dinner." Thorn nodded and put the files on the floor beside McGill, who indicated a pile on his other side and said " I'm finished with those." Thorn nodded, and McGill stretched, then shook his head.

" How are you getting on sir?" McGill shook his head again.

" I've got three pairs so far definitely unaccounted for properly, but I've another 30 days or so to go through. Even if I get to the end of the period, I'll just have a lot of names, none of which will have been checked through." He opened the file on the dead man once more, and read through the autopsy report.

" Blue eyes, five foot ten inches tall.." and suddenly stopped. He clicked his fingers.

" That's it – a shortcut! Anyone more than just short of 6 foot or under five feet nine we can discount ." Thorn nodded.

" That should help. What have you got so far?" McGill scrabbled for the six files he had already extracted, looking briefly at the first page of each. Three he quickly discarded, muttering " Too short." The other three he read more thoroughly, then placed them carefully in the centre of his desk.

" And after dinner, we'll make more progress!"

It was too late to get to Thorn's barracks or mess, so they slipped out to a small estaminet nearby that served plain food. The room was stiflingly hot and crammed with raucous men. McGill paid the few sous needed for two bowls of thick onion soup, some sort of chicken casserole and a small jug of red wine. McGill would have preferred a beer but Thorn assured him he'd be better off with the wine. They ate quickly, exchanging few words, then went back to the tiny office.

" Right, Corporal, you can help even more. We can both go through the files and discard anyone outside the size we are looking for. That should speed up the whole thing." So saying McGill let Thorn lead him into a large room that was jammed full of racks with files. Thorn pointed out the parts they were interested in. McGill started at the latest possible date and worked backwards, Thorn from where he had left off and going forwards. Within a couple of hours they had twenty men who fitted the height. They took the files to the little office, where McGill snorted.

" Haven't looked at the last lot you brought in before we went for dinner" They set to and within a few minutes had another single file put aside.

" Now all we have to do is check if these men disappeared with another at the same time and place and then the real work can begin."

They worked steadily through the files discarding one after another until around one in the morning when McGill put down the file he was looking at and reached for another. Glancing from one to the other, he turned pages back and forth, then sat back.

" Got it." Thorn paused in his reading.

" Two lieutenants disappeared near Albert on October the twenty third, one just returned from England the other due to go on leave that day. Lieutenant Charles Braintree had reported in at Amiens that day and was immediately sent to Albert. According to what we know, there was a very heavy bombardment and the train he was in got hit as it drew in to Albert. There were casualties at the railhead as well. Braintree's pay-book was found on a badly mutilated lieutenant's body.

Braintree was therefore listed as killed in action but there is another Lieutenant unaccounted for - an Owen Ralston. It appears he got on to the next train going back to Amiens and then disappeared So either our murdered man is Ralston - or Braintree."

" So how do we find out who he is?" McGill leafed through the files again. " Does it matter?"

" Well, in as far as both of their families will have been told either " missing, presumed killed in action" as far as Ralston is concerned and " Killed in action " for Braintree, I don't suppose it does. There's still a murderer wandering about, so I'd say we need to know which one it is before we can get very much further."

Thorn nodded. " Well at least we've got a couple of days to try. What's the plan sir?"

McGill thought for a moment then nodded." We'd need to interview anybody else who was on the train or at Albert waiting to get on a train. Someone might have a clue as to what happened. Anyway, bed for now I think, then a fresh eye in the morning."

Thorn yawned and stretched. " No arguments there, Sergeant." So saying, the pair donned their overcoats and headed for their respective beds.

The next morning McGill got to the pokey office by eight thirty, and found Thorn already leafing through files and checking them against a list he was holding.

" Hello – you're early!"

" Not really – we have reveille at oh six hundred, so I was here not long after seven. I've found something, though.." and he handed McGill a list.

McGill looked at it without understanding much, until he spotted Braintree's name half way down the page.

" And another." McGill took the second list and saw Ralston's name.

McGill looked up. " What are these lists for?"

"The one with Ralston's name on it is the list of people who had passes who were leaving on the train with him. Just the one's from his section, so the people who would know him best. The list with Braintree on is all the officers who checked in that day at Amiens and were sent on to Albert." McGill looked at the lists again. Braintree's list had about fifty names on it, but Thorn had crossed off a large number. McGill looked at Thorn – who shrugged.

" They don't last long out here."

" No I can see that," said McGill sadly. He looked at the second list where even more where crossed off. " It's appalling."

" Too true. A lieutenant out here lasts about six to eight weeks. They don't last long enough to learn enough to be able to survive." McGill shook his head.

" I'm beginning to see this more clearly. Braintree goes up to Albert. The train gets blown up. He finds another body of someone going on leave and takes his pay book. He leaves his own on the body. So now he has a pass to go on leave and get out of the zone where the fighting is – he wouldn't be able to get away otherwise. He gets on the next train back to Amiens. And of course no one recognises him because he isn't the person on the pay book, so no one talks to him or anything else. And because he's just arrived in any case, nobody knows Braintree either. They just know Ralston isn't there any more – so presumed blown to smithereens."

Thorn nodded. " And reported as such. Braintree they have a body for, Ralston they don't."

The two men thought quietly for a moment. McGill shook himself. "What was Braintree or Ralston doing though? Did he intend to desert – to disappear somehow? And how did he get into the house? And why?" Thorn shrugged and shook his head.

" We'll need to interview some of Ralston's section", said McGill. "At least they will have known him for some time, unlike Braintree's lot who never met him. Any idea where they are?"

Thorn sifted some papers, then extracted one. " They're due to come out of the line tonight into Albert before a week's rest behind the lines - behind Albert."

McGill placed both hands on the desk and stood up.

" We'd better go and see your Mr. Watkins. And I had better tell Inspector Brown."

The two men made their way through the building, back to Watkins' office. Thorn knocked, and opened the door for McGill. Watkins was on the phone and gestured for the two to sit down.

" Right sir, I'll tell him... He's just come in... Yes sir, of course. Goodbye sir."

Carefully replacing the receiver, he looked at it for a moment or two. He seemed to come to a decision and looked up.

"Well, McGill, I have some bad news for you. Your Inspector Brown is dead."

McGill hadn't liked the man but couldn't help feeling shocked and saddened for his family.

"How did it happen sir?"

"Rotten luck. He was well away from any fighting, and had hitched a lift in a car to take him to see his friends up near Doullens. There was some sort of dogfight in the sky and one of the Huns pulled away and was high-tailing it to get back across the lines at low level. He must have come across the car as he was being chased by one of our RFC chaps, and let rip with his machine gun. Didn't do much damage to the car but a bullet went straight through the inspector's head. Never felt a thing by all accounts. Seems as soon as the shooting started the driver slammed the brakes on and everyone jumped over the side. Of course, Brown wouldn't know the drill and was either too slow getting out, or didn't even try. In any event he's as dead as a Dodo." God, thought McGill, maybe there really is something to the lighting-three-cigarettes superstition after all.

There was silence in the room, broken by Watkins reaching for his cigarettes. McGill didn't know what to say. Watkins took a cigarette from the packet and tapped the end of it on his desk. Putting one end in his mouth, he carefully struck a match and held it to the other end, which obediently glowed red as he sucked air through it and smoke into his lungs. He took another puff, tilted his head back, coughed, and blew the smoke towards the ceiling.

McGill shook his head. "Where do we go from here?" he asked. Watkins looked at him.

"Why did you come here this morning?"

"I think we know who the dead man is, sir." Watkins gave a little jerk, and leaned forward across his desk.

"Really?"

"Yes sir. I think it's a Lieutenant Braintree. He was going up to the lines when he got bombarded and another Lieutenant by the name of Ralston was just going on leave. He was at the railhead when the bombardment started, and no one has seen him since." Watkins thought a moment.

" And of course if Braintree swapped his pay book, a body would be taken for Braintree when it was Ralston. Braintree would be able to use Ralston's pass to get away. Once in Amiens " Ralston" could just disappear." He paused. " I don't like it one bit, McGill. That's cowardice in the face of the enemy and liable to get you shot."

McGill snorted. " In this case, sir, he got strangled." Watkins flicked ash towards an overloaded ashtray.

" No less than he deserved, I'd say. What are you going to do?" McGill thought for a moment, his normally clear eyes pensive. Usually it would have been asked of Brown, but now he would have to make a decision and provide an answer.

" I suppose I better tell the Yard and await instructions. Is it possible to phone?"

Watkins nodded. " I can certainly say it's an emergency and related to the war. But what I meant was what are you going to do now you know who the dead man is?"

"I'm not 100% sure that it IS Braintree, sir. I was coming here to ask permission to travel to Albert and interview Ralston's section, who might be able to tell me something to confirm it one way or the other." Watkins glanced at Thorn, who nodded.

" Very well. Once you've spoken to your superiors I'll give you the necessary papers. But Thorn stays here. I don't want one of my best men getting blown up." Doesn't care if I get blown up, thought McGill.

So saying Watkins picked up the phone and asked to be connected to Scotland Yard. He was told there would be a two hour delay. Replacing the receiver, he motioned Thorn and McGill towards the door.

" Go and get a cup of tea or something and be back here in two hours. And don't go anywhere I can't find you. I don't want to be talking to Scotland Yard on my own." So saying he stubbed out his cigarette, which made the overloaded ashtray spill over. Cursing, Watkins used his sleeve to sweep the detritus into his waste bin. He vigorously patted his sleeve to remove the remains of the ash. A dark stain was left and Watkins cursed again.

" Bloody disgusting habit, and bloody messy too," he muttered as McGill and Thorn closed the door behind them.

Chapter 5

Two hours later they were back in Watkins' office, which by then was almost entirely filled with a blue haze of cigarette smoke. Watkins waved them to seats and continued reading one of the files that littered his desk, smoke pirouetting slowly towards the ceiling, then spreading out in all directions and falling back towards the floor. McGill and Thorn sat quietly. McGill was wondering what would happen when he told the Super about Brown's death, and Thorn was looking forward to his lunch. Watkins was reading Braintree and Ralston's files and wondering why someone would strangle either of them.

After about fifteen minutes the phone rang and Watkins put the receiver to his ear.

" Major Watkins". He listened for a few moments then held the instrument towards McGill.

The line was crackly but McGill could tell it was the Yard switchboard.

"Hello, Detective Sergeant McGill here. I need to speak urgently to Superintendent Truman." There was a pause as the operator explained the Superintendent was busy and could the sergeant leave a message. " Tell him I'm calling from France and Inspector Brown is dead. I need orders and I need them now." There was another pause which mostly consisted of an intake of breath at the other end, followed by a " One moment". McGill waited patiently. After a few minutes the receiver crackled again and Truman came on the line.

"McGill what the hell's going on?" Briefly McGill explained about Brown's death and where he had got to with the investigation.

Truman chuckled. "That's one in the eye for the Army. Well, what do you propose?"

" I was just about to get papers to go to Albert to see if I can find out any more about Ralston, sir. One way or another I was then going to come back to Amiens to see what I could find out here."

" Sounds reasonable to me. Do you need some additional help?"

" Well, sir, I'm sure I can manage on my own, but I thought you might be going to send out a replacement Inspector."

" Not at all. I've lost one already over this, and I don't intend to lose another." There was a pause. "However, you are quite right. Murders can only be investigated by Inspectors. So as of now you are an acting Inspector. I'll tell Brown's family. Can you make arrangements over there to have his body shipped back?"

" I'm sure I can sir."

" Good. Well carry on and keep me posted. Oh and McGill"

"Yes sir?"

" Try not to get shot." So saying, Truman disconnected.

McGill slowly put the instrument back on Watkins' desk and hung up the earpiece.

" Well?" asked Watkins. McGill hesitated.

" He's made me an Inspector."

" Congratulations. Is he sending anyone else out?"

" No sir. I'm to carry on the investigation on my own." Watkins nodded.

" I'd probably do the same. Give me half an hour and I'll have your papers ready."

" Sir, could you make arrangements to have Inspector Brown's body returned to the UK? Superintendent Truman asked that arrangements be made."

Watkins nodded. " Leave it with me. I'll get someone on to it." McGill rose and headed for the door. He opened it then turned back towards Watkins.

" Sir I was wondering if you had any ideas about Braintree's death. Or Ralston's. I noticed you were reading their files."

Watkins looked shrewdly at McGill. " Not daft are you, sergeant – sorry, Inspector." Watkins stressed the word. " I can't see anything in here that would suggest either of them was a target." Watkins glanced at Thorn, who shook his head." Perfectly ordinary chaps, been in the line several times for two or three weeks, had some days R&R before going on leave. Nothing to suggest anyone wanted them dead."

" Could there be a German spy about and Braintree or Ralston heard or saw something he should not have done?"

Watkins shrugged. " It's always possible, but I can't imagine what it could be. Everyone knows pretty much when and where we're going to attack by the barrage and by how it's laid down. Strangling is a strange method of killing. Anyone can do it at any time, but in practice it tends to be an impulse whilst in a rage. The stories of people being strangled in a dark alleyway are very overdone – in my experience it tends to be a knife in the ribs." Watkins paused, lighting another cigarette from the stub of the one he was holding, then jabbing it into the ashtray." One thing I would say. We had some words with the French Gendarmes after the body was discovered. They said it was usually women who were strangled by jealous lovers or husbands. So Braintree is a definite outlier as far as I am concerned."

McGill nodded, turning over possibilities in his mind. " From the reports, sir, it would appear he was carefully laid out – there was no sign of a struggle and the blankets had been pulled over him. That suggests to me that either the murderer made a really good job of tidying up – or the murdered man was already unconscious when he was strangled. According to the autopsy, he didn't have any other contusions that could have knocked him out. I'd like to speak to the pathologist if that's possible."

Watkins grimaced. " It was one of our doctors here in Amiens."

" You mean, not a professional pathologist?"

Watkins shook his head. " There didn't seem any point. The marks on the neck clearly indicated strangling." He leafed through the file on the murder and produced a short form. " Here – it plainly says, death by strangling. I don't think an actual autopsy was performed."

McGill shook his head. " Major, we need to know more about that body. Where is it now?"

" It's in the morgue nearby. "

" Can I speak to the doctor who signed the certificate?"

" I'm not sure where he is now . But give me an hour or two and I can find out." McGill left Watkin's office and made his way outside. It was cold and dull, but at least there was no cigarette smoke.

After a few minutes Thorn appeared clutching two mugs of sweet tea. He handed one to McGill without a word, then took a cautious swig of the steaming brew. As he licked his lips, staring along the road, he said " I don't envy you going to Albert". McGill turned to face him.

" Is it so bad?"

"They say there's nothing left of the town and they are all living in cellars and dungeons. It's only used because there is some sort of road system behind the town which can move men along the front. Bloody dangerous place though." McGill sighed.

" I need to be sure who it is before I go very much further. The two men will have had different connections and mates, and unless I can be sure who it is, I'm unlikely to find out who the murderer is."

Thorn nodded. " Yes I suppose you're right." The men stood quietly drinking their tea as soldiers came and went through the doors beside them. Thorn saluted smartly at any officer, whilst McGill brooded on what he was planning to do. Eventually they went back inside and found a bench to sit on. McGill turned to Thorn. " Shouldn't you be going back to your regular work?" Thorn grinned.

"Not if I can help it! I just do the charge sheets for the men they bring in overnight."

McGill frowned. " So why did Watkins give you to me? You've nothing to do with investigation" Thorn laughed. " I'd say it could be one of two things. One – he thinks I'm useless and you wouldn't find out anything so it didn't matter. And two – he knows I'm called the Ferret, because I ferret about to try to get the boys off the charges. So maybe – just maybe – he was trying to be helpful. That, of course, and the fact that nobody knows all those bloody files as well as I do." McGill raised his eyebrows.

" You think he wanted me to fail or he really, really wanted me to succeed?" Thorn nodded.

" Failure would suit him – Scotland Yard couldn't find out so you can't blame us. On the other hand, if one of US helped YOU to the right conclusion – well, you wouldn't have done it without our help. Sneaky, eh?" McGill snorted.

" I can see this lot are as much involved with politics as the Yard. Heaven help us!"

"Oh no, sir. Heaven help YOU!" They both laughed and fell silent again.

Shortly thereafter Watkins' sergeant found them and took them back to the smoke filled office. Watkins was busy with some papers he was signing and looked up as they entered.

"You're in luck! That doctor is just close to where Ralston's troop are going when they get pulled out of the line – Ville sur Ancre."

"So he's close to Albert then?"

"Yes only about 4 miles. His name's Captain Peter Binning. Young chap, not long out of training, as I recall. I've done letters of introduction to him and Ralston's troop – to their CO's of course. Travel passes and laissez passer as well. If there's anything else you need ask for my opposite number at Albert – Major John Humphrey. There's a letter here for him – you'll likely need him to get you somewhere to stay. I'm not sure that there IS anywhere to stay as such – I think it's still pretty much front line, but without the trenches. It's well within Hun artillery range so keep your head down." That certainly seemed to be the main preoccupation in France thought McGill

He took all the papers and leafed through them, ticking off in his mind what he would need to do and what he wanted. He looked up to see Watkins eyeing him.

"Thank you sir, that's extremely helpful." Watkins grunted.

"Don't thank me, I've got the ruddy top brass after me to get something finalised – and frankly you're my best bet. Thorn! Take the Inspector to the train and see him settled – then double back here and get on with your work. There's a backlog already."

McGill leant across the desk and extended his hand. Watkins looked a little surprised but stood and shook it firmly. "Best of luck" he said.

As they were about to leave the building, McGill stopped, and Thorn turned to him.

"Where's that morgue your Major was talking about?"

Thorn led the two of them round the side of the building and into a back entry hall. There was a large stairway leading down to the basement. Underground, heavy double doors stood ajar, with guards checking papers. There was a distinct chill. McGill produced his laissez passer, and the guard waved them through.

A harried man in a white coat, clutching more papers, made to pass them but McGill placed a hand on his arm and asked to see the body of the strangled man. With an annoyed grimace, the orderly led the pair down a passage and through some more doors. Once inside he shut the doors. The temperature was much colder here. There were large metal boxes stacked on trestle tables. From what McGill could see, there was only one box that was occupied.

" Not many customers, " he remarked.

The orderly shook his head. " No, this is the police morgue – so only murdered or unexplained bodies are here. Getting blown up doesn't qualify you."

The orderly removed a metal lid, and McGill saw the young man he had been looking for. I wonder if you are Braintree or Ralston, he thought. The smell was making Thorn gag, but McGill was used to it. He carefully inspected the body, then stood back a yard or so to look at the whole cadaver once more. What a strange look on his face, thought McGill. Almost a smile, a happy look.

McGill nodded to the orderly, and he and Thorn made their way back along the passageway and up the stairs. The temperature rose as they ascended. Thorn led McGill out onto the road and the pair set off towards the railway station. The whole town was heaving with men in uniform. Some were grim and scowling, others were laughing and happy.

" Not hard to tell which way they are going, " said Thorn. McGill grunted. When they reached the station Thorn took McGill to the Movements Office to see the Colonel in charge, a Colonel Bramlees. Thorn explained who McGill was, and Bramlees looked him up and down.

" So you're the chap who found out who the murdered man was. Sharp work. I hear Thorn here was a great help." McGill smiled to himself. Politics! And clearly the rumour mill had been at work, too.

" Yes sir, he was a great help. I hope to be more certain of the dead man's identity once I get back from Albert."

Bramlees looked at him. " I think IF would be better, " he said softly, then shook himself. " Still, what you need now is a train.

There's one in about half an hour. Corporal, see him aboard will you?"

Thorn saluted smartly, then did an about turn and headed out of the office. McGill thanked the Colonel, and followed him. At the door, McGill heard Bramlees speaking to him. " Well done Sergeant. Good work." Praise! Almost unheard of. He turned back to Bramlees. " Actually, sir, it's Inspector now." Bramlees eyebrows shot up. " Well, well – promotion in the field. Well done!"

McGill and Thorn made their way through the massed khaki figures, seemingly all converging on one extremely long train with engines at the front and back. Thorn pushed his way to one of the carriages reserved for officers, and bundled McGill inside. There were already six junior officers there, all very drunk and red in the face. McGill bent down out of the compartment and shook hands with Thorn. " Thanks for everything." Thorn nodded and turned away. McGill edged himself into a corner.

Chapter 6

He wondered why the soldiers were quite so drunk and yet quiet. He glanced around, but within minutes they were all fast asleep and snoring. He leant his head against the corner, shut his eyes, and tried to sleep as the train chugged and rattled slowly across the landscape.

He was awoken by the train coming to a jolting stop. As he opened his eyes he saw a couple of the young officers had also been awoken. They were looking around in a dazed manner, McGill supposed because of the drink. One of them put his head in his hands and shook. Looking out of the window, McGill could see they were still in the countryside, but a countryside he had never seen before. There were ruined farmhouses and churned up fields with men sitting in groups smoking. There were twisted pieces of metal scattered about and overall a smell of cordite.

As he looked, he saw flashes towards the horizon and then heard a muted roar as it washed over the train. Despite the noise not being that loud, all the other officers in the train woke with a start and looked around in great agitation. As it sunk in they were still in a railway carriage, they calmed down, but McGill saw their hands all shook slightly as they lit cigarettes, one after the other. No one offered any other a light. Each lit his own cigarette, hiding the flame, then put out the match before dropping it on the floor. None of them looked at any of the others or McGill. With another jolt the train set off again, crawling slowly along. The bangs and crashes slowly grew in volume. The view from the window worsened as they moved forward, passing shattered artillery and struggling horses and mules, cursed by their handlers.

McGill couldn't understand why they were not all on a train across the muddy terrain. The soldier sitting beside him was balefully looking out of the window as well. As he took a deep drag on his cigarette, he shook his head and muttered to himself. McGill turned to him.

" What did you say?"

" I said those poor buggers are where the reserves are kept. They're supposed to use the time as R&R."

" But they're just in a field!"

" Bloody sight better than in the line though." The two of them stared out of the window. McGill glanced at the others in the compartment. They were all nodding their heads in agreement, sucking quietly at their cigarettes.

Slowly the train started to pass more ruined houses. Behind them McGill could see what passed for roads that were full of craters and potholes, filled with oozing mud. Carts and artillery pieces were stuck here and there. By now the noise of the guns was all around them, and the others in the compartment were wincing and cringing as each explosion rattled the windows of the train.

" Not far now," muttered McGill's companion. " Better put your helmet on"

" I don't have one."

The soldier looked at McGill properly. " So what are you?"

" I'm a detective from Scotland Yard. I've been sent to solve a murder." The young officer looked at McGill as if he were mad, then burst out laughing.

" Which one?" he guffawed. McGill noticed the others were grinning openly.

" I can see the humour in it right enough. Had I better get a tin hat then?" The man guffawed again.

" If you want to last more than five minutes, yes, you'd better. When we get off the train stick beside me and I'll get you one."

A few more minutes and many more shudders finally brought the train into a siding of sorts. Whistles were being blown, yelling and doors were clanging open. McGill's companion flung open the door and jumped down, yelling at McGill as he did so " Come on!" McGill found himself already surrounded by a surging crowd, and it was all he could do to keep in touch with the lieutenant. As the human tide poured along the siding and out onto an open space, McGill saw there were little or no buildings standing around what passed for a station. The train they had arrived on was already being loaded up with more men going in the opposite direction. Glancing up, he saw the crazily leaning Madonna that he had heard about.

Rumour had it that whichever side knocked it down would lose the war. From what McGill could see round about him there was no chance of anyone winning anything.

Suddenly the crush relented and the men round him were starting to form into ranks, pushed and shouted at by sergeants and redcaps. A shell exploded above them to the right, and everyone threw themselves flat in the mud. McGill had only crouched down, but felt himself being pulled onto the ground amidst the dirt. His companion shouted in his ear to keep his head down. Another shell exploded, off to the left this time, and McGill felt the force of the explosion drive him further into the mud, his nose filling with ooze as his face slammed into the ground in front of him. Whistles were sounding and sergeants were kicking men all around him. Reluctantly some men rose to a crouch and headed towards a new shell hole that had appeared. The lieutenant grabbed McGill and shouted to him to follow. McGill felt the mud trying to claim him but he struggled free and followed the fast disappearing lieutenant.

More shells exploded, knocking McGill one way then the other. He could see what looked like a hole in a mountain of sandbags ahead of him, where the lieutenant had disappeared. McGill was running towards it now, but suddenly felt himself lifted in the air and slammed into the side of the sandbags. His head reeled and his breath was punched out of him as he slid to the ground again. He suddenly felt hands lifting him and throwing him through the doorway as he gasped and tried to get air into his empty lungs. As he felt himself slipping into a dark abyss, he vaguely saw the outline of a Captain dragging him along the ground away from the entrance to the dugout as more and more men piled into the space.

When he came too it was eerily quiet. Men were leaning against walls running with water, helmets tilted back. McGill groaned, sat up and looked around him. His train companion was beside him, quietly smoking. He glanced at McGill.

" Awake are we? Nice of the Hun to lay on a reception committee for you." McGill shook his head and winced as pain shot through his brain.

" Is it always like that? Who dragged me in here?"

The lieutenant shrugged." It's certainly like that several times every day. They spot the trains coming in and bombard us." He took another drag on his cigarette. " I've no idea who it was got you in here – some Captain I think."

" So why don't they let you get off the train further back?" The lieutenant laughed.

" You'd never get anyone to the front if they did that! You saw what it was like from the train. At least this way they get a mass of men within an hour or so's marching to the trenches."

McGill shook his head again despite the pain." Insane!"

" You're telling me. This whole thing is just insane."

"So how do you know where to go and what to do after something like this?"

" That's easy. The minute the all clear is sounded we'll all be formed up and marched off !" With that whistles sounded and the mass of mud covered trolls lumbered to its collective feet and headed out the way they had come in. McGill tried to stand but found his legs buckling under him. His companion helped him up. He looked McGill up and down from front and back.

" Well, you're the lucky one! Not a scratch. Who are you anyway?"

" My name's Alan McGill. And you?"

" Jimmy Sumpter. Suffolk regiment." Sumpter extended his hand and somewhat unsteadily McGill shook it.

" We'd better get moving – and we better get you a helmet!" McGill reached to his head and found his hat had gone. He grimaced.

" I've lost my hat." Sumpter laughed.

" Thank the Lord that's all you lost! Come on, we'll get you a helmet."

They trailed out of the dugout, McGill leaning on Sumpter and emerged to find that darkness had fallen. There were screams and sobs all around. The whole area was in darkness with the odd torch shining here and there. There were some bodies already being taken up and put onto carts to be taken away, and others were being treated for wounds of differing sorts. Sumpter moved through the crowds, seemingly looking for something, then suddenly quickened his step, bent down and lifted a helmet triumphantly. He slapped it onto

McGill's head, grinning widely. "There you go. Told you we'd get you one."

" So why did it's owner just leave it there?" Sumpter stopped and looked straight at McGill. He shrugged.

" Because he's dead." So saying, Sumpter turned forward again and the pair made their way into the centre of what passed for the town of Albert.

In front of the church with it's crazily leaning statue, was another hole surrounded by masses of sandbags. McGill suddenly stopped. "My bag!"

Sumpter grunted. " That's long gone too, mate."

" But it's not mine!" Sumpter laughed bitterly.

"Well, you can tell whoever it belongs to it died for a good cause."

By now they were at the entrance between the sandbags, where several guards with fixed bayonets barred the way.

" Gentleman from London to see the C.O.," said Sumpter.

" Papers." McGill rummaged in his coat pocket and produced all he had. The guard looked at them, then at McGill, and without looking round shouted " Major!"

A short heavily coated Major appeared, his moustache bristling. He looked as if he had just arrived, perfectly turned out and new to the battlefield. McGill noted none of these men were muddy or particularly dirty like the troops filing through the square. The guard handed the Major McGill's papers without shifting his gaze from McGill. The Major eyed McGill sourly.

" You might have tidied yourself up before coming here."

McGill suddenly remembered the mud and his face pressed into it. His hand flew to his cheek and came away filthy. The Major had turned away and the guard drew back his rifle to allow McGill to pass. Sumpter gave McGill his hand.

" Good luck mate. I'm off to re-join my unit." They shook hands and McGill mumbled his thanks. Another moment and Sumpter disappeared into the crowd that seemed all encompassing. McGill followed the Major down some steps that were poorly lit but at least had some light. They walked along a tunnel only about ten feet wide, which slowly went deeper underground, with doors on either side.

Every now and again it was interspersed with recesses that contained soldiers all sitting around bored. After some minutes the corridor widened out and a large metal door stood ajar in front of them. The Major pulled it wider, then entered. McGill followed and found himself in a room with officers, wireless operators and others all going about their business. The Major marched up to a tall Colonel bending over a map with two other Majors and a second, smaller, Colonel pointing out various features. The group looked up, then resumed studying the map. With a sigh, the taller Colonel stood up as far as the low ceiling would allow.

" Yes, Humphrey, what is it?" The Major saluted smartly.

" Sir – this is the detective HQ told us about." The Colonel looked at McGill then extended his hand.

" Colonel Matthews," he said. McGill shook the proffered hand.

" Inspector McGill, Scotland Yard," said McGill stiffly.

Matthews waved his other hand, pointing towards a couple of wooden chairs that stood beside the far wall. There was a small table between them. Almost like a pub, thought McGill.

Sighing once more, Matthews sank onto one of the chairs, motioning McGill to take the other. Once seated, McGill bethought himself of his muddy appearance and pulled his handkerchief out of his pocket. He started to rub at the mud that had caked onto his face. Matthews watched him silently. After a minute or so, he spoke. "Well, what are you doing here?"

McGill stopped rubbing his face, and stared at the Colonel.

" You mean you don't know?"

" Oh I know all right. You're here to cover the redcaps backsides with HQ. What I want to know is exactly what you are going to do *here.*"

McGill collected his thoughts for a moment." I've two things I want to do. One is interview a doctor, Captain Binning, who performed an autopsy on the murdered man in Amiens."

" And the other?"

" I want to interview a section of troops who were being moved out of the line a few days before he was murdered."

The Colonel looked coolly at McGill. " Have you any idea where they are?"

" Both would appear to be at Ville-sur-Ancre, about 4 miles from here, I believe. The section are in reserve, I think, and the doctor is operating on casualties before they get shipped back to Etaples." Matthews nodded.

" You'll have to walk it. You came through it on your way here in the train"

" I didn't notice any village, sir" Matthews laughed.

" No, I don't suppose you did. The Huns and ourselves have pretty much blown it to smithereens. You'll need a guide. Stay here tonight and I'll get someone to take you there in the morning."

" Thank you sir – I appreciate that." Raising his voice, but keeping his eyes on McGill, the Colonel said " Humphrey"

The Major appeared at Matthews elbow, saluting as he did so.

" Take the Inspector here and find him a bed for the night. Get him cleaned up and then bring him to me for dinner." Humphrey saluted again, and took a step back to allow McGill to rise and thank the Colonel.

Matthews waved his hand again. " Oh, think nothing of it. We don't get many visitors up here. See you at eight." Matthews stood and walked back to the table where the group were still discussing features on a map.

McGill followed Humphrey back through the metal door, and first left into what passed for a dormitory. There were about twenty camp beds around the walls with just a foot or two either side. A small cupboard stood beside each bed. The beds were immaculately made up and smartly turned down. McGill was taken aback. Humphrey sensed his surprise and pointed to one of the beds. " That's yours. I'll assign you a batman for the night. He'll bring you some water to wash in. Give him your clothes and he'll brush them up a bit." Humphrey turned to leave, turned back again, eyeing McGill suspiciously.

"Your papers didn't say you were an Inspector."

" I wasn't when they were written – but I am now." Humphrey stared straight at him, then turned away, nodding." Very good. I'll call for you in a couple of hours." He shut the door behind him.

McGill had hardly taken off his mud-caked coat when an elderly corporal appeared and saluted.

"Jones, sir. Here to get you fettled."

McGill felt somewhat strange having another man cleaning up after him. He sighed inwardly. It would all change when he got back to London.

" Thank you Jones. I need water and a towel, and I'm be obliged if you'd give these clothes a bit of a clean up." Jones looked at the muddy mess that was McGill's coat and trousers. The jacket was only tashed around the collar, as was his shirt.

" Better get that lot off sir, and I'll see what I can do."

McGill stripped, retaining his undergarments and shivering slightly as the damp and cold hit him. He reached down and took the blanket off his bed and wrapped it around himself. He handed the soiled clothes to Jones, who took them and disappeared.

McGill sat down on the bed and stared around the dormitory. Was this how the soldiers lived? Shot at, shouted at, crammed together, covered in filth? How could anyone give of their best when it was like this?

Jones reappeared clutching a bowl and a ewer filled with tepid water. A bar of carbolic soap and a towel made up the rest of his burden. McGill rose to his feet, staggering slightly.

Jones eyed him. " Did you get caught in that last barrage sir?"

"Yes I did. Lost my hat and bag. At least I ended up with a helmet", he said pointing at the muddy tin hat. Jones nodded.

"Much more use sir. I'll get you a tot to steady the nerves and a razor. I'll see if I can find a comb too. I daresay you'll want those in the morning." McGill nodded his thanks and set to washing himself. There was a small mirror on one of the tables and he checked that he had got all the mud off his face and out of his hair. He took off his vest and rubbed himself down. Just as he was putting his vest back on, Jones reappeared with shaving kit and a comb. In his other hand he held a tin mug. He laid them on the table nearest the door and disappeared again. McGill picked up the mug and looked in it. There was a dull dark fluid looking back at him. He sniffed. It was rum. He knocked it back in one.

He looked at his face in the mirror again. His bright blue eyes looked back, tired but reasonably clear. He decided he didn't need to shave for the evening. He combed his dark hair, then lay down on the bed and pulled the blanket over himself. He lay there thinking of the barrage and wondering how many had died without even getting to fire a shot in anger. He shook his head, and dozed

Almost before he knew it, he was being shaken by Jones.

" Time to get up sir. Dinner's in fifteen minutes. I've done what I can with your clothes, but I'm going to have another go at the coat if I can get it a bit less damp."

McGill sat up and was astonished to see what looked like a clean shirt and trousers, as well as a pristine jacket.

" That's amazing! How did you do that?" Jones tapped the side of his nose with a slight smirk.

" Tricks of the batman's trade sir. I was a gentleman's gentleman before this lot kicked off. I'll be back in ten minutes to take you along to the mess. The Colonel doesn't like his dinner to be late." Jones disappeared and McGill hurriedly put his now clean if a trifle damp clothes on once more. He combed his hair again, and straightened himself out.

By the time he had finished, Jones was back and eyeing him with a professional eye. He nodded.

" You'll do sir – this way."

The pair made their way along the tunnel to just beside the big metal door that protected the nerve centre of the whole operation. Jones turned sharp left and walked down another badly lit tunnel before arriving at double doors, which he opened and stood back.

McGill could hardly believe his eyes. There was a long table with silver all over it, twinkling in the light from dozens of candles. A small group of officers stood at one end drinking from glasses and chatting as if this was the most normal thing in the world. McGill turned and looked askance at Jones, who shrugged. " Mess night. Happens once a month. Otherwise they just sit down and eat."

Jones shut the door and McGill turned back towards the group. He spotted Matthews chatting to Major Humphrey, and made his way towards the pair. As he came towards them, Humphrey nodded in his direction and Matthews turned to greet him.

" Inspector! Thank you for coming. Care for a sherry?" McGill nodded without expression. Matthews reached a hand out and a white jacketed servant put a glass into it. Almost without a hesitation, the arm bent and the glass appeared immediately in front of McGill, who by now was feeling distinctly out of place and very unsure of what was expected of him. He took the glass and mumbled his thanks.

" So," said Matthews." You're here to interview some witnesses. Very thorough of you I must say. I had heard you found out who the murdered man was. Sharp work!" McGill took a sip of his sherry and instantly decided if he was ever in a position to be offering other people a drink it would be something else. I wonder how he found out about that so quickly, he thought.

McGill cleared his throat. " Yes, sir, I had a lot of help from a Corporal Thorn. I'm not one hundred percent sure yet, which is why I want to do the interviews, and I need to know about the autopsy, but, yes, I'm pretty sure I know who it was." Matthews nodded and took a small sip of his sherry.

" Can't see it makes much difference. Whoever he was he'll have been listed as missing or dead anyway by now."

" That's true sir, but being a policeman I deal with just one murder at a time." Matthews looked sharply at him, and Humphrey harrumphed. There was a small silent pause. It appeared that despite talking to each other, the other officers had been listening to what was being said by their CO. Oh God, thought McGill. That's torn it. Matthews took another sip, then a smile started to play about his lips.

" Touche! I know Sir Douglas is very keen that this gets properly investigated. Sounds to me as if somehow we've been sent a copper who will do his job properly!" The almost visible tension about him eased off and there were even some smiles and chuckles from the other officers. The doors were opened again, and two white jacketed staff appeared clutching enormous steaming silver tureens. More staff came in behind them and stood, one behind each chair. " Ah, dinner," said Matthews." Been looking forward to that all day! Inspector, would you be so kind as to sit beside me?" McGill nodded and surreptitiously put his glass with the remains of the sherry onto a side table.

The tureens held a brown soup, which turned out to be a sort of oxtail, if a bit thin. Wine was served. Grace was said. Napkins were shaken out and conversation started up again.

" Sir, if I might ask…"
" Yes Inspector."

"Well, all this silver and glass and so on. Presumably it all had to get here on one of the trains."

" Indeed it did. I don't know how much you know about the army, but this is our regimental silver. By tradition it's always in use on Mess nights. In every campaign we've fought, Mess nights have continued without a break. Some damn Hun war isn't going to ruin something like that."

McGill nodded. Matthews went on. " This is the sort of thing we're really fighting for – though God knows after this lot's over I can't see anything being the same again. Too many dead, too much destroyed. It's not like previous wars where the actual fighting was fairly localised, and people at home hardly knew what was happening. The front here is nearly 500 miles long. Every sinew of every worker back home is engaged on war work. Even women are working in factories, on buses and trams. Everything and everyone must bend towards the total effort needed to defeat the Hun. We're only a small part of it up here at the sharp end."

" I see what you mean, sir. Standards." It was Matthews turn to nod.

" Indeed. Without them we'd be no better than the Germans who raped nuns and invaded Belgium."

By now the second course was being brought in. It was a sort of stew, with potatoes and cabbage.

" So where does all this come from?" asked McGill.

" Gets brought up specially. The cook does his best but the stuff we get is frequently not very good."

" And it's cooked down here?"

"Oh, yes. We have our own cookhouse just along the corridor."

"Amazing!"

" Not really. It's all pretty primitive, but at the end of the day we need to be able to get out pretty damn quick. If the Hun decided to make a concerted attack, we'd have to be out of here in a couple of hours. So no point being too fussy." McGill goggled at the silver and couldn't help but think that if this was primitive, he was a Dutchman.

After dinner was over, the King was toasted, cigars were lit and port passed. The atmosphere turned more friendly as the alcohol did its work, and McGill found himself liking the Colonel more and more. Before the war he'd been a solicitor in London who drilled with troops out on the

Heath. When war started he'd presented himself at the War Office and was immediately made up from captain to Major. Matthews opined that he was quite lucky because it meant he didn't actually end up in the trenches, only Captains and below being sent to die immediately. As a Major he became an ADC to a Colonel at Dover Castle, in charge of making sure the ships bound for France were loaded and unloaded quickly. After two years doing that he was shipped out to take over at Albert as a Colonel.

" Extraordinary really – must have done a half-decent job. I don't know anything about fighting and so on. It's mostly making sure the men get shipped in and out as efficiently as possible, and the shells and bullets get to where they're needed. I suppose without that we'd end up on the losing side pretty rapidly."

" Usual story, I suppose sir. Your legal training is completely un-used, and you just have to get on with it."

" Too true! At least when I get back to civvy street I'll be able to run my office properly!"

By now some of the other officers were just sitting quietly. Matthews looked around, then stood up.

" Gentlemen – the toast is – The Regiment!" All stood and finished off their glasses, then turned them upside down on the table. A heartbeat behind, McGill did the same. Matthews turned to him and grinned. " Well done! I expect you'll want to get your head down now. I'll send someone along in the morning to take you to Ville-sur-Ancre –" and he shook McGill's hand before leading the way out of the Mess.

By the time McGill made his way back to his dormitory, the lights had been dimmed and most of the camp-beds were occupied. Quietly McGill undressed and got under his blanket. What a carry on, he thought.

Chapter 7

The next morning he was awoken by the sounds of bodies moving round about him. The lights were still dimmed but he could see men shaving and dressing. He felt for his watch, which he had left in his boot the night before. Six o'clock. He flopped back, staring up at the low ceiling. Suddenly Jones was beside him holding a jug.

" Rise and shine sir. The Colonel has detailed Gunner Crowell to guide you to the rest and recreation area. He'll be ready to take you after breakfast."

" Where do I get that?"

"I'll take you to the cookhouse door. You won't have a mess tin or a mug, so I'll get you one. I'll be back in fifteen minutes." Jones put the jug on the table beside McGill's bed and disappeared.

McGill groaned but threw back the covers. He sat on the edge of the bed and scratched. A passing soldier grinned at him. " That's the lice!" McGill stopped scratching and pulled off his vest. He brushed away some little black specks he saw, then pulled off his pants and tried to do the same for his lower half. He shook out his underwear then gingerly put it back on. Shuddering, he quickly shaved with the borrowed kit, and pulled the rest of his clothes on.

By the time he had finished Jones was back, brandishing a mug and a flat tin bowl. Silently they made their way along the corridor which was now full of men forming up getting ready to leave the safety of the tunnels and make their way outside. At the cookhouse there was a serving area where cooks ladled out what might have been porridge and poured tea with sweet milk into the mug. Jones handed McGill a spoon. He juggled a bit until Jones took the mug from him. McGill took a small mouthful and decided it wasn't as bad as it looked.

" Not eating Corporal?"

" Had mine nearly an hour ago, sir. You better get a move on, Crowie'll be here in minute."

McGill spooned the rest of the porridge down, then drank his tea. As he did so, he suddenly stopped.

Jones grinned." No bromide sir – not down here!" McGill finished the mug. He pulled on his coat and picked up his helmet, and walked into the tunnel.

A young ferret faced gunner was coming towards him. Jones pointed at him " That's Crowie, sir. Brilliant guide. Used to be a poacher in Lincolnshire!" Jones came to attention and saluted. "Maybe see you later, sir." Crowell saluted offhandedly. McGill noticed he was not neatly turned out, with all his buttons dull, his uniform mud spattered.

" Good morning, Crowell. I take it we have to walk to Ville-sur-Ancre?" Crowell nodded. In his flat east of England accent he rolled out his reply "Yessir, goin' take us 'bout toonarf hours I reckons – each way. Best get goin'".

Crowell turned and made his way back towards the entrance, climbing the slight slope at a leisurely pace. As they approached the steps, McGill started to hear the rumble and crash of artillery. He also noticed that the temperature dropped as he climbed the stairs. There were others behind them, heading for above ground. By the time he got outside the cold was biting, and the guns sounded much closer.

" How far away is that?" he asked.

" 'bout three moile oi'd say. Ours, though." McGill suddenly felt relieved he wasn't about to be blown sideways again.

They emerged into the dark remains of the town, with a slight glimmer coming from the east. The church was in silhouette with its crazily leaning Madonna looking like some sort of hook nose on an ancient face. Crowell pointed at McGill's helmet, then turned in the opposite direction, heading away from the rising sun into what was still a dark and gloomy place. At least it's not raining, thought McGill, as he clamped the helmet onto his head.

Crowell set a fair pace, not fast but not slow either, and at an almost metronomic, steady rate. He seemed able to sense where best to place his feet, never stepping on a shattered brick or into a puddle, whilst McGill was in permanent danger of twisting his ankle or falling flat on his face. Within half a mile, McGill was gasping as the broken roadways gave way to almost permanent mud and rubble.

" How do they get vehicles over this stuff ?" he panted. Crowell glanced behind, but never slackened his pace.

" No veehicles thisum way. All 'orses." After another half mile or so, Crowell cut away from what passed for a road, heading into the churned up mud that passed for a field. There were huge craters every few steps, some with bodies in them, although there appeared to be stretcher-bearers working to remove them. As the sun got properly over the horizon in a narrow slit between it and the lowering clouds, McGill saw that the nightmare landscape stretched as far as he could see. His boots were already wet through and clogged up with mud, he kept slipping and his walking became more and more difficult. In contrast, Crowell appeared to float over the debris and mud. After another half mile, McGill needed to catch his breath, and told Crowell so. Crowell stopped and looked about, then jumped into a shell hole.

Standing above it, McGill looked down. " Why did you do that?"

" You'm never know when one of them buggers goin' to explode." McGill looked about. It was a clear sky with only a muted mumble in the distance of guns and shells exploding.

" What buggers?"

" Them shells what ent exploded yet." McGill stared at the little man.

" How do you mean? Surely they explode when they hit the ground – or in the air beforehand?"

Crowell shook his head. " Nozir. There be hunners of unexploded shells aroun'. Bit of pertection in 'ere." McGill shook his head, but jumped into the muddy puddle beside Crowell. As his feet landed he slipped and landed flat on his back. Crowell smirked. " Need to jump un special ways."

McGill sat up, shaking his hands to clean them a bit. There was suddenly an explosion quite close, and he ducked his head in unison with Crowell. He heard the smack of what sounded like heavy rain spattering on the mud and there was a ping as something smacked off his helmet. Crowell grinned.

"Tol' yerz."

"What if we'd been up there walking?"

" I'd a spotted it – an' we'd a bin movin'." McGill didn't know whether to believe Crowell, but had to admit he'd been right about being in the hole. After five minutes or so, Crowell cocked an eyebrow at McGill who nodded dumbly and they clambered out of the hole. McGill could see people scurrying about like rats some distance away as they set off again through the mire. Within a few minutes McGill was panting again. Crowell stopped and turned to him.

" Don't go fightin' it. Jus' flow with it – an' take toiny steps." Crowell stepped off again, and McGill could see his pace was extremely short, with his feet placed flat on the ground. McGill knew he had been stepping out, his heel going down first and causing all sorts of problems. He took a couple of small steps placing his feet as flat as he could on the uneven surface, and found it much easier. Crowell glanced over his shoulder and nodded.

It took them another hour and a half to get to what passed for the remains of Ville-sur-Ancre. What was left of the buildings clung to the small river. As they approached the village, the number of soldiers lolling about smoking increased dramatically, with khaki tents scattered about. There didn't appear to be any order anywhere, and no one challenged them as they made their way through the rubble towards what appeared to be a slightly larger pile of rubble surrounded by sandbags. There were a couple of soldiers on guard outside the structure, and as McGill and Crowell approached, one of them raised a hand in greeting.

" Ello, Crowie. You 'ere again?"

" Looks like'um."

" Wotcher want?"

" This 'ere gennleman gort business 'ere."

McGill was reaching into his coat for his documents, but the soldier paid no attention.

" Major's over mess tent. Best take 'm there."

Crowell waved his hand and turned aside. McGill shoved his papers back into his pocket and followed.

They straggled past more men, some eating out of tins, heading closer to the river. After a few minutes, McGill could see a larger tent surrounded by a few smaller ones, with steam rising above them. Crowell ignored the queues lined up with mess tins, and headed straight for the table at the back of the tent. As he passed some of the men serving out indeterminate splodges, several of them waved their ladles at him and called out his name. Crowell waved back nonchalantly.

They reached the table where men who were clearly officers were sitting, tucking into what passed for lunch. Crowell threw no salute, which surprised McGill. No one had addressed any officer whilst he had been in France without saluting.

" Gotter gennleman 'ere for yer,sir." A young man looked up from his plate, then looked down again and kept eating.

" Get yourself and the gentleman some grub, Crowie, then join us." McGill made to follow Crowell, but the officer interrupted him.

" Not you – you sit here," he said waving his fork to the area beside him. The man next to him moved away to allow space, and McGill crammed himself in beside the Major.

" I'm..."

"Detective Inspector McGill, come to interview some people. Yes I know. I'm James Ruglan. I pass for being the CO around this dump." He put down his knife and stretched his hand towards McGill. "Pleased to meet you, I suppose." McGill shook it, and Ruglan picked up his knife again.

As if by magic Crowell appeared carrying two tins and eating utensils. He plonked one of the tins and a bent knife and fork in front of McGill, then made to move away.

" Sit down, Crowie. Tell us your news." Two men opposite the Major made space and Crowell squeezed in. He took a mouthful of food, chewed silently for a moment or two and then began to speak.

McGill couldn't really understand what it was all about, but it appeared Crowell was some kind of scout. The Major kept nodding as the information was doled out thoughtfully and carefully, and every now and again flicked his knife at a lieutenant further down the table who was busy scribbling in a notebook. At the flick, he underlined what had just been said. McGill ate his food stolidly. It was far from bad – in fact if he'd been served it in an East End eatery he'd not have been disappointed. It just looked awful. After ten minutes or so, everyone had finished eating and was hanging on Crowell's every word. The Major had by now lit a cigarette after first offering one to McGill, who refused.

Crowell stopped talking and the Major nodded again.

" Well done Crowie, that gives us a pretty fair idea of what's what round about. You'll be taking the Inspector to the unit then back to Albert I take it?" Crowell nodded. " Right – the Doc's out beyond Pall Mall and the troop you want is down beside Covent Garden. " He turned to McGill. " If there's anything else you need, see me after you've done your interviews. I'm sorry our hospitality isn't up to Albert's standards, but cookie gives us a pretty fair shake." He rose, and all the other officers and Crowell did likewise. McGill stood too.

" Yes sir, thank you sir" – and Ruglan was gone, leaving McGill with Crowell. All of them had taken their tins and knives and forks with them. Crowell reached across and took McGill's eating kit. By way of explanation, Crowell muttered " Gotter give it back, " as he wandered towards the servery. McGill followed. His loan repaid, Crowell waved amicably at a few of the people who called out to him, and made his way out into what had turned to rain. Turning his collar up, he set off down the remains of a road, McGill thankful he had something reasonably solid under his feet.

After a walk of ten minutes or so, the pair saw some large tents with red crosses on them. Soldiers had been hailing Crowell as they walked along, all of whom had been acknowledged by a lazy wave of the hand.

" You're well known around here," said McGill. Crowell nodded.

" Alluss in the area – brings 'em noos, like." As they approached the first of the tents, an orderly came out carrying a bucket. He approached a shellhole, and threw the contents in. McGill stopped abruptly and felt his stomach turn over as blood and bits of human anatomy spilled out into the hole. Crowell touched McGill's arm and nodded towards the hole.

" T'aint respectful. But there ain't nowhere else to put 'em". A moment later two more orderlies came out with an unconscious man on a stretcher. They wheeled away towards one of the other tents. A young, haggard, blond haired doctor emerged from the tent, drying his hands on a bloody towel. He hailed Crowell.

" Hello, Crowie. What brings you here?"

" Gennlemun ter see yer," he said, nodding towards McGill.

This was Binning, who had performed the autopsy. He turned to McGill. " You must be the detective I was told was coming for a chat."

" I am, sir. Detective Inspector McGill." Binning nodded and finished drying his hands. He looked dubiously at the towel, then threw it in a large basket that was already overflowing with stained cloths.

"Half these poor sods will die of infections from our ministrations. But what can we do? Come in to my office." Binning laughed bitterly. " Well, my tent anyway." He led the way past several more large tents. McGill could hear the groans and shouts from inside. Once past them, a smaller tent appeared and Binning threw back the flap. Inside, McGill could see very little to start with, his eyes taking time to adjust to the gloom. There was a camp bed, a table and two rickety chairs, as well as a travelling trunk. Binning slumped onto one chair and waved McGill to the other. Crowell hovered just outside the tent's entrance, and reached for a cigarette.

" Well, what do you want to know?" McGill had to concentrate his mind to make his thoughts coherent.

" You performed the autopsy on the murdered man in Amiens?" Binning nodded.

" That's right. It would have been about 36 hours after he was murdered."

" I've read the report, obviously, but I just wanted to fill in a few spaces." Binning looked at him, and shook his head.

" It was a proper autopsy," he said sharply.

" I know that, sir, I've read the report, but I just want to clarify a few things in my mind. You say the time of death was between eight thirty and ten thirty. That would imply he was hardly dead when he was found."

Binning nodded. "That's right."

" And there were no other signs of a struggle or any bruising anywhere?"

" No, not at all. In fact, he looked almost peaceful and happy" McGill stared.

" Happy? Yes I noticed that too."

"You've been to see him? How thorough! Yes, happy. I thought it was strange at the time. You would think someone being strangled would thrash about and try to escape, but there was nothing." He paused. " Apart from a slight bruise on the right hand." McGill thought back to the report he had read.

" That wasn't mentioned." Binning thought for a moment.

" No – no it wasn't. I didn't think it was either relevant or significant. "

" Might he have been striking out at his assailant?" Binning shrugged.

" He could have been. But it was a very slight bruise. At most it would have been a very half-hearted punch. But there was nothing else to indicate any kind of resistance to what was happening to him." McGill nodded, thinking to himself how could he have been happy to be strangled?

" So what about anything else that wasn't in the report?" Binning looked hard at McGill.

"Nothing at all".

McGill chanced it. " Not even the fact he'd had sex before being strangled? That would explain him being happy."

Binning stiffened." I hardly think it relevant, then or now. He'd had sex shortly before he died, yes. And I suppose that could be why he looked happy." McGill grinned to himself. Yes that would do it.

" So, Captain, he was probably naked before he had sex, would you say? And then he was strangled? Might he have fallen asleep and been taken unawares?"

Binning peered towards the roof of the tent, then back at McGill, nodding thoughtfully.

" Yes.Yes I'd say he was naked before he was strangled. Whether he was asleep or not when strangled, I can't say, but he could have been." McGill nodded and stood up. He stretched his hand across to Binning who took it.

" You've been very helpful, Captain. Thank you." Binning sighed.

" I'm just glad the poor bugger died happy." McGill nodded.

" Any reason for calling him a bugger?" Binning recoiled as if slapped, dropping his hand to his side. His eyes widened, but he said nothing. He stared at McGill, who grimly nodded to himself

" Thank you again, Captain. You really have been very helpful." McGill turned and pushed out of the tent where Crowell was still standing, his little eyes darting to and fro.

" Right, Crowie, we'd best be on our way to Covent Garden." They set off away from the tents in a different direction from the one by which they had approached. McGill guessed they were effectively taking two sides of a triangle. Crowell glided along for some distance then stopped and turned to McGill.

" D'you reckon 'e were one o' them? I 'eard what you said." McGill stopped and caught his breath, then nodded.

" Yes, Crowie, I do."

" 'An that there Cap'n knew it all along, didn' 'e?"

" Yes, yes I think he did." Crowell shook his head.

" Loike 'e said, poor bugger." Crowell turned and set off again, McGill trailing behind. After a few minutes they came to a ruined shell of a house, which had twenty or thirty men lounging about. In the way of soldiers everywhere, they were making the best of it. Some makeshift benches had been made by lashing odd bits of wood together, and inside a fire was hissing away in the remains of the hearth. The troops all yelled out to Crowell good humouredly. He waved his lazy wave.

" Wot you doin' 'ere Crowie? On a mission?" And they all laughed. Crowell grinned happily then waved his hand towards McGill.

" Detective 'ere ter talk ter you lot." The men fell silent, all eyes on McGill, staring at him with puzzled frowns. He stepped into what passed for the centre of the room, and looked about. Raising his voice slightly, he spoke.

" I'm Detective Inspector McGill of Scotland Yard. I'm here to interview any of you who were shelled at Albert on the day Lieutenant Ralston disappeared." There were murmurs and the men looked at each other. " I know not all of you were there, and I only want to speak to those that were. So if you *were* there, I'd be much obliged if you could move to this end of house. " He pointed away from the fire. Slowly, men started standing up and moving away from it. McGill watched them. If he didn't know better he'd have said they were a beaten army, slack eyed, listless and dirty. He knew they weren't beaten yet, but he couldn't help thinking they might be. Then what would happen? After a minute or two there were twelve men keeping close together beside the gable end. He turned to face them.

" Thank you for that. I have some questions about the attack as you were leaving Albert. You were about to board a train when the shelling started." Several of the men nodded, then one glanced at his mates, and spoke up.

" That's right, sir. We was just goin' on leave. It were a right to-do. Lots o' dead an' wounded."

" And you were under the command of Lieutenant Ralston, I believe." Again the look around at the nodding heads.

" That's it, sir. Poor bugger must have bought it, 'cos we never seen 'im again."

" I take it you believe he was blown to pieces in the bombardment?" They all nodded.

The spokesman repeated, " Never seen 'im again."

" What happened after the shelling stopped? Did you all just get on the train?"

"Nossir. The track was damaged, and the repair parties had to sort it."

" So how long before you moved off?"

" Not long. 'Bout arf an 'our I reckons." The heads nodded.

" And what did you do while the track was being fixed?"

" There was a roll call and we wus formed up into our sections again."

" So who took the roll call?"

" That were the thing, see, 'cos it should by rights have been the 'tenant. Well, the sergeant anyway, but the 'tenant wus supposed to be in charge. An' he just weren't there." McGill nodded.

" So you didn't see him blown up – you never saw him disappearing?" This time the heads all shook.

" Nosir. 'E just weren't there." McGill thought for a moment.

" Was he with you when the shelling started?" The spokesman hesitated.

" Not as I recall, sir. 'Ed gone to get some papers sorted." McGill began to feel a warm glow inside.

" I see. And had the train you were to get on come in when the shelling started?" Sure of themselves now the heads eagerly nodded.

" Oh yessir. Just the minute train stopped, the shelling started and the lads inside all scrambled to get out." McGill felt warmer and warmer.

" So it was pretty chaotic? You couldn't tell who was who could you?" The soldier grinned.

" Nosir. It were a right mess." McGill was sure now the murdered man was Braintree. Ralston was away from his troop when the shelling started, and the men on the train were leaping out to escape the bombardment. Shrapnel would have been flying about, not to mention bodies being thrown into the air by explosions. Until it was over, everyone would have been pressed hard into the ground as he had been the day before, eyes at least down and probably shut. No one would notice a body under another man as he took the papers. Braintree had seen his chance and taken it. All he would have needed to do was keep away from the troop Ralston had been leading, and that would have been easy in all the chaos. Even then, unless he'd been asked for papers in front of them, they wouldn't have known anything about it. The men's uniforms would have been covered in mud, and insignia would have been covered. With the numbers involved and the danger they all faced, everyone would have been concentrating on getting away.

"Did you like him? Was he a good officer?"

" Oh yessir. He done took good care of us" Heads nodded all around.

" So if he had been able to, you're pretty sure he would have come back to you?"

Again the nodding heads, if anything even more vehemently. McGill was certain Ralston wouldn't have left his men. It had to be Braintree.

" So did you go looking for him when he wasn't there with you?"

" Well, there were no point sir. He just weren't there anymore. Sergeant asked about a bit, but nobody 'ad seen him. The place where he'd gone for the papers were blown up too." McGill nodded again.

" And you never heard any more about him?"

Shaking heads.

" Nosir. 'E were blow'd up. 'E were the third 'tenant we'd had." And that was probably not a bad average, thought McGill. He knew some units had had as many in a month.

" Thank you. I'll be on my way. Good luck." The men happily grinned back and gave the thumbs up.

McGill and Crowell made their way out of the ruined house and started to walk across what had once been fields of grass, but were now just mud with holes dotted about. The odd stick poked into the air, showing where a tree or trees had once stood. Crowell seemed to dance over the earth like a sprite with McGill stumbling and cursing behind. After quarter of an hour or so Crowell stopped and turned to McGill.

" D'you wanner see Major agin'?"

" No," panted McGill." I've got everything I came for." Crowell nodded, then cut off to the right of the line they had been taking. As they walked along, McGill could hear the guns in the distance. As time went by, the noise became louder and he stopped for a moment to listen and to catch his breath. Crowell stopped and reached for his tobacco tin. He quickly made himself a cigarette, and lit it. After a couple of pulls, he took it from his mouth, then pinched the end of his tongue to get a stray bit of tobacco off. He glanced at McGill.

" Yer knows wot 'appened, dun't yer?" McGill nodded, sucking air into his lungs.

" I think so."

" 'Twere another bugger did 'im in weren' it?"

" Yes it was. But I don't know who or why yet." Crowell nodded.

" Yer will though. I sees it in yer." McGill laughed.

" How can you be so sure?"

"'Cos I sees it. An' you cares." Crowell turned away and set off towards the sound of the guns again. McGill followed him a moment later, turning away from the sun that was beginning to break through the clouds behind him. In front all he could see was a gathering dusk and darker clouds looming behind it. Flashes appeared every now and then, eventually followed by a distant boom. McGill trudged on, following Crowell's even pace.

Suddenly Crowell turned and threw himself at McGill, flattening him to the ground.

McGill started to speak but stopped as he heard a rattle of machine guns and saw spouts of mud churning up about them. A tri-plane roared over them, followed by an RFC aircraft. The aircraft were gone almost as soon as they were there. Crowell raised his head and watched them go, then sat up and followed them with his eyes as the German plane peeled off and climbed, desperately trying to get back towards its own lines. As he made the turn, the pursuing 'plane appeared to pounce, and the noise of machine guns came to them again as the tri-plane started to trail smoke, then spiralled into the ground. McGill sat up, thinking to brush himself off, then dropped his hands. He was completely covered in mud again. There was a flash as the 'plane hit the ground and a moment later a muffled crump. Crowell stood up and held out his hand to help McGill stand.

" Thanks Crowie. Why was the Hun shooting at us? We're not much of a target." Crowell smiled crookedly.

" 'Tweren't Germun bullets. Them wus ours. 'E wus shootin' from above, see – darnwards loike." Crowell wiggled his hands, showing the position of the two aircraft. McGill must have looked horrified, and Crowell's smile widened. " Best way ter escape is to fly as low darn as yer can.'E were goin' wrong way though. 'Ad ta turn, see, an' our boy gott'im." Crowell turned and moved off again, McGill shaking his head and trying to understand how things were at the front. Nothing was as it seemed. Crowell looked over his shoulder and grinned. " Kernelled never forgive me if youse end up dead!". McGill snorted, thinking the Colonel would probably be perfectly happy if he did get killed, just not on his patch.

They stopped another couple of times as the dusk started to surround them, jumping into shell-holes for shelter. It was still only late-afternoon, but the lowering clouds were stealing what light there was. The closer they got to Albert, the louder the explosions and the more the flashes from both sides' artillery came to dominate the horizon. As they approached the outskirts, Crowell stopped and looked about, almost sniffing the wind like an animal scenting danger.

" What is it Crowie? " said McGill softly. Crowell shook his head and motioned McGill to silence. Quietly he moved away from the line they had been taking, calling McGill to him with a hand signal. There was a short piece of wall that had somehow survived the war so far, and Crowell dropped down behind it. McGill crouched beside him, his eyes following the direction Crowell was looking. McGill could see nothing until suddenly there was yelling and shots, flashes and cries about a hundred yards ahead. Bullets cracked and snarled about, but they were safe behind the wall. It only lasted a few minutes, the fusillade and shouting ceasing almost as quickly as it had started. Crowell stood up and set off towards where the noise had come from. McGill followed, unsure what had happened. Crowell made an extraordinary noise as he walked, again and again, rather like a bird in pain. After some minutes walk, McGill could see figures ahead of them looking at the ground. As they got closer he could see that there were looking at bodies . As he watched, he saw a pistol raised and fired at one of the bodies. A shout came from the group. " Orl right Crowie, lay off that!" Crowell stopped his noise and he and McGill quickly found themselves in the group.

" Wotcher doin' out 'ere Crowie? 'Sdangerous ."

" This 'ere gent been ter innerview some lads aways out." The troops crowded round, and an officer pushed through, waving a pistol.

" What's going on here!"

"I'm Detective Inspector McGill of Scotland Yard. I've been out to Ville-sur-Ancre to interview some witnesses. Crowell here is the guide I was assigned by Colonel Matthews."

The officer subsided a little, and holstered his pistol." Well you can't go wandering around here – some Hun scouting parties have got behind the lines and everyone is very jumpy. You're liable to get yourself shot!"

McGill waved a hand at the bodies around them. " Presumably that was one of the groups you were after." The officer, a Captain, smiled grimly. " Yes, we got them!"

"Crowell, here, stopped about a couple of hundred yards back, or we'd have been in the middle of it." The Captain looked at Crowell. "Yes, Crowie has a sixth sense about these things. Leads a charmed life, the men say". McGill saw the twitch of a smile on Crowell's face. One of the soldiers spoke up.

"We 'eard Crowie comin' in, sir, givin' that cry of his. Can't miss that anywhere." The Captain nodded. "Yes I heard it too. Horrible noise." Bloody useful, thought McGill. At least anyone on our side would know who was coming in and wouldn't shoot.

"Anyway," said the Captain, "I can't let you wander about just now. You'd better come with us."

"Are you going back into Albert?" asked McGill.

"Not likely! We've got patrols out all round trying to round up these filthy infiltrators. We'll be out all night."

"I don't think that really helps at all. I need to get back to Albert and then Amiens tomorrow."

"Well, I daresay we could take a swing down towards the centre and hand you over to another group to get you back. It'll take a while though. Crowell you take the lead and we'll follow you."

"Where'um we's headin' if not the centre then?" Crowell asked.

"There's another patrol out down near Oxford Circus. Can you find it in the dark?" Crowell looked pityingly at the Captain, then turned and headed away to the right. The troop fell in behind him, with the Captain close at his shoulder. McGill kept as close to Crowell as he could, but the little man was jinking left and right in a random pattern and McGill couldn't read which way to go. After a hundred or so yards, Crowell stopped and waved his hands to either side of him. The other soldiers quickly fanned out, then ducked behind any cover they could find. Crowell was standing absolutely still, McGill and the Captain with him. Suddenly a star shell burst almost directly above them. McGill made to duck but Crowell yelled "Don' move!" Moments later there was a whistling as a shell passed overhead, then Crowell was diving to his left. The Captain and McGill followed, crashing into the soft muddy ground as more shells whistled overhead, but off to their right, then exploding both in the air and where they landed. Crowell, the Captain and McGill were in a shell hole with more than a foot of water in it. The shriek of shrapnel was all around them and the explosions deafened them. The barrage lasted about four minutes, then ceased as abruptly as it had started, with the last of the star shells sputtering out nearby.

" Bugger me!" said the Captain. " Thanks Crowie. We'd have been right under that."

The soldiers were cautiously getting up and making their way towards where McGill was trying to disentangle himself from some odd wire he had picked up. Crowell rummaged in one of his pockets and came up as if by magic with a pair of wire cutters. He leant down to McGill and snipped away the offending wire, which had left tears and rips in McGill's clothes.

When they were all assembled, and the Captain had checked he still had a full complement of men, they set off again, angling left to one side of Albert. Crowell was leading with the Captain and McGill close behind. I'm not going to be too far away from you, me lad, thought McGill. If you can sense the danger like that it just might save my skin. He thought he heard a noise off to one side and immediately felt a prickle down his spine as if he was being watched and whirled round. The soldier behind him pulled up short, nearly jamming his rifle into McGill's stomach.

" Watch it!"

McGill peered into the gloom to the side where he thought he had heard the noise. Could he see someone? He was sure he had heard the noise. Where the enemy patrols shadowing them? Crowell had looked in the direction the noise had come from, but paid it no heed.

After about ten minutes, Crowell gave his weird cry again, and two figures rose out of the murk about sixty yards ahead.

" Wotcher, Crowie. Who you with, then?" Crowell stopped crowing and glided towards them.

" Gennleman detective. Got ter get 'im back to HQ loike."

By now there were only a few yards between the patrol and the two figures.

" We 'ent goin' back t' town 'til dawn, but yer should be fine from here. No bastard Huns this way."

Crowell nodded, then turned to the Captain.

" We'll leave yer then. " So saying he turned back towards Albert and set off at his strange smooth pace. McGill hardly had time to say thank you to the Captain, and hurried after Crowell. After a few minutes he nearly ran into the back of him. Crowell was standing absolutely still, his hands slightly away from his sides, listening intently. McGill knew not to say anything and stood as quietly as he could. Crowell signalled McGill to lie down, then disappeared.

War is a really muddy business, thought McGill. What happens if he doesn't come back? I'll just have to wait here for daylight and hope someone can direct me.

It seemed like an eternity, but at last McGill felt a hand on his shoulder. He wretched his head round to find Crowell grinning down at him.

" All clear now. Couple o' lost krauts needed help on their ways ter hell."

"I thought it was clear this way" said McGill as Crowell helped him up.

" 'Tis now."

It took them nearly another hour and a couple more challenges from sentries, but Crowell's strange cry did the trick each time. They found themselves trudging the last half mile as troops eddied all about them, with the odd shell bursting not that far away. The night was lit up by the flashes of the exploding shells, the fires that had broken out and the torches flashing as officers tried to get their men to where they were supposed to be. When they finally reached the sandbagged entrance, Crowell turned to McGill.

" This is you. G'night." McGill shook Crowell's hand.

" Thanks Crowie. It's been an education!" Crowell's face creased into a thin, tight smile.

" 'Slong as you get thet bugger. Don' hold with that." So saying Crowell turned away and sauntered off.

McGill turned back into the dark hole that would take him into the labyrinth that was Albert HQ. He looked at his watch. It was only 10pm. They'd been walking about the battlefield for nearly fifteen hours. He suddenly felt exhausted and hungry.

As he descended into the depths, officers and men were struggling about him in both directions, no one giving him a second glance despite his filthy, torn clothes. I suppose everyone looks like that around here – apart from the senior officers, thought McGill.

Quite quickly he found himself unsure of which way to turn, and he stopped a large sergeant who was heading past him.

" I'm Detective Inspector McGill of Scotland Yard." The sergeant looked at him.

" I expects you are, even if you looks to be a bit in disguise, like. Who you lookin' for?" McGill didn't actually know, so he asked for the canteen. Without a word, the sergeant led him left, then right and they found themselves beside a big door which was opening and shutting continually. Without a word, the sergeant turned and walked away.

" Thank you!" McGill called after him, as another group came out from behind the doors and made their way along the corridors.

The canteen was as busy as it had been in the morning, with steam rising from enormous pots and sweating chefs. There was a roar of conversation. McGill decided his abiding memory of his time in France would be damp muddy clothes and steaming food. He joined a queue and shuffled forward to the serving table. The chef dipped his ladle into a pot and brought it out, then raised his eyes to look at McGill. The ladle hovered in space.

"Mess tin?" McGill looked at him blankly and then realisation dawned.

" Ah, sorry, don't have one." The chef dropped the ladle back into the slop and hung his head.

" 'Strewth. What I have to put up with." He reached down and came up with an enamel bowl, a mug and a spoon. He shoved them at McGill, then picked up the ladle again. Just before the food hit the bowl he said, " And I want them back when you're finished or you'll be on a charge."

Gratefully, McGill moved along the line. More food was piled into the bowl, and the mug was filled with hot sweet tea right at the end of the table from a clutch of urns. McGill turned and sought a place to sit. There didn't appear to be anywhere, but as he moved between the trestle tables, soldiers got up from odd places and McGill quickly took the first one he came to.

As he sat down, the conversation around him died. He put the bowl and tea down, and shifted the spoon so as to be able to eat. He glanced up at the silent faces staring at him. To his left a mud-spattered Captain turned away and made for the door.

" Evening." He dug the spoon into the pile of food, and started eating. After a couple of mouthfuls of what turned out to be something like corn beef and potatoes, the conversation started slowly about him. As he got to the scrapings in his bowl, the soldier to his right dug him in the ribs.

" You're that detective entja?"

" I am, " said McGill putting his spoon down.

" Got yer man yet?"

" Can't say as I have, but I know a lot more than I did."

" I reckon it was some Frenchie done it. Bloody foreigners."

" It was almost certainly an Englishman."

"Why'd you say that?"

" Because no Frenchman would have had access to the building."

The soldier snorted, and turned away. The English can never trust Johnny Foreigner, thought McGill. He sat for a moment longer then rose and took his borrowed items back to the chef. The man was still busy ladling food into mess tins, and took the items back with a grunt of acknowledgement.

He wandered out into the passageway again and wondered how he was going to get cleaned up and exactly where the bed was he had slept in the night before. He saw a Sergeant reading some papers and asked him about baths and so on. The man looked at him with astonishment.

" No baths here sir. Bowl of hot water if you're lucky. The senior officers have hip-baths, but I wouldn't know how that works." McGill didn't know what to say and felt himself beginning to be drowsy from fatigue and relief at getting back safely.

The Sergeant saw it and took pity on him. " Look, sir, come along with me and we'll see what can be done." Obediently McGill followed as they set off down yet another passage. After a few moments they came to a narrow door. Inside was a sleeping area akin to that which McGill had been in previously. These beds were not pristine like the night before, but all untidy. There were a few beds unoccupied, and the Sergeant pointed." Take that one. It's first come first served down here. I'll see if I can rustle up some water." He turned and left McGill struggling out of his coat. As he flailed about he hit something on his head. With a clatter his helmet fell to the ground, eliciting curses from the other beds. He'd completely forgotten he had it on.

Underneath the coat his clothes were reasonably clean. The worst bits were the bottoms of his trouser legs, and he removed them and laid them on the bed. He thought he should have gone back to see Matthews, but he was just too tired. He took his jacket off then his shirt. A wave of tiredness swept over him and he decided to leave everything until the morning. He stretched out on the bed and pulled the cover up to his chin. Before he knew it he was fast asleep.

When he finally awoke he looked at his filthy clothes. He had no brush or anything to clean the mud off. Looking around he spotted a bowl, presumably left for him the night before. It had some water in it, so he splashed his face and ran his hands through his hair. He started smacking his clothes in an attempt to remove the mud that still clung to them, but gave up after a while, and simply pulled them on. They were still damp from the day before.

Grasping his helmet, he sallied forth into the busy corridors. By luck more than judgement, he came to the mess hall again, and made for the table with the chef who had helped him the day before. The chef looked at him keenly.

" You can't make a habit of this, you know. You need to get your own kit." McGill nodded and a sharp pain lanced through his head. He gasped, but said " I know. I hope to be gone by tomorrow."

" Huh!" The chef reached under the table and handed McGill the same items as he had the night before, then splashed porridge into the bowl. McGill shuffled along and took the tea he was offered. He made for the closest gap, and sat down. Another pain went through his head but he ate his porridge and drank the tea, and felt somewhat refreshed.

He decided he had to see Matthews, and made for what he thought was the main command post. After a couple of wrong turns he reached the outer doors and walked into the room in which he had first met Matthews. There was no sign of him, but other officers were working there and Humphrey looked up as he came in, a frown on his face. It turned to disgust as he saw the mud and the generally unkempt appearance. Humphrey, of course, was immaculate.

" Is Colonel Matthews about?"

" Sorry," said Humphrey. " He's been called to a meeting at HQ. Won't be back until tomorrow." McGill nodded.

"I wanted to report to him but I have some other things I want to do before heading back to Amiens."

" I daresay he'll be back late tonight, but he certainly won't want to see you until the morning. I suggest you get on with your enquiries and report back here tomorrow at this time."

McGill turned and made his way back towards the entrance of the complex. At least there were signs telling you which way it was. Once he got there he jammed his helmet on his head, and went out into the dull day.

As soon as he was outside, the noise assaulted him again. The boom of the guns seemed further away, but he supposed it only meant a different part of the line was under fire. His plan was to visit the station with a view to understanding what had happened and how. As he walked the short distance to what remained of the station, he heard the skirl of bagpipes. Instinctively he straightened his back and started walking with more purpose, swinging his arms. Round the corner came a row of pipers, followed by what looked like a complete regiment of Scots. They were small men, probably from the cities, but all looked wiry and determined. He pulled aside into a doorway, and was joined by a Major, complete with heavy coat turned up against the cold. As the men passed and made for their destination, the Major muttered to himself. " Makes the hair on the back of your neck bristle." McGill nodded. " If they came from Glasgow, I wouldn't want to be the Huns who came across them in the trenches at night."

The Major laughed. " Nor would I!" He looked properly at McGill and was about to upbraid him for his general dirtiness when he noticed he wasn't in uniform. " What are you doing here?" He asked, curiously.

McGill stuck his hand out. "Detective Inspector McGill, of Scotland Yard." The Major shook the hand.

"Major Derek McIntyre. You must be the detective looking into that murder. I hear you're the chap who found out who it was. Well done!" McGill reflected again on the difference between being a constable and an inspector. It was almost as if the elite wouldn't allow anything below them any kind of credit for intelligence or ability. Brown certainly hadn't.

" Thank you."

" What are you up to now?"

"I was just going to have a look at the station." McIntyre grimaced.

" Not much of it left I'm afraid. I'm going that way, I'll walk with you."

The two men fell into step and silently walked towards the end of the street. The station was just to one side of it. When they reached it, McIntyre looked at McGill and asked if he knew who he needed to speak to. " You can't just go wandering about – you're liable to get shot!"

"No, I never thought of that. I just wanted to see where the train had been on the twenty third of October."

McIntyre snorted. " No one's going to know that. Your best bet is just to have a look around. Come – I'll introduce you to the OC and he'll likely give you one of his men to help." McIntyre led the way into the ruins of the station, then turned towards a sandbagged gap that had two guards.

"Major McIntyre and Detective Inspector McGill for Major King" The guards saluted and one of them yelled " SERGEANT". After a moment a bruiser of a man appeared and looked at the two intruders. He saluted the Major. "Come this way please, sir." McIntyre and McGill followed the sergeant down a flight of steps, then left along a short corridor. At the end and set to the side was a heavy wooden door. The sergeant knocked, opened the door and stood back to allow the Major and McGill access.

Inside was stuffed with desks and officers reading or writing on mountains of paperwork. At one end there was a blanket strung across the corner of the room. McIntyre made for this, and twitched it aside.

" Can I come in, Bonar?"

" Derek! How nice to see you! What brings you here?"

McIntyre lifted the curtain fully, and McGill ducked his head, wincing at the pain that hit him, and walked into what was quite a cosy space. McIntyre followed.

At a table sat one of the smallest men McGill had ever laid eyes on. His feet barely touched the ground, and, on further inspection, McGill decided both the table and the chair had been cut down to accommodate his height. King stood up, came round the table and shook McIntyre's hand, then turned to McGill. His head appeared too large for his body, but his eyes were alive and intelligent.

"Well, well, I suppose you are the hero of the hour. You must be the detective."

" Indeed I am, sir."

" And what are you doing with my friend McIntyre here?"

" Well sir, I have a theory as to how the murdered man got to Amiens and I just wanted to have a look around the station area. If you could tell me anything about the trains that were here on the twenty third of October, especially the one that was bombarded, I'd be very grateful."

King laughed. " All I can tell you is it got blown up! You have no idea how little control we actually have over things here."

" I appreciate that sir. But I'm really looking to check on the way things are done after such a bombardment, and how easy it would be to get on a train going back to Amiens."

King settled himself into his mini chair again, and folded his hands on the table in front of him. He shouted " Sergeant!" The man who had brought them to the room popped his head round the corner of the blanket. " Sir."

" Three teas please."

" Sir."

King turned towards McGill." Please take a seat. I can tell you all about that. The first thing that happens is there is a roll call in the sections of each regiment that was on the train. So, for example, we have a list of which regiments are coming up from Amiens and how many men there are in each train. If there's a hiatus, it's the individual sections responsibility to check the roster and report any missing to the officer commanding."

" I see – that makes sense. So what's done to find the missing men?"

King laughed." I can see you haven't been out here very long. If a shell lands anywhere near you there isn't anything to find. We have hundreds who literally disappear into thin air every day. Of course, there are *bits* of them – scattered all over the place. But there isn't actually a body to identify or bury in many cases."

McGill nodded sombrely." So for example a missing lieutenant would be reported to the OC and presumably any papers found would be handed in."

King nodded. " Yes, that would be right. It would be the same for anyone missing."

McGill thought for a moment. " So you have a check on people arriving. What about the other way around. How do you check those leaving?"

" Nobody can get on a train without a specific order and travel warrant. So anyone going back to Amiens would need a leave pass (assuming they were going there on leave) and a warrant to travel on the train. Both would be in their own name. We check the orders and collect the warrants as they file onto the platforms." King chuckled. " Ha! Well we call them platforms but of course now they are just bits of mud beside the tracks! The point is every person who leaves has to leave their travel warrant with us. That's how we track them in and out."

A grin spread across McGill's face. " I don't suppose you have the warrants from the twenty third of October do you?"

King laughed again." As a matter of fact we do. We keep them here for about six weeks then they get shipped off to Amiens. Of course, once they leave here they often get blown up or destroyed, but by that stage it doesn't really matter." McGill slapped his thigh.

" Perfect! Can you let me see them?"

" Of course. Do you need a hand?" The curtain was suddenly lifted and the Sergeant and a corporal came in clutching steaming mugs of tea.

" Ah, perfect timing! Sergeant, Inspector McGill wishes to see the travel warrants for the twenty third of October. Could you ask someone to take him and show him?"

The Sergeant handed King his tea, then took a step back and saluted. " Very good, sir."

The three men fell silent and sipped their tea. McGill wondered idly whether *this* tea had bromide in it, and whether in fact the two mugs he had drunk in the mess did. It would explain the somewhat muzzy feeling he had in his head, he supposed.

After a few minutes the edge of the blanket was raised again. A young lieutenant – my God, thought McGill, he looks about twelve! – poked his head round the corner. " Sergeant said you wanted to see me sir."

" Ah, Miles, do come in. This is Detective Inspector McGill from Scotland Yard. He's investigating that nasty murder in Amiens. He wants to see the travel warrants we collected on the twenty third of October. Could you take him along and give him any assistance he needs?"

" Certainly, sir."

McGill stood up and put his mug down.

" I probably won't see you again, McGill, but I wish you luck. If there's anything I can do just ask."

" Thank you very much, sir. It's been a pleasure."

King looked surprised. McGill explained. " You're the first person I've met since I've been out here who actually seems to know what's going on." King laughed. " It's only a façade!"

McGill shook McIntyre's hand and thanked him for his help. "That was a pleasure too," said McIntyre.

The young lieutenant led the way back along the corridor until they reached a metal door with a heavy bar across it. Miles lifted it and put it to one side. He swung the door open, then reached inside and switched the light on. Rows and rows of racking sprang to life, crammed with boxes and papers.

" My God," said McGill. " How many are there?"

Miles shrugged. "We have up to fifty trains a day going out with up to 1000 men. So at any one time we could have over two million travel warrants here". McGill felt crushed. He would never find what he was looking for amongst all this.

" Is there any kind of filing system?"

"Not really. We can look by day, but thereafter it's just a mass of warrants."

McGill sighed. " I'm going to need some help."

Miles grinned. " That's what I'm here for."

The pair moved off through the racks, looking at the dates. Towards the back of the room, they found a rack marked "23/10/1917". McGill looked balefully at the mass of papers.

" Are they not even in trains or alphabetical order?"

Miles shook his head, then said, " Well I suppose the earliest trains in the day will be at the bottom of the pile." McGill sighed.

" I think all we can do is start at the bottom and at the top and work towards each other."

Miles laughed. " I'll start at the bottom as befits my station!"

They each pulled out a box. McGill was sure his heart was going to drop when he looked inside the box and saw the mess inside, but in fact there were neatly tied bundles of papers. He took one out and saw it would be relatively easy to flick through each bundle to spot the names.

As Miles extracted his first bundle, he looked across at McGill.

" What am I actually looking for, sir?"

" The name Ralston." He paused. " Ralston and Braintree. But mostly Ralston. Both lieutenants."

They set to and after an hour or so of silent page rustling had managed one box each. McGill wiped his brow. He felt hot and shivery, but pulled his second box off the rack and started going through it.

Miles glanced across at him.

" Are you all right, sir? You look unwell."

McGill shook his head. " It's nothing – probably just a cold coming on. I haven't been warm for a week!"

Miles laughed and pulled another box out. There were still another half dozen to get through and at this rate it would take them nearly the rest of the day to check all of them. McGill couldn't see any shortcut. He just wanted confirmation that Ralston – or rather Braintree – had left the area that day.

They ploughed on and at a little after one o'clock they had each done two and a half boxes. McGill shook his head to try to clear it.

" Come on Miles, we need some air – and food!" They made their way out of the room and Miles barred the door again.

As they made their way towards the entrance, McGill noticed the noise rising.

" Bombardment under way sir. Better stay down here for now," said Miles. McGill nodded and they stood leaning against the wall of the tunnel. Miles reached into his jacket pocket and pulled out a tobacco tin. He offered it to McGill, who shook his head. There was an extra loud bang and the tunnel shook, some earth falling down from the roof between the supports.

" We have to dig people out quite often."

" I can imagine. I really wouldn't want to be buried alive." Miles laughed.

"There are more ways to die here than there are prayers for survival!"

After ten minutes or so the explosions in the immediate vicinity stopped and the dull booms moved further away.

" That's it over for now, " said Miles. " We can nip out and get a wad and char."

They walked out into the fresh air. McGill immediately saw that the rubble and earth had been re-distributed by the bombardment. There were men scurrying about helping the injured and stunned to their feet, whilst the less fortunate were stretchered off. He shook his head and searing pain shot through it, making him gasp.

"Are you sure you are all right sir? You look pretty ropey to me."

" I'm fine, I'm fine. Just need some grub."

Miles led them a short distance from the station where an open air canteen was dispensing thick sandwiches and hot sweet tea. They lined up in the queue and shuffled forward. Miles produced his mug and McGill sighed. " I don't have one."

" Not to worry sir, keep my place and I'll get you one."

Miles disappeared and McGill continued to shuffle forward. Even before he got to the chef doling out the sandwiches, Miles was back and handed McGill a somewhat battered mug. He looked at it. " If my helmet's anything to go by, this came off a dead man." Miles nodded. " That's how most of us keep our kit in one piece."

They reached the sandwich area, and were handed a thick example of army catering. McGill opened his sandwich. Spam and margarine. Did the army know how to make any other kind, he wondered? Apart from corned beef. He bit into it but he could hardly taste anything. They reached the tea urns and filled their mugs and moved off out of the way. McGill swigged his tea. It was sweet and hot and at least he could taste it. He wondered about Miles who seemed cheery but so young.

" Been out here long?," he asked.

" About five months, sir. I'm lucky really. I got sent here as soon as I arrived so I've never been in the front line." McGill laughed.

" You don't think this is the front line?" It was Miles' turn to laugh.

"Oh, no, sir, this is WELL behind the front line!" My God thought McGill. What must the front line be like then? They ate in silence for a short while.

" Where are you from, Miles?"

" Warwickshire, sir. My two brothers came out before me. I haven't seen either of them. I know one's relatively nearby but there's no visiting hours! We've exchanged letters though. I hope to see them both next time I have a 48 hour pass."

McGill thought for a moment." You mean they'll have a pass at the same time?"

Miles laughed. " No, I'll find out where they are and go there."

"You'll give up your leave to see them?"

" Of course. We are a very close family."

" I hope you all make it," said McGill fervently. He had no siblings and couldn't imagine that kind of bond.

They finished their meal and headed back to the station. They set to again and within a few minutes Miles gleefully waved a piece of paper in the air. " Ralston!"

McGill reached across and took it. It was Ralston all right – but the wrong one. He sighed and shook his head. As he did so his shoulders and neck hurt. He hunched and then expanded and braced his shoulders.

" You won't believe this, but it's the wrong one. I should have said we are looking for an Owen Ralston." Miles looked crestfallen as McGill handed back the offending warrant. Miserably they started their search again.

Two hours later there were only a couple of boxes left. Wearily they pulled them off the rack and started to rummage.

" Bingo!" McGill turned to Miles to see him waving another warrant. " Lieutenant Owen Ralston!"

McGill eagerly took the paper and read it quickly. Yes, this was what he had wanted. Quickly he got out his notebook and took the details down. Another confirmed fact. He sat back, exhausted.

" Well done Miles. We got what we came for. Any chance of a drink anywhere?"

Miles grinned and reached into another pocket. Out came a hipflask. He popped open the top and handed it to McGill. " Cheers!" McGill took a swig and started coughing.

" Bloody hell! What is that?" Miles laughed as McGill handed the flask back

" My old nanny makes it. Whatever it is, it's about ninety percent proof!" Miles took a cautious sip, then pushed the top back on. McGill was still shaking his head which didn't help in the least.

" Some nanny!"

" Oh yes. She's Scottish from the Islands, I believe, and the moment she came she made it very clear there would be no nonsense from we three boys. We really enjoyed helping her make the still in one of the potting sheds! She had one of the gardeners put a lock on it and blanked out the window. Even when we were quite young she allowed us to have a sip. Needless to say we adore her!"

McGill marvelled at how people lived. A nanny, at least two gardeners and presumably house staff as well. And this boy seemingly oblivious to Death that scythed down those all about him.

They left the store, Miles clanking the bar into place. They made their way out of the tunnel and into the gathering gloom. McGill wasn't sure what his next step was, so he bade Miles farewell who shook his hand with a cheery grin, then sauntered off.

Chapter 8

The station as ever was heaving with soldiers. McGill had no further business there apart from perhaps seeing where the bombardment on the twenty third of October had been. He decided he knew enough about Ralston. What he didn't know was much about Braintree. As he walked along his legs felt heavier and heavier, and his head started to throb, with the occasional stab of pain if he moved it too sharply. He trudged back to the underground bunker complex, the sky lit up with flashes and booms in a never ending display of hate. God, I can't stand much more of this, he thought. How do they cope with it? The guards checked his papers and let him through. He made his way to the canteen. Now that he had a mug he was able to get a tea without recourse to borrowing one. Nursing it in his hands, he set off in search of his billet from the night before.

He opened several doors until he found a room that looked like the one from the previous night. The beds were all unmade with several occupied by exhausted, dirty men. McGill chose an empty one and sat on it. He drank his tea and suddenly felt incredibly tired. He reached down and took off his filthy boots, then lay on the bed, fully clothed.

His sleep was full of dreams of bodies being thrown into the air, and nearly all looking like Braintree. Except of course it wasn't Braintree who had got blown up - it was Ralston. Some of the bodies had undefined faces, as if nobody had bothered to draw them in. Then the dream changed. He was running away from something. Every time he turned to face the threat, there was nothing there – just something a bit like when a stick is pulled out from water. It had been there but it just wasn't there anymore. When he finally awoke he was sweating and shivering. He pulled his boots on and staggered out into the corridor. He made for the canteen and took a tea – he couldn't face any food. He got some very strange looks as he sat hunched over his mug. His teeth chattered and he felt alternately hot and cold. The tea finished, he pulled himself to his feet, ramming his mug into a pocket, and staggered out into the corridor. He made a conscious effort to steady himself, and lurched towards the stairway that would take him into the fresh air.

He wasn't sure why, but he wanted to see where the bombardment had been on the twenty third of October. He made his way unsteadily back towards the station area as the "Morning Hate" crashed and boomed behind him. I would never get used to that, he thought. He trudged on, head down, and was surprised when he found himself pushed aside as a column of infantry marched up from behind the station. He looked dazedly about, and then started to make his way around the remaining buildings.

He heard his name called and turned towards the sound. It was Crowie coming towards him. McGill stood where he had stopped, swaying slightly.

Crowell came up to him, grinning crookedly. His grin disappeared as he looked into McGill's face.

Taking him by the arm, Crowell led McGill to a pile of rubble and sat him down.

" What youm doin' 'ere? Youm ill, man!" McGill groaned.

" I just wanted to see the area where the trains were blown up on the twenty third of October."

Crowell shook his head. " Blouidy fool. Youm in no state to be out 'ere. Youm get yersef killed."

Crowell hauled the much larger man to his feet. My God , he's strong, thought McGill as he let himself be led around and away from the station. After what seemed an eternity, Crowell sat him down on another pile of rubble.

McGill looked about curiously.

" Thism it."

"Where the bombardment was?"

" Yers."

McGill looked again. There were a few twisted rails that had been flung aside. Everywhere there was mud and shell holes filled with water. Some tracks that looked as if they were still in service snaked away into the distance and McGill could see signs of activity on a line half a mile or so away. He stood to get a better look, and nearly fell over as he tried to take a step. Crowell grabbed him and started retracing their steps.

"'Ope youm blouidy saisfoyed. Nothin' there but blouidy mud." McGill groaned and concentrated on putting one foot ahead of another. Once they were back at the remains of the station, Crowell sat McGill down and called to a soldier on guard who disappeared briefly. Moments later, he re-emerged with King beside him.

" Well, well, a sick detective. Crowie, Bickerstone, get him back to HQ and put him to bed. If you'll take my advice, McGill, you'll stay there for a few days." McGill groaned as the two soldiers hefted him onto his feet again and half dragged, half walked him in the direction of the town.

McGill could still hear bangs and crashes of artillery, and every crash and explosion appeared to be going off in his head. The intensity increased. Suddenly McGill noticed there was a growing silence as the three men got into the first part of the dugout, then down the steps and along the first part of the corridor. Crowell kicked open a door which gave onto a dormitory, and the two soldiers sat McGill on a bed. McGill stared stupidly at his feet as Crowell took his boots off. Crowell swung McGill's legs round onto the bed, and gently eased his body backwards until he was lying flat. He pulled the blanket from under McGill and laid it over him.

McGill was already asleep as Crowell and Bickerstone looked at him before turning away.

"Thanks Bicky," said Crowell. "O'id better report to Colonel. Bluddy fool!"

McGill's sleep was desperately troubled and at some point he got up and took his clothes off as he was sweating so much. He pulled the filthy blanket over himself and felt his body cool as pain swirled around inside his head. He shivered and dozed. He felt steadily worse each time he awoke. Desperate for a drink of something he roamed the room until he found a basin with some relatively clean water in it and drank, gagging on the soapiness but relieved at the liquid. He dozed and slept through the rest of that day and the night.

When morning came, McGill pulled on his filthy clothes and staggered out of the room and along the corridor towards the bunker's entrance. As he emerged the guns were still pounding away from both sides and the continuing shocks and crashes made him wince. He had to get back to Amiens, to some sanity so he could think about what he now knew and so he could get better. His mind simply wouldn't work in Albert, and his head felt distinctly woolly and gummed up.

As he came up and into the daylight, the rattle of gun limbers going by, the tramp of marching feet and the shouts of NCOs assaulted his senses, almost making him stagger. The rain of the day before had settled into a straight drizzle. He put out his hand to the nearest pile of rubble which crumbled as he put his weight on it. He crashed into the mud and filth, sending his head spinning. He hauled himself upright and staggered away from the noise of the guns towards the road to the station and out of the remains of the town.

He had only been going a short while when a lorry came up behind him hooting furiously. McGill jumped aside, and found himself nearly up to his knees in stinking mud. By now his head was aching and he laboriously pulled himself out onto the road again. As he did so, a motorbike messenger skidded and slewed towards him. The bike came to a stop beside him.

" You goin' somewhere , mate?" McGill could hardly focus on the rider, as stabbing pains flashed behind his eyes.

"Amiens" panted McGill.

" I'll take you to the rail'ead – hop on." Thanking his lucky stars, McGill straddled the pillion, and clutched the rider's waist.

" Go easy, mate, I ent made of wood!" So saying the rider let the clutch in and the bike chugged off along what remained of the muddy road.

They passed troops marching in both directions, and after about ten minutes, with the bangs and explosions slowly receding, the remains of the station came into view. The rider brought the bike to a stop beside a sergeant who was directing marching men in different directions.

" 'Ere! Sarge! This bloke wants to get to Amiens." McGill managed to get off the bike and stand on both feet, swaying slightly. The sergeant eyed him suspiciously.

" You got papers?" McGill fumbled in his pocket and produced the laissez passer from Watkins. The sergeant took it and looked at it.

" Wot you doin' in Albert then?"

McGill shook his head to try to clear it. He only succeeded in making it hurt more.

" I'm investigating a murder."

The sergeant burst out laughing and the rider grinned.

" Oh, that's a good 'un! There's thousands every day and you've to investigate? Well good for you!" So saying he handed back the paper and pointed to a train that was standing in the sidings.

" Get yourself over there and tell the redcap Sergeant Willis sent you. He'll see you right."

McGill turned to thank the rider, but he had already let his clutch in and was heading away. McGill tentatively raised his hand, but let it drop. It felt too heavy for him to hold up.

Making his way towards the line of redcaps beside the puffing train, McGill felt his limbs grow even more heavy. He had no difficulty being allowed onto the train, but of course there was nowhere to sit, and he was crushed into a corner of a compartment with about fifteen other men. He heard a whistle, felt a jolt, and the train began its journey away from the front. He felt relief that he wouldn't be coming back.

The journey to Amiens was only about twenty miles, but the train took over two hours as it huffed and puffed across the broken land towards its destination. It frequently juddered to a stop for no apparent reason, jerked forward for another few miles, then stopped again. McGill could hardly move or breathe and felt steadily worse as time went on. Just when he thought he would be unable to stand for any longer the train gave one final heave and stopped in Amiens station. When the carriage door was opened, the mass of men flooded out onto the platform. The release of pressure caused McGill to slump down into a seat, panting. No sooner had he recovered somewhat than another group of men started to enter the compartment. McGill struggled to his feet and almost threw himself out of the carriage. He landed on top of two soldiers trying to get in, one of whom punched him on the head, sending him sprawling onto the platform.

" You wanna watch it mate. You could get hurt doing that." McGill looked up to see a burly redcap looking down at him.

" Sorry " mumbled McGill as he staggered to his feet.

" Wot's wrong with you then? " asked the redcap as he gripped McGill by the elbow.

" I'm ill."

" So wot you doin' 'ere then?"

" I'm investigating a murder." The redcap let McGill's elbow go as if it was red hot.

" You'll be that Scotland Yard bloke from London, 'ent ya?" McGill nodded.

The redcap sneered. " Solved it 'ave ya?" McGill shook his head, sending daggers of pain through his brain.

" Not likely to either, from wot I 'ear. Get goin' before I arrest ya."

McGill didn't argue and headed after the streams of men making for the exit.

He staggered out of the station and stopped. The men behind him cannoned into him, swinging him around and ignoring him as they headed off for whatever pleasures awaited them.

His head by now was bursting and he started shivering. He pulled his filthy coat tighter about him and turned the collar up, but the shivering intensified. He took a couple of steps forward, flailing like a drunk, and a lorry narrowly missed him, the driver shouting abuse and blaring his horn. McGill swung back to the side of the road and was pulled along by the hordes as they made for the town centre. Slowly the numbers around him dropped as individuals reached their destinations.

McGill had no clear idea of where he wanted to go, just putting one foot in front of the other. He tried to make his brain work with no success. He needed somewhere to lie down, but couldn't focus properly on the buildings around him. He thought he saw a sign saying " Hotel" across the road and swung towards it as a drowning man will clutch at straws. His legs wouldn't obey him as his body was wracked with huge spasms. He forced one foot to move towards the other side of the road, and gritted his teeth to move the other. Nothing happened and he felt himself unable to stand anymore. As if in slow motion he fell forward into the mud, just as he heard a car screech towards him. A figure loomed over him as a hand felt his forehead before blissful oblivion claimed him.

McGill woke with a raging thirst and a gently throbbing head. The shivering had stopped and he felt better than he remembered. He couldn't hear the far away boom and crash of the heavy guns any more. He no longer wanted to be a soldier – he'd seen too much of what went on, and too much stupidity. The courage and bravery of the fodder in the trenches was beyond his understanding. No wonder the French had mutinied but he marvelled that the British had not.

He had little memory of where he was or what he was doing in a warm bed. Looking about, he saw his clothes were lying carefully folded on a padded chair. They were clean and fresh, and looked as if they had been mended. He looked around the room. Thick curtains were keeping most of the light out, but he could see this was no ordinary billet. He threw back the covers and swung his legs over the side of the bed. The motion made his head spin, and he sat on the edge of the bed for a moment until it stopped. Then he rose and staggered across to the dressing table. There was a ewer and he splashed water from it onto his face. Pulling his clothes on he wondered how had they become clean. And where was he anyway? he staggered out of the room onto the hall landing. He was in a substantial house by the look of the number of corridors and rooms that led off from where he stood. Gripping the handrail, he made his way haltingly down the stairs. He opened the first door he came to and found himself in a heavily swagged and upholstered sitting room. He tried another and found himself in a dining room. He supposed he was in the hotel he had been trying to get to. He finally found a door that opened onto another flight of stairs. The smell of food was wafting up towards him. He clumped down towards the smell. He followed his nose and finally stood in the doorway to the kitchen, swaying slightly. There was a girl in the kitchen, sewing. She put it aside, and poured a mug of steaming tea, adding milk and two teaspoons of sugar, before handing it to him. He took two swigs, scalding his mouth, but the pain acted like a tonic, clearing his mind and made him think clearly for the first time in days.

The girl looked at him. " You arr bettair? Madame said I was to call hair when you came down"

" Where am I?"

" You are in ze 'ouse of Madame de Bonnefoix," said the girl, as if it was the most natural thing in the world.

McGill took another swig. The last thing he remembered was collapsing in the mud, and the hand on his forehead. That was in Amiens. He had been trying to get to the hotel on the other side of the road.

" And am I in a hotel in Amiens?" The girl looked very puzzled then her face cleared and she laughed.

" Ah non, monsieur. Madame she tell me she pick you up outside ze Hotel de Ville!" It was McGill's turn to be puzzled.

" Not a hotel?" The girl laughed again.

" Non non, monsieur! Ze Hotel de Ville is - 'ow you say -where zer officials are – for ze town!"

McGill didn't really understand, but decided his head was still not strong enough to comprehend. " So where am I?"

" I tell you already! You are in ze 'ouse of Madame de Bonnefoix!"

" In Amiens?"

" Of corse! Where did you sink?"

" What day is it?"

" Is sursday." McGill pondered for a moment. The last thing he remembered, apart from the mud, was arriving in Amiens on Monday.

" So I've been here three days?"

" Mais oui. But now I must tell Madame." So saying she pushed past McGill as he leant against the doorway.

There was a stout wooden chair beside the cooking range. McGill made his way towards it and sank into it just before his legs gave way. There was a clatter on the stairs and a smartly dressed woman in her thirties appeared, closely followed by the kitchen girl. He rose shakily, holding onto the chair.

" Monsieur, I am Isabelle de Bonnefoix. May I ask your name?" The accent was only gently foreign. She's a fine looking woman, thought McGill.

" My name is Alan McGill. I am a detective from Scotland Yard in London. And I am very grateful for your hospitality." The lady inclined her head slightly.

" My pleasure and my duty," she said. " I am glad you are not a deserter". McGill was taken aback.

" Why would you think that?" She shrugged and made a mou with her mouth.

" Men who collapse in the street who are in a filthy state tend to be escaping from something"

McGill shook his head. " I'm sorry if I've been a nuisance – I was travelling back from Albert, but I must have picked up some fever. I shall not delay my departure". Madame de Bonnefoix waved her hands.

" Not at all Monsieur, you will stay until *I* say you may leave. But Albert – Mon Dieu you are lucky still to be with us at all. Marie…" which was followed by a string of French words. Marie nodded and headed towards another door. Madame turned to McGill again, smiling." You will eat now Monsieur, and then rest again in your room until dinner is served at eight o'clock. I would be pleased if you would be with me at that time."

" I would be honoured, Madame," said McGill with a slight bow, which made his head spin again. He gripped the chair hard.

Madame looked at him searchingly. Satisfied, she said " Bon! Until this evening".

" Madame, I must inform my superiors of the situation. If I write a telegram, would you have it sent for me?"

"Mais bien sur! Let me have it tonight." So saying she turned and went back up the stairs.

Marie reappeared clutching a leg of ham, bread and cheese. She pointed at the table and McGill dragged his chair across the floor. A long carving knife and some eating utensils were placed beside him. Marie turned to the range and pulled a pot across onto another part. She lifted the lid and stirred briefly, peering into the depths.

McGill cut himself a hunk of bread and a goodly slice of ham. His hands were still shaky, but the thought of decent food after the rations he had been eating made his mouth water. He took a bite of the bread and followed it with a piece of ham. He still had some tea left and took another mouthful. Marie turned to him, leaning back against the range. McGill looked at her then busied himself with his food. A few moments later, a steaming bowl of soup was placed at McGill's elbow. He grunted his thanks, even as he spooned it into his mouth. He suddenly found he was starving and cut himself another slice of ham. He glanced up and saw Marie smiling.

" What? " he asked through a mouthful of food.

" You arr vair 'ungry!"

" I can't rightly remember when I last had a proper meal." Marie nodded.

McGill was just starting to wonder how all this good food was available in such quantity, when he suddenly felt very, very tired. The warmth in the kitchen and the food were combining to tip him over the edge. He leaned back in his chair, stretching his legs and arms out. He meant to revive himself, but allll he managed to do was accentuate his fatigue and he slipped back into oblivion.

Marie looked at him, then quietly cleared the food and plates away. She and Madame had tended him for the last few days, and they had both discussed his handsome features and well-built body. She fetched a blanket from a cupboard, and gently tucked it round him. McGill snuggled into its warmth and dozed on.

He was awakened by a hand gently shaking his shoulder. He opened his eyes to see Marie bending over him.

" M'sieur, it ees time for zer dinair. You must 'urry to shange." McGill focussed then struggled upright.

" But I have nothing to change into."

" Madame says you are to wear ze clothes I 'ave put for you. Zhey are on your bed."

McGill made his way up the two flights of stairs and into his room. He missed it first time but in the second room he entered he saw evening clothes laid out.

There was hot water in a jug and he quickly shaved and dressed. He'd never been one for evening clothes, but as he caught sight of himself in the mirror he paused and decided his height and demeanour made him quite the thing – even if the clothes were a touch small. He also reflected that he was feeling considerably better. Just as he turned to admire himself again, a gong sounded, and he hurried to make his way to the ground floor.

To his astonishment there was a man standing by a large gong. His left hand held the gong-stick. His right was merely a folded and pinned sleeve. Looking at him, McGill could see he was a butler of sorts and probably in his late forties. The man pointed to a door with his stick, and McGill passed through.

Just as he entered, a door on the other side opened and Madame de Bonnefoix appeared. She was magnificently dressed with jewels and her hair softly cascading to her shoulders. She smiled at McGill, who quickly moved to hold her chair for her.

" Merci" she said with a nod and another smile.

McGill took the other seat. He glanced at the table which was laid with crystal and silver and – to McGill's horror – innumerable forks, knives and spoons that he knew he had little idea how to deal with.

Madame saw his look, and not unkindly laughed. " Monsieur – do not worry. Start outside and work in!"

The butler and a footman appeared carrying a tray between them. The footman had no left arm. McGill served himself some of the steaming soup and Madame did likewise. The butler busied himself serving wine, then stood behind Madame's chair. McGill watched

Madame lift a spoon and did likewise. She smiled at him again as she dipped the spoon into her soup.

McGill was curious about the servants, but felt he could hardly ask whilst the butler was in the room. He kept glancing at the man, who looked straight ahead without moving. Madame saw his glance and put down her spoon.

" I see you are wondering about Rene. He worked for us before the Bosch defiled our country. He and my husband joined the army together and he acted as his valet. They were at Verdun together where he lost his arm. My husband – well my husband was not so lucky." A shadow passed across her lovely face, but she quickly shook it away.

" So, thankfully, he came back to help me."

" Your house is wonderfully well appointed, Madame"

" I am very lucky. My husband was a very rich man with many properties and farms as well as other businesses. The Government has effectively taken over the businesses, but I still have all the rents and produce from the farms. I spend my time trying to help in the *departement* all the poor widows and orphans."

" And do you have children yourself?"

" Sadly no." Another shadow crossed her face." My husband could not produce children."

"I'm sorry" said McGill.

She waved her hand again." It may be better that I have none. Especially if we lose this war."

McGill nodded." Madame, what I have seen makes me disbelieve everything I was told in England. There is chaos and confusion everywhere, and no plausible way forward. If we do win, it will be because the Huns are in a worse state than we are, not because we achieve success."

The butler glanced at McGill and then looked away again. He agrees, thought McGill. He's been at the front too.

The butler moved to take away Madame's soup bowl as she put her spoon down and indicated she was finished. The footman behind McGill reached round in front of him and took his bowl away too.

As he did so, McGill felt a wave of weakness and pain smash through his body. He grabbed the side of the table with both hands.

Madame was out of her seat and beside him before the feeling left him. He felt himself sweating, and was grateful for the napkin dipped in water she pressed to his forehead.

" Monsieur, I have asked too much of you. Rene..." The butler moved to take McGill by the arm and the footman did the same on his other side. McGill was no lightweight, but the two Frenchmen were clearly much stronger than he thought, for they were easily able to help him out of the chair and up the stairs back to his room.

McGill collapsed on the bed and the butler took his boots off and started to undress him. McGill waved him away, and slowly undressed himself. He climbed back into the bed, feeling totally drained. Just at that point Madame appeared at the door followed by Marie with a tray.

" Monsieur, I apologise. You are worse than I thought. Marie here will feed you some chicken and vegetables and then you will sleep again. I will call the doctor to be here in the morning to see to you once more. Then we shall see."

McGill was too weak to protest, and he struggled to sit upright. Madame on one side and the butler on the other dragged him into a sitting position, then a tray was placed on his lap, and Marie sat on the bed beside him. He made to pick up the fork, but found he couldn't make his hand move. He looked up into Madame's face with a look of shame and fear, and her concern and compassion for him was clear. She took his hand and held it briefly, before cupping his face with her own hand, and looking deep into his troubled eyes.

" Pauvre petit. Marie will feed you. You will be better." So saying she left the room, and McGill turned his heavy head towards the fork that Marie was now bringing to his mouth.

" Marie – why am I so weak?"

"Monsieur you 'ave wot you Tommies col zhe Trench Fever. When we bathed you, we found many lices on you bodee. But we kill them all and wash your clothes and as Madame says, you will be bettaire." McGill took the mouthful and chewed slowly.

" You bathed me? With no clothes on?" Marie laughed but McGill felt himself redden. He was no prude but the thought of the two women washing him in the bath took him aback.

But Trench Fever? He hadn't been in any trenches, just in the billet underground at Albert. He supposed the whole place would be crawling with lice as the troops came and went. He took another forkful, and felt the pain and weakness edging away. As the last mouthful went in he felt himself slipping away to sleep again, and this time gave in to it.

Chapter 9

The next morning he was wakened by the doctor shaking him.
" Monsieur, I must attend you!"
McGill looked behind him to see Madame and Marie hovering. He sat up. The doctor took his pulse, then pulled the skin beneath his eyes downwards with his thumb, first the right then the left.
" Well Monsieur, you must rest a few days more – but then you will be cured. Madame.." then a string of French McGill didn't understand.
The doctor turned back to McGill, and shook his hand with a small bow.
" I will come again in two or three days' time. By then I expect you will be wanting to leave." So saying he took Madame's hand, lifted it to his lips and left.
" Well Monsieur McGill, you must stay some time with us it seems. That will be…pleasing." McGill lifted his hand in acknowledgement, just as Marie reappeared with a tray. There was milky coffee, butter, jam and bread.
" The coffee has a cognac in it for strength. If you feel strong enough you may come down stairs for lunch. Otherwise Marie will bring it here. I must attend to some business today, but I shall return for dinner. If you care to, we will have a quiet meal together."
" Thank you Madame – you are most kind. I must send my telegram. If I may have paper and pen I will write it now. It would be a pleasure to take dinner with you. I hope I will remain upright long enough to finish it with you this time."
Madame laughed then nodded." Yes I think so. The Trench Fever is also called the five day fever and you are now on the fifth day. At worst you will be much improved tomorrow." So saying she pulled her gloves on and left.
Marie slid the tray over his knees then left as well.
McGill breathed in the tang of the laced coffee and wondered at his luck. After all he might have ended up robbed and left for dead

on the street. Who was the person who had hovered over him in the street? It wasn't a woman, he was sure of that.

He moved the tray to one side, then padded slowly across to the dresser. Yes his warrant card and wallet were lying there. He hadn't even noticed them yesterday. He felt a stab of dizziness lance through him as he turned back to the bed and he grabbed the edge of the dresser. Not right yet old son, he thought to himself. Marie came back in with paper and a small travelling writing desk. She laid it across his lap, then opened it and pointed to an array of pens and pencils.

Later, McGill made himself get dressed and take the stairs to the kitchen, clutching his message for his Superintendent. There, Marie was busying herself with pots and pans, whilst the two men he had seen the night before polished silver. One held down the piece whist the other applied polish and then rubbed until it was gleaming. McGill marvelled at how the men appeared to be adapting themselves and working as one whole as opposed to two halves.

McGill sat in the same chair as the day before and laid his paper beside his place. Marie served a steaming plate of what appeared to be ham and vegetable soup. The two men stopped immediately, and moved to places that were already set further up the table. Rene reached for a jug and offered McGill some with a gesture. McGill nodded and was astonished to see dark red liquid splash into his glass. Of course, he thought, wine. Marie served two more plates to the men and then another to herself, sitting down near McGill. Rene had already poured her half a glass of wine, which she topped up with water.

" Bon appetit," said Rene, tearing a chunk of bread from a large loaf in the middle of the table. McGill stretched across and did likewise. He dunked the bread into the soup and bit off the soggy end. Looking more closely at his bowl, it was clear the dish was more of a soupy stew than a soup plain and simple, and from the first taste he was sure he was going to enjoy it.

They ate in silence, stopping only to refill their glasses. McGill felt the wine mingling with the cognac he had had in his coffee, and felt, too, the good it was doing him.

After lunch, McGill sat quietly beside the range as the others went about their various tasks. Rene gestured at the paper, and McGill handed it to him. " Tell Madame, " he said speaking slowly," I will pay the charges." Rene nodded and climbed the stairs. After half an hour or so Marie chased him off to his room and told him he must rest. Rene would call him when supper was ready.

McGill slowly walked back up the stairs and lay on his bed. It wasn't getting the case solved but at least he now had time to think.

He now knew that the dead man was Lieutenant Braintree. He had obviously got on the train back to Amiens using Ralston's papers. The next thing anyone knew he was lying strangled. Why would someone strangle him? It was usually men who strangled women. The reason for taking away the clothes and identification was clearly because there was some link between Braintree and his killer. But Braintree was carrying Ralston's papers when he left Albert. Why steal them? Unless…suppose Ralston's body was claimed by his relatives, and when it arrived back in Blighty they said it wasn't Ralston. Then there would be a much more thorough investigation. No, much better just to make it all disappear and leave a cold trail. The killer wanted Braintree dead, that was clear. The two, murderer and victim, must have agreed to meet. If someone wanted Braintree dead they could just have followed him to the front and shot him. No one would have bothered about one more body amongst the thousands. It had to be in Amiens because that was where the murderer was. McGill was more convinced than ever that Braintree knew his killer. And why was the murder in that particular house? How had the two, murderer and victim, got in? The occupants of the house had been interviewed but it seemed they knew nothing. He drifted off.

He didn't hear the door open, nor the careful footsteps as they came towards the bed.

Isabelle de Bonnefoix stood looking down at him, her face a mask. She stood motionless for several minutes, then carefully pulled a blanket higher up the bed and tucked it around him. Her face softened, and with a final glance at his sleeping face she silently made her way from the room, shutting the door behind her. Once in the corridor, she felt herself exhale and a shiver pass through her body. She shook herself and made her way to her own bedroom. I think the light blue dress, she said to herself.

Before McGill knew it, there was a knock at the door and Rene came in. McGill waved his hand at him to indicate he was awake. Rene jiggled his hand which was holding a piece of paper, left it on the dresser and then withdrew. McGill struggled to his feet and staggered across the room. He opened the note.

" Monsieur McGill – please do not trouble yourself to dress for dinner. Tonight we will be quite informal." McGill sighed with relief. At least he could get into his own clothes.

When the gong sounded for dinner, McGill was just taking the first step at the top of the stairs. He carefully made his way to the dining room, to be greeted by Madame de Bonnefoix as he entered.

My God, thought McGill, if that's informal I'm a Chinaman. Isabelle de Bonnefoix was wearing a waisted light blue dress which clung to her figure, and set off her eyes. She smiled at McGill, took his arm and led him to a chair. She moved gracefully to the other side of the table and sat with a discrete susurration. McGill felt a stirring in his groin and his face reddening at the same time. Madame de Bonnefoix smiled at him, seeming to know the effect she was having on him, and looked demurely down at her cutlery. Taking her napkin, she carefully spread it across her lap, smoothing the perfect white cloth as she did so.

McGill didn't know what to say, but was rescued by Rene and the footman appearing with a tureen of steaming soup.

" We are having only strengthening food whilst you are here, monsieur. Nothing light. Only food that will build you to health."

" You are most kind Madame. I am already feeling better through your insistence on rest and good food!"

Madame de Bonnefoix smiled again as she took a ladle of thick meaty soup. "Marie makes a wonderful potage." Rene moved round to McGill who took two ladles. He was ravenous again. Madame de Bonnefoix saw and smiled once more.

There was a hare pate followed by lamb and fruit. She ate sparingly but McGill ate well, and by the time they were finished he felt not only stronger but overflowing with good food. They had talked of this and that, nothing of great consequence, but a gentle way to spend a pleasant evening.

At the end of the meal, Madame de Bonnefoix rose and gave McGill her arm.

" Now, Monsieur, I think if we are to be together for some days I should call you Alain, and you must call me Isabelle." McGill gave a small bow.

" I should be delighted and honoured, Madame – Isabelle." Isabelle gave a little tinkly laugh, and placed her free hand across her waist, and onto McGill's hand. He felt a shock run through his body and his face reddening again. They walked from the dining room into the main drawing room, where they stood awkwardly for a few moments, until Isabelle gently extricated her arm and went to sit beside the fire. She pointed at the chair on the other side of it, and obediently McGill sat.

Rene brought Isabelle a steaming cup. " Tisane," she said, " For my health. It helps me sleep as well. Would you care for one?"

" Not for me, thank you. Perhaps just an ordinary tea." Rene withdrew and Isabelle stirred her tisane, looking over it at McGill.

" So detective Alain, what is your next move?"

McGill paused. " The answer has to be here in Amiens, so I shall resume my enquiries here. I need to interview the people who were living in the house where the murder took place and see if there is anything further that they can tell me. At the moment, all I know is who the murdered man was and how he got back to Amiens." Isabelle nodded, and sipped her tisane. Rene came back in bearing a tray with McGill's tea, complete with milk and sugar to add to taste. He poured and stirred the two sugar lumps pensively.

" Madame – I mean Isabelle. You have wonderful food here and so much of it. We have shortages in the shops at home and there is talk of rationing of food being brought in. How do you have so much?"

Isabelle smiled and McGill thought he would melt in those eyes."We grow everything we need – and more. There are no shortages here. I have always believed that that is one of the reasons the dirty Huns invaded us – to feed their growing population." McGill nodded. It would make sense.

" Yes we import much from the Empire and other places. The German submarines have made things difficult."

They sat in companionable silence for a short while, both of them watching the fire and sipping their respective teas. After a little time, Isabelle glanced up at McGill, who, sensing the movement, turned towards her. Their eyes met for a moment until Isabelle dropped hers, and said quietly " Alain, in the evenings I used to play Ecarte with my husband sometimes. Would you care to play?"

" I know little or nothing about cards. But I would be happy to learn and maybe give you a game or two."

Isabelle inclined her head, rose and went to a dresser. McGill could hear the slight rustling of her dress and his eyes followed her as she glided across the room. Her back was towards him, and he gulped as her buttocks swayed under the material. She opened a drawer and took out a pack of cards, then rang for Rene. She spoke briefly to him in French, then turned towards McGill again.

" He will bring a table for us." McGill nodded. The two were silent, Isabelle standing, McGill sitting, studiously avoiding each other's faces. Rene came in carrying a small table, and McGill marvelled again at his dexterity with just the one arm. He bowed slightly and withdrew. Isabelle pulled a chair closer to the table and laid the cards on it. McGill looked up at her and caught her watching him with a strange, serious look on her face.

Picking up the cards again, Isabelle shuffled them. " Alors! We begin..."

An hour or so later, McGill had mastered the rudiments of the game but found himself unable to keep up with Isabelle's superior technique and female intuition. A wave of fatigue came over him and he sighed.

Isabelle glanced at him sharply." I have tired you. You must go to bed. Perhaps tomorrow we will take a small walk if the weather is good." So saying she rose, followed by McGill. In the hall she turned to him and held out her hand. "Bon nuit, monsieur Alain. I have much enjoyed the evening." She turned and went through another door, leaving McGill to climb the stairs wearily, and thinking only of her.

The next day dawned clear and bright, and McGill and Isabelle went for the promised small walk. The colour was slowly coming back to McGill's cheeks and he felt the warmth of Isabelle at his side as she held his arm tightly. Rene had been instructed to follow in case McGill had another turn. In the afternoon, after his nap, there was a telegram waiting for him.

" Glad you survived. When better let me know." Not much for what he had been through, but still.

In the evening, McGill and Isabelle ate quietly together again. McGill wasn't sure if it was just the Florence Nightingale in her, but she seemed to care for him. She had a lovely smile which crinkled her eyes, and made McGill's stomach tighten. They played cards again that night, and by the third night McGill was beginning to win the odd hand. Isabelle clapped her hands with glee when he won the first one. Their walks increased in length each day, Isabelle with her arm through McGill's and Rene trailing behind.

Three days later the doctor came to examine McGill again and pronounced him fit and ready for work again " In a few days."

On the fourth night after the cards were put away, Isabelle looked full on at McGill's face. A sad look came over her, and her eyes seemed to lose some of their sparkle.

" Alain – I - I know you must go to find your murderer. You are well now. I shall miss you. I have much enjoyed you being here."

McGill bowed. " Isabelle, I cannot thank you enough. If you hadn't found me, I don't know what would have happened. I too have enjoyed my time here very much. I cannot repay you."

"There is no need. I must go tomorrow early for a few days on business."

" Then I shall leave in the morning."

They shook hands, and Isabelle, looking up, peered into McGill's eyes. She nodded as if to herself, then let his hand go and glided through the doorway. McGill sat again, watching the dying embers of the fire. Rene appeared and gestured at the fire. McGill shook his head, and rose to go to bed. Rene offered his left hand, and, grinning, McGill shook it with his left hand. Rene nodded, smiled briefly, then stood back to allow McGill passage.

Once in his room, he undressed slowly and stood looking out of the window. The sky was cloudy, but suddenly the moon flashed out, and bathed the garden in a wan light. There was a movement to one side, but as McGill looked at it the usual happened and it disappeared. He glanced away again, knowing that at night the sides of the retina are better to see things with, but there was nothing there. Had he imagined something? Shaking his head, he got into bed. My God, he thought. What a woman! I bet her husband was a very happy man. He closed his eyes and felt himself drifting away.

It seemed only moments later but could have been hours when he felt the covers being lifted and the bed move. Still drowsy, he turned to see what it was and suddenly felt cool lips on his. He came fully awake.

The kiss lengthened and McGill felt himself growing and thickening, his prick stubbing against silky smooth flesh. A hand drifted down his body and gripped him, causing him to gasp. The kiss stopped.

" Isabelle, I…"

" Shh. We have only tonight. It has been a long time. And my husband never loved me enough."

McGill wrapped his arms around her and stroked her back. She shivered slightly and snuggled closer into him. He kissed her again, then moved his hand round and down between her legs. She sighed and opened herself.

Later, as they clung together, Isabelle started to talk quietly.

" My husband only married me because I was beautiful and would bring him prestige. He preferred men though we did make love sometimes. It was always quick and brutal. In a strange way I was glad when it was only Rene who came back, but of course it has meant I am besieged by old men looking for one thing only. But with you I felt quite different – as I did as a young girl of 18. And you looked so beautiful when I saw you asleep the first time in this bed."

"I'm so sorry. You should have only had good things in your life and happy times."

" Hush. *This* has been a happy time." So saying she reached for him again and kissed him hard.

Later still McGill told her about his life and the bitterness he felt at the way he had been treated in his job. Isabelle listened gravely. She kissed him, holding his head between her hands and looking hard into his face.

" You must not hate them. It will only take away your soul." She kissed him again." And you have a beautiful soul."

McGill felt loved and wanted for the first time in many years.

Later, as he slept, Isabelle gently disengaged herself and slipped out of the bed. A wan beam of light fell across his face, and she saw him again as she had the first time in that very bed. She tenderly moved his hair as she would a child's. She sighed quietly and picked her nightdress up from where she had discarded it. Wrapping it around herself, she looked once more at the sleeping McGill, remembering the feel of him inside her. She hugged herself, alive and tingling for the first time. She had never known a lover, only a brute. Silently she turned from the bed and left the room.

Chapter 10

When he awoke next morning, he reached for Isabelle, only to find nothing where she had been. He sat up and looked to make sure she was gone. He flopped back in the bed. He felt sated and happy. He wondered whether he should stay, until he remembered Isabelle saying they had only the one night. Groaning, he swung his legs over the side of the bed and planted his feet firmly on the floor. With a sigh he stood up and prepared himself to meet the day.

In the kitchen, Marie had made him a strong coffee with a cognac in it. She smiled at him as he greedily ate two croissants. Once breakfast was finished, McGill hesitated, at a loss to know what to do next. Marie came to his rescue.

" Madame 'as gone on business," she said firmly." You will 'ave to walk into Amiens." McGill nodded, rose, and made his way back to his room to gather his remaining things.

He could have sworn the smell of Isabelle was still there as he looked at the rumpled bedclothes. Even as he did so, he understood that it really had been just the one night, that in a way he had been used – ever so nicely, but used all the same. A twisted smile came to his face as he donned his coat. He felt the lump in his pocket that was the mug he had been given, and he grimaced. He may have been used, but he was still very lucky. He made his way downstairs to find Marie waiting for him in the hall. She shook his hand formally and said "Adieu" gravely. Equally gravely, McGill shook the small hand and said "Goodbye". Marie opened the door and he stepped outside. Before he could take a step, the door shut behind him.

As McGill turned from the door, he felt a wave of regret pass through him. He had never been a lady's man, and felt he should have at least left a message. But Isabelle had made it abundantly clear she didn't want him there anymore, and Marie's message that Madame had already gone out precluded any lengthy goodbyes.

From a window two floors up, Isabelle de Bonnefoix followed McGill's progress as he made off down the drive, out through the gates and along the road. He looked back once. She pulled back from the window. Then he turned to his path once more and was gone from her sight. She sighed and tears sprang to her eyes as her hand slid down the curtain, then left it and came to rest between her thighs. There was still a healthy tingle there, a sweet soreness, mixed with a new aliveness beneath her fingers. A smile spread through her tears.

McGill didn't recognise where he was. After all he didn't even remember getting to this place, so he walked on. Soon enough he came to a cross roads and would have stood there all day if a lorry filled with wounded hadn't come past. McGill flagged it down, and jumped on the running board.

" You going into Amiens mate?"

" Too bloody right I am. Want a lift?"

McGill swung the door open and jumped into the squash of two other soldiers and the driver who were already taking up all the space on the front seat.

" So what you doing out 'ere then?" asked the driver.

" Been ill. Got a job to do in town."

"Oh yes? And what might that be?" McGill hesitated. He didn't want to let on he was a copper, and he didn't want to say what he had to do.

" Provisions" he said. The driver nodded. " Thought it must be something like that. Not a lot of English civvies around 'ere. Not in one piece any road."

Within a few minutes they were approaching the town proper, and McGill noted the masses of khaki everywhere. He needed to find the officer in command of billeting, and he didn't know where to start until...

" You got a billet, mate?" asked the driver.

" No I haven't. I need to find one."

" Not easy, but I'm going past Headquarters anyway. I'll drop you there." So saying, the driver swung to the left down a cobbled street which gave on to a large square. McGill saw the Union Jack fluttering above an enormous building with steps. There were streams of men of all ranks going up and down, as well as messengers toing and froing. Chaos again, thought McGill.

The truck pulled up and McGill opened the door and almost fell out. The occupants of the front seat took up their normal, comfortable attitude and the lorry drove off.

McGill made his way towards the entrance of the building, but had not even managed to put a foot on the first step when a bayonet appeared at his midriff.

" Goin' somewhere, mister?"

McGill reached slowly for the warrant card in his pocket and the paper signed by Watkins. He offered them to the soldier, who simply shouted over his shoulder – " Sergeant!" The bayonet never moved.

Down the steps came a sergeant with buttons that flashed even in the dullness of a drab December afternoon. Eyeing McGill he took the proffered documents, scanned them and handed them back.

" And wot would you be wantin' 'ere then sir?" There wasn't a trace of warmth in the question and McGill realised no one wanted him interfering with *their* patch.

" I need a billet. And I need to send a telegram to Scotland Yard." The sergeant glowered at McGill.

" I suppose you better come in then." So saying he turned on his heel and headed back up the stairs.

Reluctantly the soldier lowered his rifle, and McGill followed the sergeant into a cavernous entrance hall with the sound of echoing boots on marble and shouts for odd men. Indicating a door to the left, the sergeant knocked and entered without waiting for an answer.

It was much quieter once McGill shut the door behind him. The room was fully a hundred feet long with rows of men sitting at desks with piles of files and paper about them. More men were walking up and down between the rows, dropping off papers here, collecting others there, then disappearing through another door at the side. At the far end sat a Captain at a nearly empty desk, and the sergeant headed towards him.

The sergeant jumped to attention in front of the desk, throwing a perfect salute.

The Captain went on reading the paper he had in front of him, then glanced up.

" Permission to speak, sir?" The Captain waved his hand and sat back in his chair. He looked at McGill, then back at the sergeant.

" Well?"

" Sir, this 'ere is one of them detectives from London. Askin' for a billet sir And to send a telegram." The Captain nodded, and reached his right hand down to a drawer in his desk.

" Not just any billet, Captain, " said McGill. The Captain paused in taking a file from the drawer.

" Oh really? And why would that be then?"

" I want to be billeted in the house where the victim was found". The sergeant's eyes widened and swivelled towards McGill and the Captain looked as if he had been hit over the head.

" You what?"

" I want to be billeted where Lt. Braintree was found dead." The Captain paused again.

" Who's he?"

" The man who was strangled recently." The Captain's mouth dropped.

" Braintree? How do you know that? He didn't have any identification." McGill smiled.

" Just one of the things Scotland Yard knows how to do. Now I'd be obliged if you would get me into that house."

" But that's impossible! The house is already full, and I can't just foist you on them!"

" Do I need to speak to the General?" The Captain looked as if he would gladly strangle McGill, debating whether the detective might just be able to speak to the General. He finally dropped his eyes. He reached into another drawer and pulled out a pad of forms. He slammed it on the desk and reached for his pen. Slowly and deliberately he unscrewed the cap, then stuck it on the end of the pen. Glancing up at McGill, he filled in the form without any sense of urgency, signing with a flourish. He handed the form to the sergeant.

" Make sure that gets registered, then get him out of here." The sergeant took the form, saluted, wheeled about and headed for one of the men at the desks. McGill followed, then turned to say thank you. The Captain was watching him, and the words died in McGill's throat. He swung back to follow the sergeant.

By the time McGill had caught up with him, the clerk was looking goggle eyed at the form.

" Is 'e bleedin' serious?" asked the clerk

" I most definitely am," said McGill. The clerk looked up and sighed.

" Well, it's your bleedin' funeral, mate," and started rummaging amongst the files on the floor at his feet. He eventually found what he was looking for, slammed it onto his desk, and flung the cover open. Rifling through some pages, he stopped at one, glancing at the form again. Carefully he transcribed the information, handed back the form to the sergeant, closed the file and dropped it onto the floor. He sat back and folded his arms, looking at McGill without a word. The sergeant tilted his head in the direction of the way out and set off towards it.

The sergeant marched in front of McGill until they reached the top of the steps. McGill pulled his coat tighter about himself, and stuck his hand out for the form. Reluctantly, the sergeant extended the hand holding it.

" And the telegram?" The sergeant nodded towards a small door to the right.

McGill made his way into the room which had more desks and soldiers handing out telegram forms to runners who rushed off to deliver them. McGill spotted a "send" form which he picked up and made use of the pencil attached to the desk. He handed the form to the person who appeared to be in charge, who looked at it. He looked up at McGill.

" Back at work? Is that it?"

"Yes thank you – that's all that's needed." The man added the form to the top of an upturned pile of telegram forms, just as a runner came and collected the whole bundle, turning it right way up.

McGill turned away and exited the room. He spotted the sergeant who had left him and approached him.

" Which way? " asked McGill, pointing at the address on the billeting form he was holding.

" No bloody idea, mate." So saying the sergeant turned back into the centre of the building, leaving McGill with no idea where to go.

He started to walk down the steps and reached the bottom just as the soldier with the bayonet swung towards him.

" Get a billet then didya?"

" Yes thanks. Any idea where this is?" McGill handed over the form, and the soldier rested the butt of his rifle, bayonet pointing skywards, on the ground, so as to take the form with both hands.

Frowning, he mouthed the foreign names, tilted his helmet back and scratched his head.

" Coo. Never 'eard of that. "

Another soldier appeared and looked over the guard's shoulder.

" 'ere, Nobby! You know this place at all?" McGill could instantly tell Nobby wasn't the usual cannon fodder. He held himself with an assurance and a confidence that spelled " toff." He took the form from the soldier and read the address. He looked up at McGill with surprise. When he spoke McGill was satisfied to hear his surmise confirmed.

"I know where this is", he said. " There was a man murdered there." McGill nodded.

" Yes a Lieutenant Braintree." Nobby looked even more surprised.

" I didn't think he had been identified". McGill nodded again.

" Yes, I've got that far anyway. Now I need to find out who killed him." Nobby handed McGill the form back and shook his head.

" It's bad enough the Huns murdering us without some nutter going about behind the lines at it." McGill nodded again, warming to Nobby, who was neither talking down to him nor peeved that he was on his patch. On an impulse, McGill stuck his hand out.

" Detective Inspector Alan McGill – Scotland Yard." It was Nobby's turn to tilt his helmet back.

" Well, I've heard about you, " he said as he gripped McGill's hand and shook it. " Private Nobby Murgatroyd at the moment" McGill grinned.

" And usually?"

" The Honourable Francis James St.John Murgatroyd" McGill laughed. " And of course that's why I get called " Nobby"

" I can see why you would prefer that!" The two men grinned at each other. " Can you tell me how to get to this place?"

" I can do better than that. I've got a 72 hour pass from tonight and I can take you there. It's about a mile or so from where we stand." Nobby glanced about and then yelled " Sergeant!" The same man who had left McGill at the top of the steps reappeared . He did not look happy.

" Wot you want Nobby?"

" Sarge, Inspector McGill has requested I show him where his billet is." The sergeant looked as if he was about to explode, his eyes bulging and his face reddening.

" Oh 'e did did 'e? Well, your job, is to stand 'ere on guard 'til I sez you can leave, and I 'ent about to do that."

" But sarge, he's got a laissez passer signed by the provost marshal and another from the General."

The latter was the first McGill had heard of it, but he kept his face absolutely still, whilst the sergeant wrestled with his anger and his sense of orderliness. It would never do to go against the General's wishes.

Throwing his hands up, he turned on his heel and went back inside the building. He came out again and shouted " Well be bloody quick about it!"

Grinning, Nobby shouldered his rifle, and swinging his right arm marched away from the steps. McGill fell in beside him and the two men marched off together towards the centre of town.

The house where the murder had taken place was in a small side street off a main road. There were shops and a couple of small bars and cafes nearby. There was no difference between it and the other houses in the street. According to the reports, there had been four men billeted in it at the time of the murder. McGill guessed the owners had long since left for safer areas, and the Army had simply commandeered it. Nobby knocked on the door, then tried the handle. The door opened and the pair entered. The only sound was a sudden snort from upstairs. McGill guessed it was one of the inhabitants sleeping off the night before.

They looked into all the rooms on the ground floor. One had a camp bed in it and was very untidy. Another was a sitting room. They finally found the kitchen towards the back of the house and Nobby set about making tea. McGill sat quietly watching him.

" Won't you get into trouble when you don't report back?"

" No, don't worry. I'll just say you wanted to be shown around – the sergeant isn't going to make trouble. It would only rebound on him. The non-coms are all a bit scared of me in a strange way. I know quite a few of the higher ups and they can never be sure I won't tell on them." McGill nodded." In any case, I always wanted to be a detective!" McGill's eyes widened.

" Well, you've the right background for an Inspector! I was only a detective constable a couple of weeks ago, and now I'm an acting Inspector. 'Course, when this is over they'll put me back to sergeant or maybe even constable, but it's rather a good feeling to have made it to a position of proper responsibility."

Nobby put the two teas on the table and sat down." I wouldn't be too sure about that. If you find out who did it they'd be hard pushed to justify you being demoted again. And if you don't, well, they never expected anything to be found out, and here you know who the dead man is." McGill snorted.

" Maybe – but I don't fit in. The Inspectors and the Super are all upper class and they look down on the likes of me." Nobby shook his head.

" When this lot's over things will change. Your lot, if you'll pardon the expression, won't stand for what went on in the past. They've put up with too much. And lots of them have been made up to officers because so many of the original ones are dead. They won't take kindly to being looked down on. It's been a great leveller, this war." McGill shrugged his shoulders.

" I don't know. I was a copper on the beat in the East End of London before the war, and I had better know my place or I was for the high jump. I doubt that will change much." Nobby grinned.

"Tell you what. Let's meet up five years after it's all over and swop stories!" McGill laughed.

" At the present rate of progress neither of us might make it!" He reached for his tea, and as he lifted it to his lips, the door crashed open and a red-eyed, grizzly man in his underclothes stood there pointing a pistol at them.

" Hands up! And don't move!" Gingerly, McGill lifted his left hand in the air as he put the tea back on the table with his right. Then he slowly raised it too. Nobby hadn't moved a muscle, but had left his hands on the table in plain view. " Come on! You too!" Slowly he put his hands above his head.

" Now then, who are you and what are you doing here?" Nobby spoke first.

" This is Detective Inspector McGill of Scotland Yard and I'm Nobby Murgatroyd from the billeting section. I showed Mr. McGill the way here."

" So what's he doing here?"

" I'm here investigating the murder that took place." The figure blanched. Then a puzzled look came over his face.

" You're not Aubrey Murgatroyd's boy are you?" Nobby nodded.

" Well why didn't you say so? I'm Charles Woodville." The gun dropped to the man's side, and he sat down. He put the gun on the table. " Your father and mine were old School chums. We've never met, but father goes on about Aubrey and his larks when they were young." Nobby reached across and shook the proffered hand.

"I'd heard there was some chap who could have been an officer in the area who had joined as a private." McGill wondered as he always did at the cocksure nature of the statement. There were literally hundreds of thousands who had joined as privates – but only someone from their own class counted at all. He sighed inwardly.

" Well, that chap is me," said Nobby." They won't let me go to the front though. I keep asking and they keep knocking me back. The powers that be like having me around so they can feel superior for once." McGill noted the bitterness in the statement, and was reminded of his own desire to get to the front. Not so sure now though, he thought.

Woodville turned towards McGill. " So how's the investigation going?" McGill grinned to himself. The certainty that McGill would tell everything was clear. These people never learn, he thought.

" I'm not really at liberty to say, sir. The investigation is on-going. I can tell you who the murdered man was." Woodville started.

" Ruddy hell! That was smart work! How did you do that?" McGill smiled. " I'm sorry, sir, I'm not at liberty to divulge that. But I can tell you that I am here to interview whoever was living in the house when the murder was discovered." Woodville stared.

"You think one of us did it?"

"Not at all sir. I simply need to check the statements that were made after the murder was discovered. Just in case there are any discrepancies." That'll show him, thought McGill grimly.

Woodville looked at Nobby, who was sitting impassively. He turned back to McGill.

"You DO think one of us did it!"

"No, sir, I do not. But one of you may have seen something or heard something or even thought something which at the time would mean nothing to you, but which, with what else I know may make sense." Woodville stared at McGill again, eyes bulging. He rubbed his stubble.

"Hmm well, it's quite simple. Percy came back in after his leave and found the body in his bed."

"Which room was that in?" Woodville rose and made for the stairs, McGill and Nobby trailing behind. At the top of the stairs he turned right and opened the first door he came to. Flinging it open, he stood back, allowing McGill to take a step inside before he looked carefully all around.

"Was the bed where the body was found in the same position as it is now?" Woodville glanced over McGill's shoulder.

"Yes, I'd say so." McGill resumed his visual survey slowly.

The room itself was unremarkable. It was fairly small, and had all the usual furniture expected of a town bedroom, but the addition of an untidy young subaltern had overlaid the original. There was clutter and mess everywhere, and the clothes McGill could see were in need of laundering.

"He's away at the moment?" Woodville nodded, even though McGill couldn't see him.

"Indeed, he's on duty at the train station but he should be back quite soon. His shift is oh-eight-hundred to sixteen-hundred hours"

If Braintree had been strangled anywhere other than in that room, thought McGill, the murderer would have had to get him into it and onto the bed. If he was clothed before he was killed, he'd have had to be stripped. No easy task. McGill felt that Braintree had probably been naked when he was killed. From the reports, there was no sign of a struggle. If he'd been knocked out before being strangled, that would explain it. On the other hand, with the delay in the Military Police getting there and the removal of Braintree's body from the bed, there was no real certainty there hadn't been a struggle. Indeed, the room looked as if there had been a couple of pigs fighting in it recently. And Braintree by all accounts had been carefully laid out with his hands crossed on his chest. Almost a loving gesture. McGill turned to Woodville.

" And where were you when the body was discovered?"

" Me? I was on duty. I didn't get back until very early the next morning."

" So when did you leave the house?"

Woodville looked at McGill, then replied slowly. " I expect it was about lunchtime. I went out to get something to eat, then reported for duty at fifteen hundred hours."

" How far away from the house were you?" Nobby started involuntarily. So that's what being a detective meant. Never believe anything without a fact to back it up.

Even more slowly, Woodville said "About twenty minutes walk."

" So you could have walked back and killed him, then gone back on duty?"

" I suppose I could – but I didn't. And I don't much care for the implication."

McGill shook his head." It's quite straightforward sir. Anyone who COULD have done it needs to have their story checked. You COULD have done it. So I'd be obliged if you could let me have the names of anyone you were on duty with who can corroborate what you say."

Woodville's eyes bulged and his face reddened. " Damned if I will!" Nobby put his hand on Woodville's arm.

" Just tell him Charles," he said quietly.

Woodville bristled, but glanced sideways at Nobby. Then he deflated a bit.

" Harrumph! Well, there was Dougie Gordon and Gerry H…There was a Major I didn't know, I think his name was Barker. And the Colonel of course – James Bramlees." There was a look of triumph on Woodville's face.

" Any sergeants?" Woodville laughed.

" Why do you want to know that?"

" Because, sir, all the people you have mentioned are clearly either friends or of your background. I'd like an impartial witness." McGill thought Woodville was going to hit him. He watched as the emotions fought with each other, until finally Woodville spat. "Grimes - Sergeant Grimes"

McGill nodded. Nobby was shocked, but said nothing. Being a detective meant getting to the truth – however unpalatable to achieve it. He didn't think he could be like that.

The three men trooped down the stairs, saying nothing. They went back into the kitchen, where McGill and Nobby sat again, but, with a malevolent glance at McGill, Woodville picked up his gun and went back to his room, slamming the door behind him.

Nobby winced. " That's not a happy man," he said quietly.

" Good" said McGill." With a bit of luck he'll tell the others what's happened and they might give me the truth without dragging it out of them."

" You don't really think he's involved, do you?" McGill shook his head.

" I'd be very surprised if he was. I just wanted to make a point."

" Oh, you did that all right. You'll be the talk of the Mess next time they all get together. Not accepting a chap's word? My goodness!" McGill laughed.

" That's the first preconception you lose when you become a detective! No one ever tells you the whole truth – and people frequently lie."

A moment later another door slammed and a voice shouted "Hallooo!"

Nobby looked at McGill. " That'll be Miller, I expect." McGill rose and opened the kitchen door.

" Excuse me sir, could you come in here a moment?"

There was a rustling in the hall as Miller took off his great coat. "And who the hell are you?"

" I'm Detective Inspector McGill of Scotland Yard." There was a silence, and then the sound of boots walking towards the kitchen. McGill stood back and a young man, smartly turned out, edged past him.

" Are you Captain Percy Miller?"

" Yes I am. Are you the chap come about the murder?"

" Indeed sir. I understand you were the person who found the body? Would you mind just telling me about it?" Miller looked from McGill to Nobby and back again.

" Mind if I sit down?"

" Not at all, sir." Miller sat in the chair recently vacated by Woodville, then clasped his hands together, looking down at the table.

" Where do you want me to start?"

" Well, let's say when you came off the train, what did you do?"

" I was with a couple of chums who'd been on leave as well. We were all fairly drunk."

" How many of you were there?"

" Three of us. There was myself, John Trent and Christopher Bannerman. We didn't have to report back until the next morning, so we went to the Café de la Gare and drank a few more brandies."

" What time would that be?"

Miller looked at McGill." These are different questions to what I was asked before." McGill smiled grimly.

" I daresay there will be lots of questions you haven't been asked. Go on."

Miller, thought for a moment. " I suppose the train arrived about twenty hundred hours, and we were in the café for about an hour or so."

" What happened when you left?"

" Well, John and Christopher had to get back to their unit which was on the other side of town, so I came back here on my own."

" You didn't stop off at all on the way? How long would that have taken?"

" Popped in to the estaminet at the corner for a nightcap and picked up a bottle of brandy. I suppose it would have been about ten pm. I was only there long enough to down the glass, and then made my way back here." McGill nodded.

" That would tie in with the redcap report that they were told of the murder about ten thirty. How did you tell them?"

" After I found the body, I went back out into the street and got a hold of a private who was walking by. I told him to bring a redcap as someone had been murdered."

" Then what did you do?"

" I went back inside and drank the brandy."

" You didn't hear anyone or see anyone or anything?"

" No nothing. I waited about an hour then went to see what had happened to the military police. When I got to their post there was chaos – a group of soldiers had been sent on leave and they were tearing up the town. When I finally got to speak to a sergeant he said they would be along as soon as they could, but it would probably be the morning."

" So how long were you out of the house?"

" About an hour I suppose. When I got back I just wanted to sleep so I turfed the body onto the floor and pretty much passed out on the bed."

"So there was no one in the house from when you went out until you got back?"

" Not as far as I know. I suppose someone could have come in and gone to their room without my knowing. In any event when the MPs arrived next morning, it was Woodville who answered the door. I was still asleep. It was a redcap who shook me awake."

" And what did they do?"

" Not very much really. They just asked me about finding the body, and spoke to Woodville. There were only the four of us here."

" So you, Woodville, and Captains Fleming and Fields were who they spoke to?"

" Yes I would say so. Fleming and Fields were on duty overnight, so there was little they had to say. Woodville came back in about oh-two-hundred and went straight to bed. I didn't hear him come in."

McGill nodded. The redcaps had done a pretty poor job from what he could see.

" I think that's it for now, Captain." Miller rose to go.

" Oh, one more thing. Was the door locked when you came back?"

" When?"

" When you came back from leave about ten p.m." Miller thought for a moment. He rubbed his chin then grimaced.

" I'm not really sure. I'd had a lot to drink, but I don't remember actually unlocking the door."

" Where do you keep your keys?" Miller reached into his right hand pocket and pulled out two keys.

"It's just that when we came in today the door was open. Do you usually leave it open?"

Miller shook his head. " Only when one of us is in here. And even then we lock it if there's no one up and about." McGill nodded again.

" So the assumption would be someone had a key to get in, then left the door open. Tell me something. When you discovered the body, what did you do?"

" Well he was just lying on my bed with the blanket up over his face. I probably prodded him a couple of times and shouted at him to get his own bloody bed, then pulled the blanket back"

" Back – or off?" Miller thought.

" Back. I just raised it enough to see his face. I saw the bruising and marks around his neck immediately. I knew he was dead." McGill nodded again.

" So you didn't know he had no clothes on and you didn't think to sleep somewhere else after you came back in again." Miller shook his head.

" No I didn't know he was naked until I tipped him off the bed. I needed the blanket. And all the other doors would be locked anyway." McGill stiffened.

" The other doors were locked? Why wasn't yours?" Miller shrugged.

" I don't know whether it was or wasn't. I can't remember."

" Did you lock it when you went out to get the redcaps?"

" No, I don't suppose I did. I did lock the front door though. I clearly remember having to unlock it when I came back."

" Someone else could have locked it behind you."

" There wasn't anyone else there to do it." McGill thought for a moment.

" Let me put something to you. Suppose the murderer was still in the house when you first came back. That would presume he had keys, both to the front door and to your room. You find the victim, then go out. Our murderer would have had time to strip the body and make his escape very easily, locking the door behind him." Miller nodded

" Yes he would. But no one else has any keys apart from those who live here."

" Where did you get your keys from when you first came here?"

" I got them from the billeting office…" Miller paused. " They must have keys to all the houses."

McGill looked at Nobby, who shrugged. " I don't know if they do."

" So why didn't I get a set when I asked to come here?" Nobby shrugged.

" Well there wouldn't be a room available – they're all taken including the parlour."

" But why no front door key?" Miller was looking from McGill to Nobby and back again with a puzzled look on his face.

" You've been billeted here? Where are you going to sleep?" McGill smiled grimly.

" I didn't suppose I was going to. I'll just be sitting up in a chair I imagine." There was silence for a moment or two, then McGill let out a long sigh.

" Right, well, you've been very helpful Captain Miller. Thank you."

" Sorry I couldn't be more help."

" Oh, but you've been very helpful. You've given me at least two further lines of enquiry to follow up." Nobby started.

" Two?" McGill nodded

" Who had the keys of course."

" And what's the other one?"

" Who saw the murderer leaving and locking the door not long after midnight." There was silence.

" How are you going to find them?" asked Miller.

" Oh that will take a little time and patience. But someone saw him leave. They just ignored it though. A man locking a door? Must live there. " The other two could see the point, but were sure it was a needle in a haystack. Nobby sighed and shook his head again.

" Well rather you than me, Inspector. That's a long job." McGill smiled.

" But it's what I do. Find the man with the keys and I'll find the murderer."

Miller stood and left the room. McGill thought over what he had learned. There was still no apparent reason for the murder, but he felt sure he was closer than before. It had to be someone with access to the keys from the billeting office. And he was convinced someone had seen the murderer making his escape. There would have been lots of people around, he felt sure. It was just a question of finding the right one.

Nobby was staring into space. After a moment or two he unbuttoned his top left pocket. He pulled out his watch and studied it briefly, grinning.

" I'm officially on leave as of five minutes ago. Fancy a drink, Inspector?"

" My thought exactly." So saying the two stood and headed out into the street.

Chapter 11

They walked towards the estaminet at the corner. It was packed with troops and had a blue fug from the tobacco smoke. Mustachioed waiters bustled about with trays of glasses and shouted orders to the men who were toiling mightily behind the bar. Nobby pushed his way through the crowd and managed to get two foaming beers. Conversation was impossible without shouting, so the two made their way outside into the street. They stood quietly after the din in the room behind them.

" Cheers – and thanks," said McGill. Nobby raised his tankard in acknowledgement, and they both took a long swallow. McGill wiped the back of his hand across his mouth and let out a contented sigh. "Wine is all very well, but a beer is much more satisfying." Nobby nodded and took another swig.

" So what's your next move?," he asked.

McGill thought before replying." Somehow I need to talk to as many people in this area as possible to find out if anyone DID see a man at the door that night, and I need to find out who has access to the keys."

" Well, I can help with that one if you like. I've got three days off, but I was only going to drink too much. We could start at the billeting office and find out what's what."

McGill drank again, and nodded." I'd like that," he said quietly. "Another?"

" Thought you'd never ask!"

The next morning McGill awoke in the kitchen of the dead man's house, with Nobby in the seat across from him, still snoring. McGill rose stiffly and shook his shoulder. Nobby opened his eyes and then rubbed them vigorously . The house was quiet as McGill started making tea, whilst Nobby opened cupboards to see if there was anything to eat.

" Nothing," he said contemptuously.

" Never mind – we'll get something across the road. Might even have the chance to ask them some questions. I'd dearly like to know who Miller sent off to the redcaps, even if only to verify the timings." McGill handed Nobby a steaming mug of tea, and they sat nursing the mugs as if their lives depended on them. After a minute or two McGill rose and headed to the bathroom. The face that looked out at him from the mirror was haggard still, with a strong stubble spreading over his features. He shook his head and wondered what Brown would have said if he had turned up at the Yard looking like this. He couldn't decide whether he cared or not. When he got back to the kitchen Nobby took his place in the bathroom, and McGill continued to sip his tea.

By the time Nobby reappeared, McGill was ready to start asking for witnesses. They made their way across to the estaminet, which presented a completely different mien in the daylight. Morose waiters were polishing glasses and brushing the floor, whilst others were cleaning the tops of tables and putting chairs in their proper place. Nobby, who clearly had a command of French, ordered something to eat, then sat at a table. In no time two large bowls of milky coffee were put in front of them, swiftly followed by bread and jam, and, a crowning glory, two small cognacs. They set to with a will, Nobby sipping his cognac whist McGill poured his into the coffee.

Nobby looked quizzically at him.

" Little trick I learned whilst I was ill." Nobby picked up his glass and poured it into his own coffee, then took a healthy slug of it. He coughed.

" I see what you mean, " he said, eyes watering.

After some minutes, McGill heard steps on the stairs behind him. He turned to see a large man walking heavily down from above. Nobby waved his knife in the man's general direction.

" That's the owner. If you want to ask questions, you should start with him." McGill nodded.

" Does he speak English?"

" A little, but I can help with translation."

"Useful chap to have around," said McGill, and rose to meet the new arrival.

McGill was surprised to find that despite his own height, he was looking at the man's chin rather than into his eyes. He spoke slowly, as Englishmen always do to foreigners.

" Monsieur, I'm sorry to interrupt your day, but I am an English detective here to try to find out about the man who was murdered in the house down the road." The owner, who had a broad face and bulging eyes, looked at McGill as though he did not understand what was being said. McGill was about to appeal to Nobby, when the owner called to one of the waiters for "trois cognacs", and indicated that McGill should take his seat again. A waiter hurriedly placed another chair at the table and the large man subsided into it. No sooner had he done so than the three cognacs arrived. Raising his glass, the owner said " Salut!" and downed it in one gulp. Placing his huge hands on his knees, he looked at McGill and then at Nobby. Shrugging his shoulders, he said " Et alors?"

McGill wasn't sure what he meant, but Nobby jumped in in English. " Monsieur I am Nobby Murgattroyd and this is Detective Inspector Alan McGill from the famous Scotland Yard in London. You will be aware that a body was found in the house across the street and that he was strangled. Inspector McGill is here to find the murderer."

" And I, Monsieur, am Jean Francois Dutronc – at your service", said Dutronc in heavily accented English, extending his hand and inclining his head slightly. " I applaud you English for trying to find the murderer, but monsieur, I understand you don't even know who the victim is". McGill shook his head.

" I'm afraid you are misinformed, Monsieur Dutronc. The victim was a Lieutenant Braintree." Duntronc stared at McGill.

" And it was you, Inspector, who discovered this?"

" It was." Duntronc raised his eyebrows.

" In that case I congratulate you, Inspector. What is said about the Scotland Yard is clearly true! Emile! Encore trois cognacs!" McGill and Nobby had not even finished their second and the third was already on the table. Duntronc drank his as before, smacked his lips and sat back in his seat.

" Alors – what can I do for you?"

" Monsieur Dutronc, I am convinced that the murderer had keys for the house, and that he locked the door after him when he made his escape. I am looking to find anyone who may have seen him doing that." Dutronc shrugged.

" How would I see that? I am here inside at night."

" Not you Monsieur, anyone at all. If you could perhaps ask around. I'm sure there are people who live in this area who will have been aware of this man." Dutronc nodded.

" I will ask – but at night everything here is very busy, very many people. I think it unlikely anyone will remember such a thing." So saying he rose and extended his hand again. " M'excuse, messieurs, but I have work to do. Your petit dejeuner is on me." He shook hands with them both then turned and made for a door behind the stairs.

Nobby toyed with the remaining cognac, then shot a glance at McGill.

" Quite a man."

" He is – and I'll bet he finds our witness. He's the sort of man who doesn't like his patch muddied. He'll want to keep it clean. We should go – we need to see who had access to the keys." So saying, McGill rose, followed by Nobby, and they set off down the street.

As they made their way along the road, McGill asked " Which way is the station from here?"

Nobby pointed off to his left. "About fifteen minutes walk that way."

" We need to time it properly, but it can wait. Keys first!"

By the time they got back to the billeting office, the building was once again its busy self. The sergeant who had seen them off the day before with such ill will merely grunted as the pair passed into the interior. Nobby guided McGill back to the far end of the large room where numerous clerks were making entries on files then flinging them on the floor, to be collected by others moving to and fro. There was a different Captain at the desk McGill had been to the day before, who was not taking part in the general mayhem, quietly reading a file and making notations on it. McGill and Nobby stood in front of the desk. The officer raised his finger to indicate they should wait a few minutes. The pair stood awkwardly until the Captain closed the file, sighed, and carefully put it to the right side of his desk. " Yes?"

" I'm Inspector McGill from Scotland Yard…"

"Oh yes, the murder wallah. What can I do for you?" McGill explained what he was looking for, and the captain's eyebrows shot up.

" You think it was one of us?"

" Not exactly, sir, but someone who had access to the keys. We don't know the motive yet, but I'm fairly confident that if I find the man with the keys, I'll have found the murderer." The Captain scratched his head.

" Well we don't keep spare keys if that's what you mean. One set gets handed back and we pass it on to the next person billeted there."

" Was there a changeover at all at Rue Lepin about that time?"

The Captain scratched his head again. " Have you spoken to Sergeant Bain? No? Well he would be your man. He's in charge of change overs." Peering about, the Captain spotted Bain and pointed at him. "Tell him he's to give you anything you need – any questions, just refer him to me." Nobby saluted and McGill shook the Captain's hand. As they turned to leave, the Captain spoke again.

" Oh and McGill.." McGill turned back." Well done finding out it was Braintree. Not sure it helps that much but the redcaps were completely all at sea."

" Thank you, sir. All part of the job!" That's the first time anyone has praised my work, thought McGill. Maybe being an Inspector wasn't so bad after all.

Bain's desk was as untidy as the Captain's had been tidy. McGill explained what he was after, and Bain, after glancing towards his Captain, who nodded imperceptibly, shook his head.

" There was no change over for quite a while before the murder, sir. Those officers billeted there have been there a long time – train men. They've kept things moving at Amiens for more than a year." He shouted, " CORPORAL!" A weasel-faced man appeared as if by magic at his side. " Bring me the Rue Lepin file. Take a seat Inspector. Private just you stand there." McGill pondered that the hierarchy would never change. Nobby was a toff – a pretty decent one, mind you – but as long as he was a private he'd just get ordered about like he, McGill, had been when he was a Constable. It was going to be hard going back to that after his temporary elevation.

A few minutes later, the file was on Bain's desk. He opened it, glanced briefly at it, then closed it and passed it across to McGill without comment. McGill opened it in turn. There were details of what the property was, how many it would sleep, who would be entitled to use it and some financial details that were of no interest. Then there were pages of names and dates. The most recent, he saw, was his own dated the day before. He grinned to himself. Whatever else they were, the people in this office were quite efficient with their paperwork. Working his way back, he saw Woodville's name, then Miller, Fleming and Fields. Before Fields there had been quite a number of changeovers. As he read, something tickled the back of his brain. Nothing coalesced. Sighing, McGill closed the file and handed it back.

" So there's been no one new there since Woodville joined them?" Bain took the file and looked through it.

" No. But recently we've pretty much always kept it for people who were working at the train station. It's close to it and suitable for middle ranking officers. See here, all these officers were at the station." McGill looked at the page Bain was indicating.

" So what happened to them all?" Bain shook his head.

" Quite a few have been killed. But some have gone on to be senior officers." The tickle in McGill's brain became an itch, but still nothing would form into a coherent thought.

" So where are they now? Do you have a list of them?"

" Hmm not as such, but I could check for you."

" I'd be much obliged, sergeant. It's probably nothing but there must have been keys the murderer used, if my idea is right. And to be honest, I don't have much else to work with." Bain grinned.

" Give me some time. I see you are at Rue Lepin. That caused a bit of a stir I can tell you! I'll send word once I have something." McGill rose and he and Nobby made their way back out of the hive of activity. The sergeant at the door grunted again as they left. They made their way back towards Rue Lepin. As they walked, the itch in McGill's brain grew stronger. He suddenly pulled up and Nobby took a couple more steps before turning to look at him with a puzzled frown.

" Nobby, I don't know why but there's something scratching away at my brain about all this, but I can't get it to mean anything." Nobby raised his eyebrows.

" When did it start?"

" When I was looking at the names in that house before Fields."

" Did you recognise any of them?"

" No, it wasn't that. It was something else. It was something to do with the keys. Suppose someone just said they had lost the keys. What would happen?"

Nobby shrugged."I suppose we'd just get another set cut"

" Exactly! " McGill paused." They wouldn't even need to say they'd lost the keys – they could simply have got another set cut."

" But why?"

McGill shook his head. " I don't know. But somebody had a set, I'm absolutely sure."

They walked on. As they approached Rue Lepin, McGill touched Nobby's arm.

" We should time the walk to the station. We can try to talk to some of the people Woodville mentioned." So saying, Nobby led the way at a good pace as McGill checked his Hunter. Not long after they turned a corner and saw the station at the end of the street. Nobby pointed, and McGill took his watch out as they walked quickly to the main entrance. When they reached it, Nobby paused as McGill read the time.

" Just shy of fourteen minutes."

" It would only be four or five in a cab."

" Indeed. But whoever did it must have taken well over an hour, however he got there."

They went into the station which was crammed with soldiers moving both to and from the platforms. Looking about, they saw the sign saying " Movements Office" and made their way towards it.

Chapter 12

There was a queue, but McGill produced his laissez passer and shouldered his way inside. It was even worse there with harassed movement officers handing out chits and soldiers bawling their names and begging for the paperwork that would let them away from the chaos and mayhem for a short time. McGill pushed himself to the counter and grabbed a sergeant across it.

" Are you Grimes?" he shouted.

" Who wants to know?"

"I'm Detective Inspector McGill of Scotland Yard. I need to speak to Colonel Bramlees!"

" I'm Grimes". He moved along the counter a short way then lifted a section. McGill hauled himself through. Grimes was about to block Nobby, but " He's with me" let him in.

Grimes turned to the door behind the counter and motioned McGill and Nobby to follow him. As the door shut behind them, the noise dropped to a level which enabled normal speech. They were in a sort of corridor which had desks in it, but also several doors leading from it. Grimes was about to lead them further along when McGill stayed him with a hand on his arm.

" Hang on a minute sergeant. I need to talk to you too."

Grimes turned with a frown on his face and looked McGill straight in the eye.

" What about?"

" Do you remember the body that was found strangled in Rue Lepin?

" Yes I do. Poor bugger. It's bad enough getting ruddy great artillery shells landing on top of you without some sod strangling you." McGill nodded. He smiled grimly to himself at the sergeant's words. Everybody used a homosexual epithet to describe the murderer and his victim.

" Can you think back to that night and who was here then?" Grimes frowned again. McGill prompted him: " Was Captain Woodville here?" Grimes nodded.

" Yes – yes he was. We had a full complement that night. Major Barker, Captains Gordon and Home, and Colonel Bramlees – oh and Captains Fleming and Fields were on duty in the main signal box."

" So, could you say they were all here all the time?" Grimes thought for a moment.

" Well, I can't be certain because trains need to be checked and the like, but probably no one would have been out of the office for more than half an hour."

" If I said to you was somebody away for, let's just say, an hour and twenty minutes?"

Grimes shook his head." No sir. Definitely nobody away as long as that. It's all hands needed here all the time, and anyone who was away for that kind of time would have been noticed without a doubt."

McGill nodded. " Thank you Sergeant. Can you please take us to Colonel Bramlees now?"

" This way sir." So saying Grimes led McGill and Nobby further down the corridor, and stopped outside the end door. He knocked and waited a moment until he heard " COME!"

He opened the door, and walked through, followed by McGill and Nobby.

Bramlees was behind an enormous desk, and stood up as they came in, reaching for a file from a cupboard behind him. He turned back and seemed pleased to see McGill again.

" Hello! Back again?" McGill explained what he was doing back in Amiens. Bramlees sat down, flicking his eyes between McGill and Nobby. When McGill finished speaking, he looked at Nobby . "And you are?" Nobby explained he had been detailed to show the Inspector around. McGill grinned to himself. Clearly Nobby had no difficulty bending the truth to suit himself. All part of the upper class mentality, thought McGill. " So what can I do for you Inspector?"

" I'm trying to piece together some information in respect of the night when Lieutenant Braintree was murdered."

Bramlees nodded. " Yes, that was smart work as I said before." Twice in one day, thought McGill.

" Thank you sir. I'm just trying to make sure that the other people that lived in the house at Rue Lepin can be ruled out of my enquiries. From what I understand, only Captain Miller was just returning from leave that night. Captain Woodville was on duty here until 2 a.m. or so whilst Captains Fleming and Fields were actually on duty all night here. Sergeant Grimes has said he doesn't think it possible that anyone slipped away for an hour or so. Would you say that was right?"

Bramlees nodded. " Yes I would. We had a bit of a flap on and we were all busy pretty much the whole time. Anyone missing would have left a gap that we would have noticed for sure."

" Do you mind if I ask how you come to be here during the day at the moment, but you were on duty that night?"

" Ah well, that's easy. I change over once a fortnight with Colonel Mickerson. I was on overnight at that time. I go back on again in a few days."

" I see. So you would be pretty sure none of your people nipped off at all?"

" Absolutely." McGill sighed. He hadn't really expected anything else. Unless both Grimes and Bramlees were lying, that ruled out quite a number of possible suspects. That's Police work, thought McGill. Once you have eliminated all the impossibles, you have to start on the possibles.

" You wouldn't know anything about keys for the house in Rue Lepin by any mischance?" Bramlees looked at McGill with a frown on his face.

" In what way?"

"Well for example, suppose Captain Miller had lost his keys a while ago and had to get them replaced?" Bramlees thought for a moment.

" Actually, I think he did lose his keys. No wait a minute it was Woodville. About six months ago, I seem to recall. Grimes?"

" Yes sir, I think he did. It was when the General was here inspecting us and the Captain needed to go back to his billet for something. He was about to set off and started asking if anyone had seen his keys."

" Ah yes, I remember now". The itch in McGill's head subsided and the pleasant feeling of something having been scratched took it's place. " He always keeps his keys on his desk when he is here on duty, so as not to ruin the line of his trousers. Anyway, the General was here on an inspection before heading off to see the Field Marshall. I remember some flap or other when the General was here with Woodville – something with his uniform?"

" That's right sir," said Grimes. " He spilled tea down the front just after the General arrived, and wanted to get cleaned up. But he couldn't find his keys, so just went to the washroom and did as best he could."

"So what happened about the keys?"

" That was the funny thing, sir. When he came back, he was detailed to check a particular departure, and by the time he got to his office, his keys were in one of his drawers."

" He must have looked for them, surely?" Grimes shook his head

" Can't rightly say sir. I suppose so." McGill thought for a moment.

" Can you give me a list of everyone who was on duty here the day Woodville lost his keys?" Bramlees looked at Grimes.

" Should be able to sir. It'll take a few hours though." McGill nodded.

" I'll pop back later if I may." So saying he shook Bramlees' hand and turned to the door. Nobby saluted and followed him.

Once outside and away from the station, McGill stopped and looked about him. Spotting a small bar he headed for it with Nobby beside him. He ordered two cognacs and threw some coins on the bartop. Nobby could see from his eyes that McGill was miles away, and didn't interrupt his thoughts.

When the drinks arrived, McGill sipped his meditatively, then sighed as he put it down.

"Nobby, I'm pretty sure about the keys now. We'll need to talk to Woodville again, but it's clear there was time for a set of keys to be made the day the General visited. The question is, who took them?"

" There must have been lots of people in and out of Woodville's office all day – it could have been anyone" McGill shook his head.

" I don't think so. Somebody must have wanted the keys for a reason. Why? And once they had the copies, how did they know where the keys were for? It could only be that whoever took them knew where Woodville lived. Or had some way of finding out." McGill took another sip of his drink " And if he wanted the keys, he would have had to know when the house was empty. Otherwise the residents would ask questions. Yes – Mr. Woodville has definitely got some questions to answer. The night Braintree was killed, how did the murderer KNOW that the house was going to be empty? The only connection is the movements office at the station." McGill stopped, then went on slowly again. " So the person in charge of the rotas at the station would know when the house would be empty, and who was on leave and such like. So either he's our murderer, or he knows who is." McGill downed the rest of his drink, then motioned to the door. " He just doesn't know he knows. Come on Nobby, work to do!"

So saying the two men fell into step and headed back towards the station.

Things hadn't improved in the short period they had been away. The platforms were crammed with men and the movements office was still besieged with shrieking men. McGill muscled his way back to the counter, and spotted Grimes doing his best to keep order. Grimes came over to him and opened the flap again. McGill and Nobby gratefully squeezed through, then through the door at the back.

" Sorry, sir, " said Grimes, nodding towards the door that led to the front office. "Not had a chance to get that information for you yet."

"It's all right sergeant, I can appreciate that. I just had some more questions if you don't mind." Grimes made a gesture signifying assent, and McGill continued." Who makes up the rotas here for when people are away off duty or on leave?"

" I do sir – under the supervision of Captain Woodville." McGill glanced at Nobby, who had gone pale.

"I see. And how does the rota get communicated to the relevant men?"

"Well sir, there's a notice board in the canteen area, but I leave a note for each officer on his desk every time there's an alteration."

"So everyone passing through the canteen would have access to that information.?"

"Absolutely sir"

"And does that information get passed on to anyone outside this office?" Grimes nodded.

"It goes up the line to HQ sir."

"Would that be Amiens HQ or elsewhere?"

"Amiens sir." McGill nodded, with a sinking feeling in his stomach. If everyone at the station and at HQ could know about movements there would be dozens of suspects – not just a few. Still, Woodville was becoming more and more a suspect – perhaps questioning him would lead to something.

"Now think back to the day that Captain Woodville lost his keys. I think you said the General had just left when the Captain was trying to find them. By the way, which General are we talking about?"

"Our General sir, General Trellawney." McGill looked at Nobby.

"That's our General all right – General Sir St.John George Trellawney. He's in charge of Amiens garrison and everything that happens here." Grimes was nodding.

"Would he be in the building you were guarding Nobby?"

"He would" Grimes was nodding. "Yes," he said, "He's at Amiens HQ." McGill frowned as he concentrated.

"So Sergeant, let me just get this straight. Your General comes here for an inspection, and during that time – at least we assume so – Captain Woodville's keys go missing. Sometime later they reappear in a different place to where he had put them. Now, Captain Woodville is in charge of the rota for station duties, and that rota goes to HQ. Do you happen to know who gets it there?"

Grimes shook his head. "I don't know exactly but it goes to the manning section. They need to know where everyone is at any given time."

"So how does it get there?"

" Well, whenever it's re-done, I get four copies made. One for the canteen, one for the Colonel, one to be filed away and one for HQ. I get one of the runners to take it to HQ." McGill nodded slowly. I'm beginning not to like this, he thought.

" And the rota has the names of people away on leave as well as the shifts they are required to be here?"

" That's right sir."

" So anyone who had access to the rota could see, for example, that the night Lieutenant Braintree was killed the occupants of Rue Lepin would not be there. Miller wasn't due back until the following day, Woodville wasn't off duty until 2am and the other two were to be at the station all night."

Grimes nodded slowly. " Yes sir, I see what you're getting at. But I can't see how that helps."

McGill smiled grimly. " Oh that's simple. Whoever stole - AND COPIED – Captain Woodville's keys knew the house would be empty. Somehow he persuaded Lieutenant Braintree to meet him there, and strangled him. What I can't see is why. And more importantly, if Braintree was effectively absent without leave, why would he go to Rue Lepin in the first place? He'd want to get away from the area, I would have thought." The three men stood pondering. McGill shook himself.

" Is Captain Woodville on duty at the moment?"

" He is sir – do you want me to take you to him?"

" Yes please" Grimes turned and walked down the corridor. " One moment, please sergeant." Grimes stopped and turned to face McGill again. " You said that Captain Woodville's keys were not on his desk when the General left after his inspection, but that they were found - what – a couple of hours later?" Grimes nodded. " Did anyone else have access to the Captain's room in that period?"

Grimes thought hard. " Can't think of anyone sir."

McGill prompted gently " Anyone who was with the General for instance?" Grimes shook his head.

" He only had his ADC, Colonel Southworth with him for the inspection. Of course General de Bonaventure was with him too, but not for the inspection."

" de Bonaventure? Who is he?"

" He was just accompanying our General that day. Normally he commands the reserves between here and Albert. They were both going to see the Field Marshall."

McGill nodded. " So there would be three people who had the possibility of lifting the Captain's keys – quite apart from anyone here ?" Grimes looked reluctant to agree, but finally nodded slowly.

" So how does the inspection work?"

"Well, the General arrives in his car and is met by the Colonel, who brings him in and shows him what we do."

" So the General and Colonel – Southworth you said? – walk around with the Colonel being introduced to the various officers, looking at the different functions and so on, then he climbs back in his car and drives away?"

" Yes sir that's pretty much it."

" But this time General de Bonaventure wandered about as well with them?"

" Well he did for a short while."

"So he didn't actually do the whole inspection – just a small amount? Did any of them ask any particular questions?" Grimes scratched his head.

" That's right sir – I think he went off after we were in Captain Woodville's office. Can't say as if anyone asked anything in particular, sir. When we visited the canteen, the General asked to try the tea, but that was all."

With a sinking feeling McGill asked " Did he look at the noticeboard, can you remember?" Grimes puffed out his cheeks and exhaled noisily.

" Not so's I recall exactly. The officers were all standing in front of it drinking their tea." McGill felt sick. The only way out he could see was to walk away now. Sadly, as he told himself, that wasn't his way. And if he could bring down one of those toffs that would suit him perfectly fine. His career would be over if he made any accusation based on his surmise as opposed to hard evidence, always assuming he got away with his life. One more murder to conceal the first wasn't such a long step. McGill nodded and indicated Grimes should lead on. He glanced at Nobby who had now gone a horrible greenish colour. Nobby laid his hand on McGill's arm and whispered to him " You can't really think the General has anything to do with this, do you?" McGill whispered back, " I sincerely hope not. But I've got a terrible feeling about all this."

Grimes knocked on a door, and opened it. " Inspector McGill for your sir"

Woodville was behind his desk with his jacket off, leafing through pages and pages of information. He looked up on hearing the name, and a deep scowl came over his face.

" What do you want, McGill? Can't you see I'm busy?"

" It won't take long I assure you sir. It's just about when you lost your keys to the house."

Woodville leaned back in his chair, a look of astonishment on his face." What on earth has that to do with the murder? I only mislaid them briefly." McGill shook his head.

" Not according to what I've learnt sir. They disappeared whilst the General was here on his inspection. From what I understand you found them a couple of hours later in one of your drawers."

" That's right – they must have been there all along."

" I disagree sir. I believe they were removed, copied and then put back."

"But that was months ago! How can that have anything to do with Braintree?"

" How many times in the last six months has the house been completely empty?"

" What? What are you talking about?"

" It's very simple. How many times in the last six months has the house been empty? You are in charge of the rota here – look it up please."

" I can't just drop everything like that and go off after a wild goose! There's a file somewhere with all the rotas in it. Grimes! Dig it out for the Inspector would you? Now leave me in peace to get on with something important!"

" I want to know now when all four of the residents of Rue Lepin will be together so I can speak to you all at the same time."

Woodville sighed, then scrambled in one of his desk drawers. He pulled out a bit of paper and tossed it across to McGill.

" Work it out for yourself! Now leave me alone!"

Grimes had been hopping from one foot to the other and quickly ushered McGill and Nobby out, shutting the door firmly behind him. Resentfully he looked at McGill." You've no call to go upsetting the Captain like that. He's a busy man!"

McGill glared back. " Busy he may be, but interfering with my enquiries can get him thrown into prison." Grimes looked shocked. " So get me the file with the rota sheets in it and I'll try to forget all about him. Which way to the canteen?" Grimes waved a hand in the opposite direction to that which they had come, and made off towards another door. McGill and Nobby made their way in the direction Grimes had indicated, and finally found the canteen. It was simply the back of the main station kitchen with a room that was accessed only from the movements office. There was a counter beyond which military chefs sweated away making tea and sandwiches. Nobby sat down whilst McGill got two teas and put them on the table. As he sat down, he thought Nobby was looking over his shoulder at something. He turned but could only see the backs of several men. By the time he had turned back, Nobby was looking earnestly at him.

" You don't mind making enemies, do you?" said Nobby. McGill grimaced.

" If you ever become a detective you'll find out it's the only way to make progress. You can't be anyone's friend when you may have to get them locked up – or hanged." Nobby nodded.

" I can see that – but I'm not sure I could manage it."

McGill sighed. " Believe me it's easy. People tell you so many half-truths and downright lies, wasting your time, that you get angry and start hating them. It can't be helped, but when people know you are deadly serious – and it's not some game you are playing – they become much more helpful. Your lot are the worst – they just tell the likes of me anything they feel like." Nobby snorted.

" Don't put me in amongst them," he said sharply. " I've seen what it's like from the other side, and I don't like it any more than you do! I'm a different person to what I was before I became a private!"

McGill looked at him, weighing him up. Then a grin spread slowly across his face.

" Yes, I can see you are. Good for you!" Mollified, Nobby grinned back, then toasted McGill with his tea.

" Fancy a sandwich?" McGill smiled.

" Now you're talking!" Nobby made his way to the counter and returned with two rounds of thick sandwiches. " What's in them?"

" It's bound to be marge and spam – or corned beef. I've never had anything different out here!"

They both bit greedily into their sandwiches and both started to laugh as they realised it was indeed marge and spam between the coarse white bread. Just as they were finishing Grimes appeared with two files which he put on the table in front of McGill.

" That's it sir – everything's in there."

" Thank you Sergeant. I'll bring it back when I'm finished." McGill handed Nobby a few coins and said, " Get us another two teas will you Nobby – I'm parched after that sandwich." Nobby lifted the coins and went back to the counter, whilst Grimes disappeared through the door.

McGill opened the rota file and started to leaf back. The sheets were roughly every two weeks with long lists of officers and men with their on and off duty times. The men were listed from the most senior officer down to the lowliest private. Nobby came back with the teas and McGill took a sheaf of the lists out of the file and handed them to him.

" Have a look for when the house was definitely completely empty. I don't suppose it has happened more than a few times over the last six months, but we need every occasion." Nobby started sifting through his pile and McGill turned back to the main file.

Chapter 13

He started from the day when the murder occurred. Quite clearly the house was completely empty from three pm, and due to remain so until after 3am the following morning. It was only Miller's early return that had been unexpected, which shortened the time the house was empty. The rotas showed the same pattern every two weeks, but for different periods as the times the officers were due to be on duty changed. After half an hour or so, McGill sat back in his chair and sighed.

" Looks like we had an empty house for six or so hours at least every fortnight and once a month for twelve hours." Nobby nodded.

" That's what I make it too."

" So now all we need to do is see if anyone in the house noticed anything funny on any of these dates, and then we will know that whoever stole the keys was using the house for some reason."

" Bloody strange. Why would anyone want to use the house?" McGill grinned.

" Rendezvous!"

" But why? Officers have all got their own places and we privates wouldn't have the freedom to come and go as we please."

" There can only be one reason – whoever was using it couldn't risk being seen in his own billet."

" You mean like some Captain sleeping with the General's wife?"

McGill shrugged. " Or some Captain sleeping with the General." The blood from Nobby's face drained leaving him ashen.

"I know about that sort of thing, of course, but I can't imagine anyone out here being involved in that."

" Homosexuality? Why not? It's a toff's disease. Rich men pay for their catamites in the same way they pay for a whore." Nobby shook his head.

" I just don't believe it."

" Well, I hope you're right, because I have the most awful feeling I'm getting into very deep water indeed." McGill made some notes of dates and times, then took the sheets back from Nobby and put them back in order in the file. Closing it with a snap, he looked across grimly at Nobby.

He picked up the other file and checked the names against those he already knew. There was nothing there. He shut the file and carefully placed it on top of the other one.

" Nothing there?" asked Nobby.

McGill shook his head. " Nothing I didn't know already. It's always nice to get confirmation, though. Do you mind giving those back to Grimes for me? I'll wait here." Nobby picked up the files and headed towards the door. McGill watched him go, and thought to himself how easily he had slipped into the role of the superior officer. I won't be doing this for very long, but I'm damned if I'll behave like Brown.

Nobby reappeared and McGill rose.

"Ready?" Nobby nodded.

" Where to now?"

"Let's have another go at Woodville. Then I want to talk to Miller about his keys."

The pair started to make their way back to Woodville's office, when McGill suddenly stopped outside it and turned to Nobby.

"What?"

" Can we get a list of times when Braintree was in Amiens – or at least on leave?"

Nobby shrugged. " Of course. They'll have the records at HQ." McGill nodded then knocked and entered without waiting for a shout.

Woodville looked up as they entered, then threw down the pen he was writing with.

" Not you again! What is it this time?"

" I've been through the rotas, thank you sir," said McGill pointedly." Just a few questions about some of the dates."

Woodville sighed, then glared at Nobby. " I hope your father never finds out about your new friends! What do you want to know?"

He showed Woodville the list of dates in his notebook. " Can you remember anything about those dates sir?" Woodville looked at the list, and then back at McGill.

" They're all the dates of changeovers. Why?"

" Look carefully sir. The point is the house at Rue Lepin was empty on each of those dates for at least six hours. Would you know if anything was out of place, missing or different when you got back to it?" Woodville snorted.

"Like what?"

" Tea cups left lying about, doors unlocked, oh, I don't know, beds unmade, a funny smell, anything."

Woodville thought for a moment.

"Well we're always a bit like ships in the night, and people are always leaving stuff lying about. But there were a couple of times I got back late one night and there was a sort of sweet smell. I remember it because I thought it reminded me of something, but I didn't give it too much thought" McGill's heart pounded.

" What was the smell like? A woman's perfume? Incense? What?" Woodville thought for a moment.

"It was a bit like the smell you get when you have been to a barber's and had a jolly good shave. They put some sort of scent around your chops. So you have a mixture of shaving soap and scent."

" Male or female?"

" How do you mean?"

" Does it remind you of a man or a woman?" Woodville hesitated.

" I suppose a man. " He shivered slightly. " But of a woman too."

McGill leant his hands on Woodville's desk.

" So it might remind you of a sodomite?" Woodville shivered again and went bright red.

" Now look here, no one in that house is anything other than a thoroughly normal healthy chap. It's totally defamatory to suggest anything else." McGill shook his head.

" I'm not suggesting for one moment that anyone who lives in the house is homosexual. But someone who *is* could have been using the house for assignations." Woodville looked horrified.

" Good God! Do you mean they just dropped in, engaged in their disgusting practices then left? That's simply and utterly revolting! If you find out who it is just let me and a couple of the lads have him for an hour or two. He won't be so keen to try that again!"

" Oh, I'm quite sure of that sir. But at the moment I'm not far enough on to be able to say who it might be. What I am sure of is that that's why you lost your keys that day. Someone had a plan – or at least an urgent need – and if there hadn't been a murder, I daresay it would have gone on until the war ended." Woodville shuddered.

" God I hope they didn't use my bed!"

" Oh no sir, they used Captain Miller's. What I don't understand is how they got the key to his room."

Woodville thought for a moment. " I think I can tell you that. Miller left his keys in the house some time ago when he went on leave. Some chum of his was passing through and Miller arranged for him to stay. It was just after the day I found my keys again." McGill nodded.

"So whoever stole your keys, goes into the house, sees Miller's keys and copies them as well." Woodville shook his head.

" It's incredible. So why didn't they use my room?"

" That's a good question. Possibly to confuse. Or maybe it's a nicer room."

Woodville thought for a moment. " Or it could just be more private. Mine overlooks the front. Percy's is at the back."

McGill nodded. " Makes sense. So they get into the house using your keys, find Miller's and decide his room would be more discreet. And it would tend to confuse as well." The three men were silent for a few moments, mulling over the scenario. McGill nodded again and stood up.

" Right. I'll see you all at the house at nine pm tonight. According to the list you gave me, you will all be available. Please have Sergeant Grimes tell the others." So saying McGill turned and left, followed by Nobby.

As they walked along, McGill was deep in thought. Nobby stayed silent, letting McGill go over what they now knew. After a few minutes, McGill slowed and stopped. He turned to Nobby.

" Don't take this the wrong way, but why are you still tagging along with me using up your leave?"

Nobby grinned. " I haven't got anything else to do apart from get drunk and this is much more fun! As long as you don't mind."

"Not at all. You've been really helpful. I need someone to talk things through with. When Brown was around the minute I said anything he rubbished it, but then stole any of the ideas which seemed right. Most of the work I've done the last year or so has all been credited to him. So I learned to keep my mouth shut. Now, I'm finding it a boon to be able to talk again."

" Talk away! So what do you think happened?" McGill shook his head.

" I'm not sure yet. We're pretty sure someone stole Woodville's keys and copied them, as well as Miller's. We know Braintree was strangled and it can only have been by someone who had keys – unless Braintree somehow had keys and invited the strangler in. I'm pretty sure the murderer let himself out and then locked the door. All we need to know is who had the keys made and who locked the door. What worries me is that there is circumstantial evidence that somebody in the General's inspection party could have stolen the keys."

" You can't think the General had anything to do with it!"

" I don't know. But the evidence so far puts him in the location at the time. Those are the facts."

Nobby sighed. " If you're going to accuse any of that party, please make sure I'm nowhere near!"

McGill grinned. " Don't worry. I'm hoping to be miles away myself!" And they both laughed.

By now they were quite close to Rue Lepin, and McGill swung towards the estaminet at the corner. The huge Patron was sitting on a chair near the entrance when they went in, and waved them over.

" Messieurs, I 'ave news." McGill felt the excitement course through him. " There was an English officer who left the house with a suitcase. It was dark and my informant could not say what rank 'e was, but an officer for sure with a big coat and a peaked kepi."

McGill glanced at Nobby." And who saw this, Monsieur?" Dutronc spread his hands wide.

" A lady. She was helping a soldier into my etablisement. Ze reason she noticed him was because he put ze case on 'is shoulder, rather than carrying it by ze 'andle." McGill slapped his leg.

" I knew it! If only she had seen more. Could I speak with her?"

Dutronc smiled." Not at this time of day Monsieur. In about two hours or so she will come here." McGill pulled his watch out. There was time to speak with the residents and then interview the woman afterwards.

As they made their way out of the bar, McGill suddenly pulled up sharply, causing Nobby to barge into him. McGill turned to face him.

" You know, Nobby, we don't know anything about the murdered man."

" How do you mean?"

" Well, all we know are things about him after he was dead. I've no idea where he came from or what he did before the war."

" Did you not see his service record?"

" Exactly – I did. But I didn't bother to look at his home address or anything. I was too focussed on finding out what had happened that I neglected to see or find out *why* it might have happened."

Nobby pushed his cap back on his head and stood arms akimbo.

" I see what you are getting at. There might be something in his background that could lead you to his killer."

" There could indeed. For example, I'm almost sure he was homosexual. He could have been killed by a jealous lover or by a person who hated homosexuals. We'll need to speak to the Yard and see what they can come up with. In the meantime we need to get another look at his service record – that at least would give us his home address and some sort of connection." The pair turned towards the house once more and were surprised when the door opened as they approached.

It was Woodville. " In you come – we're all here waiting to be accused of God knows what!"

As they entered McGill tried to defuse the animosity. " I have no intention of accusing anyone of anything – unless I can prove it."

" Well you can't prove anything against someone who hasn't done anything!"

"Your idea of nothing may be different from mine... sir," said McGill drily.

Woodville whirled round.

" Just you watch it sonny! This is an area under Military rule and I don't take kindly to being accused of homosexuality and the like."

McGill stared back at him.

" As I said....sir... I would only accuse someone where there was incontrovertible proof."

Woodville glared but turned back and led the way into the kitchen, where the other three were sitting quietly round the table.

" Go on then, ask away," said Woodville as he threw himself into a chair.

McGill and Nobby remained standing and McGill started to speak.

" Thank you all for being here. I just need to make sure of a few facts and it's easier if you are all together." McGill started walking backwards and forwards.

"Firstly, I have established, I think with some certitude, that the murderer had a separate set of keys made and used them to gain access to the house several times. It seems on at least two occasions in the last six months a sort of sickly sweet smell was noticed. Apart from Captain Woodville, did anyone else notice it?"

The three others looked at each other.

"What sort of smell?," asked Miller.

" Woodville described it as like after having a good shave at a barbers."

Fields put his hand up. " Yes, I noticed that once. Smelled a bit like a scent shop"

McGill nodded.

" Any idea of the date, sir?"

Fields pondered. " Can't be sure but about six or seven weeks ago."

McGill turned to Woodville, and raised an eyebrow.

" No not then – much earlier. About three months ago."

" Captain Miller?"

" Sorry, can't help. I'm terribly prone to colds and can hardly ever smell anything" – and with that he produced a handkerchief and blew his nose hard.

" What about when you came back from leave and found the body?"

" I had the most beastly cold." McGill smiled grimly to himself. The murderer clearly had all the luck.

" Fleming?" Fleming shook his head.

" Never smelled anything – sorry." McGill checked the dates and the disposition and timings of the men. Fleming had always been the last back to the house, whilst Woodville had been the first. Any smell would have gone by the time Fleming got back.

" Can we have a look at the times when the house was empty, and see if we can pinpoint the dates that the smell was here?" McGill took his notebook from his pocket, and flicked through it until he came to the page on which the dates were that the house had been empty.

The four officers crowded round.

" Here's the date of the murder," said McGill. " You didn't smell anything when you came back Captain? We already have Captain Miller's word that he smelled nothing."

Woodville had gone red again, and mumbled something.

"Didn't quite catch that, sir?" Woodville glared at McGill with unalloyed hatred.

" I said I brought a lady back and wouldn't have been able to smell anything, damn you!"

"Ah, I see," said McGill, enjoying Woodville's discomfiture." So she had a strong perfume? What time did she leave?" McGill thought Woodville would explode as he gripped the edge of the table and seemed to be panting. McGill took pity on him and said, " An hour later?" Woodville nodded. " Did you see her out, sir?". Woodville shook his head, looking mortified.

My God, thought Nobby. This detective lark can be pretty hard pounding.

McGill turned to Fields. " So would that make the date you smelled the scent .." he glanced at the dates ".. Thirteenth September?" Fields thought for a moment then nodded.

"Yes I suppose it would be. I wasn't well, and came back early." McGill glanced at the dates and times again. Woodville had been on leave, Fleming was at the station overnight – and presumably Miller had a cold. He glanced at Woodville.

" Can you make a stab at a date? Say August the second?" Woodville nodded. " Yes it could be – I'm not sure of the date, but the house was definitely empty."

"And before that? Twenty first June?"

" Can't say. Could have been."

McGill straightened up. " Right, that's really helpful. Just one last thing. Is there anything – anything at all – you can think of that you haven't told me. It doesn't need to be an event or a fact, it could just be an impression, a feeling." He looked round the faces. They were all blank, until a shadow passed across Miller's.

" Captain Miller?" Miller shuffled his feet a bit then cleared his throat.

" I can't say for sure, but I felt once or twice that someone had been in my room when I was away. There was nothing moved or taken, it was just…. an impression." Maybe one of his cold's had been less severe those days, thought McGill.

McGill nodded. " Thank you. And thank you all. That's a great help. I'll leave you in peace now." He picked up his notebook and turned away.

" Good riddance" muttered Woodville. McGill stopped, then walked on. What was the use.

Once outside, McGill turned to look at Nobby.

" I don't like this anymore than you do, but it has to be done." Nobby nodded.

"I know. If we want the truth we'll need to break a few eggs."

" We?"

" Oh yes, definitely we!" McGill put his head back and roared with laughter at the grin on Nobby's face. He slapped him on the back and headed towards the estaminet.

Dutronc was in the process of throwing a very drunken soldier into the street as the pair approached. He slapped his hands in a dismissive gesture of the sodden heap that was lying on the ground in front of him.

" Ah, messieurs les detectifs! Ze lady you are looking for has just come in. She is upstairs at the moment, but I have told her of your enquiry, and she will talk to you as soon as she is finished." The three entered the barroom and Dutronc reached across to the stacked bottles, extracting a brandy. Rummaging under the counter, he dexterously removed three glasses, and poured generous measures. Knocking his own back instantly, he handed the other two to McGill and Nobby. McGill raised his glass to Dutronc as he turned away and took a sip. Nobby looked quizzically at McGill.

" Do you suppose he ever drinks slowly?"

McGill laughed. " I doubt it very much! And I wonder how many he's had since we left him this morning. Yet he doesn't seem in the least affected by it."

A table suddenly emptied and the two men sat at it. A few minutes later McGill noticed an overdressed woman coming down the stairs supporting a Tommy who was having difficulty remaining upright. She deposited him with a small group. She glanced about and saw Dutronc pointing. She made her way towards McGill's table.

" Monsieur? My name is Josette. Monsier Dutronc has asked zat I speak wiz you." She sat down and arranged her dress in order to display her not inconsiderable charms to best advantage.

" Well, Madamoiselle Josette, thank you for seeing us. Can you just tell me what happened on the night of the murder?"

Josette shrugged her bare shoulders. " I see ze man coming from ze 'ouse, but carrying un bag on 'is shoulder – like zis." She matched the action with the description. " I do not see 'is face, but 'e was vair well dressed – not like zer Tommies. He wore an ol' coat, but I see 'is sharp trousers." McGill glanced at Nobby who spoke rapidly in French. Josette replied, then Nobby grinned.

" She means his trousers were very well pressed," he said

McGill nodded." Do you know if you had ever seen him before?" Josette shook her head.

" Non monsieur. I only notice 'im because of ze way he carry zer bag" McGill nodded.

" And what was the time?" She shrugged again. " I do not know, but it mus' 'ave been before midnight. A hint of a smile crossed her painted face. " Ma boyfren come for me and we go 'ome. Zat was when I see 'im." Good grief, thought Nobby. A whore for a girlfriend? Whatever next?

" Well thank you Josette. At least we know our theory is broadly right." Josette inclined her head and stood up to move away. Almost immediately her arm was taken by another soldier and after the briefest of discussions, the two headed towards the stairs.

" No peace for the wicked," murmured Nobby. McGill had followed the woman with his eyes, thinking of Isabelle for the first time since he had left her house. The difference between the two women was not as stark as he would have thought. They both carried themselves with grace and style, even if Josette's was somewhat rougher. He grunted to himself as images of his last night with Isabelle churned through his mind.

" At the risk of putting a damper on things, where are you going to sleep tonight?" asked Nobby.

McGill hesitated for a moment. " Ah, I see your point. I can hardly go back to the house can I? What do you suggest?"

" What's your next move in the case?"

"I need Braintree's service record and I need to know more about him."

" The answer's simple then – we go back to HQ, get a hold of the service record then hole up in a room somewhere!"

McGill grinned." Could be worse I suppose!"

They headed out towards the street and turned towards Amiens HQ. They walked in silence, and McGill pondered all he now knew. Instinctively he didn't want to believe the General had anything to do with it. Despite being a toff, or perhaps because of it, he felt it unlikely the General would do such a thing. On the other hand the soldier leaving the house had clearly been an officer - well-dressed Josette had said. McGill really hoped it was someone on the General's staff. A thought came to him, and he turned to Nobby.

" Where did the suitcase come from?"

" Sorry?"

" The suitcase. The bag. The bag the well-dressed soldier used to hide his face."

" That's a thought. Nobody mentioned anything being stolen from the house." They walked on in silence once more.

When they reached the HQ building, one of the guards hailed Nobby.

" It's all right " he called back. " We need to speak to the officer in charge of records." The guard nodded and waved them through, and McGill thanked his lucky stars for Nobby.

Once inside the building, Nobby pointed towards the back where a door lay open and a set of steps led downwards. Servant's quarters, thought McGill.

They walked down the stairs and were immediately into a warren of corridors. Nobby never hesitated, but led McGill towards a door that stood ajar, with soldiers entering and leaving in a steady stream. Once inside, Nobby made for a desk wedged in the corner. He stamped to attention in front of a drowsy looking Major, and saluted smartly. The Major looked up.

"Detective Inspector McGill from Scotland Yard, sir. Here to request the service record of Lieutenant Braintree."

The Major sat back in his chair, and eyed Nobby as he stood rigidly at attention in front of him, then turned to face McGill. He paused for a moment, then pulled open a drawer in his desk, reached in, and took out a thin file. He checked the name on the front, and tossed it onto the desktop.

McGill was somewhat surprised.

" How did you have that to hand so easily?" The Major's expression never changed.

" Once you knew his name it was only a matter of time before you asked for it."

McGill reached past Nobby, and picked up the file. Without a word he turned and left the room. He heard Nobby stamping and saluting again, then doing an about-turn and marching to join him.

By the time Nobby arrived, McGill had the file open and was leafing through the slender contents. He turned first to the last page and there saw the latest entry which detailed Braintree's murder. It had been added as an afterthought, as the entry before had been of his presumed death at Albert. " I hope to God no one has contacted the family," said McGill. " How would you like it if you were told your son was " missing in action, presumed dead," only to be told a month later, oh, wait a minute, actually he was murdered later in Amiens by a person or persons unknown"

Nobby looked at the entry.

" It doesn't say anything has been done. Look at the previous entry. DAT and the date."

" What does that mean?"

" Death advice telegram." McGill looked at Nobby, then at the file again. He sighed. "KIA killed in action and MIA missing in action are the other two."

" Can you find us a room somewhere?" Nobby pointed up, turned and made his way through the streams of men towards the stairs. They joined the flow and were carried up to the ground floor. As they came through the doorway, Nobby peeled off left and went through another door into a passageway. It led to the back of the building, with doorways off to either side. Glancing up and down the corridor, Nobby tried a door. When it opened he stuck his head into the room. He quickly entered, and motioned McGill to follow him. Inside the room there was a desk and three chairs. Nobby turned the light on then sat in one of the chairs. He waved expansively.

" Welcome!"

" Not bad Nobby!"

McGill sat in one of the other chairs, and opened the file again. He checked the dates of Braintree's leaves, and cross-referenced them with the dates the house in Rue Lepin had been empty. They were a perfect match. He noted the details in his notebook. It didn't take him long to read the whole file, but there was nothing else of interest. He jotted down Braintree's home address. Somewhere in Suffolk. Then he shut the file and dropped it on the ground beside his chair. He slouched lower and looked across at Nobby.

" Time for bed. I'll need to contact the Yard tomorrow." Nobby nodded.

" And I'll need to report back for duty," he said gravely. McGill sighed.

"You've been a great help Nobby," he said quietly.

" Glad to have been of service," said Nobby.

With that they both shut their eyes and did their best to sleep.

They were both dozing when the door was opened and an elderly Captain spluttered.

" What's this? What are you doing in my office?"

Nobby leapt to his feet and saluted.

" Sir, this is Detective Inspector McGill of Scotland Yard who wanted to ask you a few questions."

The Captain looked suspiciously at McGill then back at Nobby.

" Harrumph." He moved to sit behind the desk. " Well get on with it then."

McGill didn't know what to say, and the silence threatened to lengthen until Nobby spoke again.

" The Detective wanted to know if you were on duty the night of the twenty fifth of October, sir."

" What? What on earth does he want to know that for?"

" Elimination from enquiries, sir."

The Captain eyed McGill who nodded emphatically.

" As a matter of fact I was in HQ all night on duty." McGill nodded again, bent to pick up Braintree's file and headed for the door.

" Thank you sir," said Nobby, saluting smartly. He did a rapid about-face and lunged through the door, pulling it shut behind him. He gestured wildly back the way they had come the night before and set off at a brisk pace with McGill behind him. Once they were back into the main hallway, Nobby stopped and let out his breath.

" That was a close one!"

" Well done Nobby. That's one very confused Captain I'll wager."

" Not as confused as I was when he came through the door." They both laughed and McGill waved the file. " We'd better give this back". Nobby took it and with a "Wait here" disappeared through the door that led down to the basement.

McGill stood in the magnificent hall watching the comings and goings. He checked his Hunter and saw it was only a quarter to seven. Whilst he was debating what to do next, Nobby reappeared. "Breakfast" he said and led the way to the canteen.

They ate silently, both wrapped in their own thoughts, and when they were finished, they continued to sit quietly thinking about the last few days.

" So do you think the General has something to do with this?" asked Nobby quietly.

" I did – but I'm not so sure now. There are quite a few people it could have been – lots of opportunity, but nothing definite in the way of motive. I need to speak to my Superintendent and see what I've to do." Nobby nodded, sighed and stood up.

" I'm sorry but you'll have to be on your own now. I'm back on duty at mid-day and I'll need to get spruced up before then." He held out his hand. " Good luck."

McGill rose and clasped Nobby's hand." Thanks – I'll need it!"

" Look me up after the war – I'll buy you a drink!" McGill nodded.

" Of course I will." Nobby let go of McGill's hand and headed out of the canteen. He wondered what to do and decided he better see Watkins. He made his way to the Major's office, knocked and entered.

Chapter 14

Watkins was in his customary pose of cigarette in hand and a full ashtray on his desk. My God, thought McGill. Either he smokes even more than I thought or he's left a full ashtray from last night.

Watkins looked up. Seeing McGill he stubbed out his cigarette, knocking ash and stubs onto the file he was reading. With a curse, he emptied the ashtray into his waste paper basket, then swept the ash on the file towards it with his sleeve.

" Bloody cigarettes! You don't smoke do you, McGill?"

" No sir – never have."

" Lucky you. They make such a bloody mess." Flapping the file up and down on the desk to get rid of the last few bits of ash, Watkins composed himself. " Sit down McGill. What can I do for you?"

" Well sir, I probably need to speak to Superintendent Truman again if you don't mind. Could you arrange that?" Watkins nodded and reached for his telephone. He barked instructions, then hung up and leant back in his chair.

"It'll be an hour or so."

"I'll leave you for an hour then, if that's suitable." Watkins nodded and waved McGill away.

He walked through the hall and back outside. It wasn't a bad day, he decided, as he looked at the scudding clouds. At least it was dry. He looked at his watch again and mentally registered the time he would need to be back, then set off down the steps and walked off along the street. He stepped out vigorously, happy that he was going to be handing back the making of decisions to a higher authority.

As he walked back to HQ, a wan gleam of watery sun broke through. There were several officers standing chatting on the steps as he ascended. One Captain seemed to be checking his watch vigorously. Something tickled the back of McGill's brain, but he dismissed it. The dim sunlight seemed to reflect his mood, and he even had a smile on his face as he re-entered Watkins' office.

Watkins motioned him to sit as he smoked and read. After a few minutes the phone trilled and Watkins picked it up. He listened briefly then held it up to McGill. He stood and reached across for the instrument. He cleared his throat. A series of clicks and whistles cleared and he heard " Scotland Yard"

"Superintendent Truman please. It's Detective Inspector McGill." There was a silence at the other end, followed by " One moment please"

Truman came on the line. " Hello McGill. I was going to try to contact you today."

" Yes sir, I've been busy and I wanted to bring you up to date." Truman jumped in.

" Don't say another word McGill. Get yourself back here immediately."

" But sir..."

"No buts! Just get back here at once – and don't talk to anyone about the case." McGill was astonished but mumbled that he would.

" And come straight to find me whatever time you get back. The Yard will know where I am if I'm not here." The connection terminated, and McGill was left staring at the mouthpiece.

Watkins looked at him curiously." Problems?"

McGill carefully hung the earpiece on its cradle and slowly put the telephone on Watkins' desk.

" I'm not sure. I've to return to London." Watkins' eyebrows shot up, but he quickly recovered and pulled open one of the drawers in the desk. He took out a pad and started scribbling on it. After a minute or two he tore off the sheet and handed it to McGill.

"Movement order to get you back to London. Good luck!"

McGill took the order and shook Watkins' hand. " Goodbye sir – and thank you." Watkins waved his hand.

" Think nothing of it – you did an amazing job, even if you haven't found the actual murderer." McGill was about to reply, when Truman's stricture flashed across his mind. He nodded and made his way out of the Major's office.

His journey back to London was uneventful in so far as being herded, squashed and generally discomfited is uneventful. He had had to wait for a boat from Boulogne, so reached Folkestone around three in the morning. A biting wind was whipping the seas into spitting spume at the harbour, and he was glad when he eventually secured a space in a carriage and the door slammed shut. The train jerked off shortly afterwards and he found himself standing on the platform at Victoria just after five am. He decided some food and tea would do him good, and he attached himself to the long queue which was snaking towards trestle tables manned by well-dressed women. They were handing out tea and sandwiches, the tea thick and dark as it spouted from the urns. McGill thanked his lucky stars for the mug in his pocket, reflecting that he had lost everything, including his neighbour's case. Apart from his helmet and mug of course. It was painfully obvious that these two items were all that really mattered to a soldier. As his mug was filled and he was handed a sandwich, he glanced at the lady serving him. She smiled briefly, then turned to the next in line. He heard her voice and he felt a leap in his heart as he heard Isabelle again. Unhurriedly he walked from the line and stood staring into space as the troops eddied around him. Slowly he ate the sandwich and sipped the scalding tea, sad at the thought that his adventure was probably over.

When he was finished, he made his way to where the omnibuses were parked and took the first one that offered him a journey that would take him near to the Yard. He still had a couple of hundred yards to walk from where it dropped him, but he was glad of the air. As he reached the building, he squared his shoulders, and made his way to where he knew Superintendent Truman's office was. He had no expectation that he would be there – it was hardly eight o'clock after all – but he would be able to find out where he was.

He knocked on the door that was Truman's outer office, where an Inspector held sway with a Sergeant. Only the Sergeant was in, and he looked up from what he was reading as McGill came through the door.

" You must be McGill. Sit down. Superintendent Truman left a message you were to wait for him here when you arrived."

" I'm still an Inspector, even if only acting," bridled McGill. Unsure, the sergeant stood to attention, a baleful look in his eye.

" Thank you," said McGill. " I'll sit here." He sat down and the sergeant did the same, picking up what he had been reading.

They didn't have long to wait. The door opened as Truman came in, and the Sergeant and McGill both stood to attention. He was a tall man but much fleshier and heavier than McGill. He also did not have McGill's muscle tone. His eyes were rather far apart, but his reputation was that they were all seeing. The gossip was he would one day head the Force. He was about to ask if there was any word about McGill, but then spotted him.

" Ah, McGill – very good. Come in, come in! Sergeant, two teas please." McGill could feel the Sergeant's reluctance to make a tea for someone who had been a constable only a couple of weeks before, but he overcame it.

Truman led the way into his office, then firmly shut the door, and gestured McGill to a chair. He took his place behind the desk, folded his arms across it, and looked searchingly at McGill.

There was a silence. Truman sighed, and sat back in his chair.

" What have you done to make Field Marshall Sir Douglas Haig send me a private letter?"

McGill was astonished. " I have no idea sir. I've never met him." Truman snorted.

" You may not have met him but he thinks highly of you. He specifically asks you be allowed to continue your investigations. That was smart work finding out about Braintree, by the way. Fairly rubbed the military's nose in it, I can tell you."

" Thank you sir. But sir, if I am to continue my investigations, why did you want me back here?" Truman looked at him, and without taking his eyes off him reached into a drawer in his desk, and tossed a file towards him.

" Read it."

McGill stretched across and picked up the file. There was no name on it or reference –the spaces for that information were blank. Curious, he opened it, and was met by a picture of a young man. He glanced up at Truman.

" Braintree." McGill nodded, then scrutinised the photograph properly.

What he saw was a gentle young man, almost self-effacing, with eyes that seemed soft as a does. The photograph was a studio portrait and the man was striking a pose, but it was not a manly pose. His clothes were somewhat flamboyant and he was looking into the camera almost yearningly. I was right, thought McGill, a homosexual.

He turned the photograph over and started to read the next page. There were details of Braintree's education at a minor public school, and of his parents. He was the elder of two children, the other a girl. There was a small picture of her. If Braintree looked girlish, his sister was quite the opposite. McGill sighed to himself. What tricks the gods played on people.

The father was landed gentry, owning quite some acres near Fressingfield with tenant farmers. The picture of he and his wife showed a man living in the last century, and his wife had a hungry look about her. The report made quite clear that there were rumours of Braintree's sexuality, but no outright proof. There were details of his military career. There was nothing much McGill did not know.

He closed the file and put it back on Truman's desk.

"Well?"

"There's nothing much there I don't already know, or at least guessed." Truman nodded.

" So why would this be delivered to me by a high ranking Colonel on the Field Marshall's staff? With a private sealed letter containing instructions it was to be handed to you in person. And with further instructions you were to be allowed to continue?"

" I've no idea sir." Truman rose and came round the desk, then leaned back against it.

"This has a horrible smell of politics about it. What can you tell me about your investigation?"

Slowly McGill started on his tale and when he got to the end, Truman was silent for a few moments. He rubbed his chin.

" So who do you think did it?"

" I really don't know sir. I have a suspicion someone on General Trellawny's staff was involved, but so far I can't tie anything down. And I still can't find any motive." Truman rubbed his chin again, as if it was itchy, then sighed and moved back behind his desk.

" What's your next move?"

" I don't really know sir. I suppose I should visit the parents, but other than that I don't really have anywhere to go. They might give me some information which I could follow up, but I can't exactly see it myself. And I need to speak to General Trellawney. I'm pretty sure the keys were lifted the day he carried out his inspection at Amiens station."

Truman nodded." All right, do that. Haig says specifically in the letter that any findings are to be reported directly to him and not to me. It's against all procedure, but there is a war on, so this may be a military matter – it could be something to do with spying, I suppose. In the circumstances you had better do as he asks."

" Thank you sir."

" Here's the letter for you that came with the file."

McGill took the letter, broke the seal and extracted the single piece of notepaper. There was just two lines. " Ask about General de Bonaventure. Don't tell anyone."

" Anything interesting?" asked Truman.

" Can't say as I rightly know sir. I've to ask about.. a particular officer."

"Ask who?" McGill shrugged.

" I've no idea sir. I suppose the war office, but I don't know."

" I expect who you ask is rather up to you, I suspect. You'd better get on with it." There was a pause, McGill thinking.

" This all started with General Trellawney when he did his inspection at Amiens station about six or seven months ago. "

" So who is Trellawney?"

"He's the officer commanding the Amiens area, sir." Truman threw his hands up.

" Bloody hell! This is serious stuff, McGill! Are you sure you want to continue with this? It's liable to be the end for your career. And that's only if they let you stay alive."

McGill nodded." Sir, I know how bad my position is. I've felt sick about it for some time, but I can't just walk away. Unless you order me to." Truman thought for a minute, sighed, and tweaked his nose.

" I don't have much choice. You know as well as I do that once a man has killed, the next one is easy. Haig has specifically asked that you continue the investigation, and I can't refuse him. Just watch yourself, McGill. I don't like the military using my men to do their dirty work. If things get too hot, you have my permission to withdraw. All right, off you go. And McGill."

" Sir?"

"Get yourself cleaned up before you go anywhere else."

"Yes sir. And thank you sir." Truman snorted again.

" Just keep me out of politics and away from spies! My life is hard enough without those kinds of complications!"

McGill made his way out through the first room, nodding to the sergeant who still looked at him with distaste. He was astonished at the turn of events, and more bewildered than he had been in France. How did Haig know where he had got to, and why had he sent the file on Braintree? Come to that, why was he saying de Bonaventure should have questions asked about him?

Wearily he made his way through the busy streets back towards his house in the east end. He let himself in and moved through it, feeling content to be in his own place. He took his coat off and hung it in the hall. He made his way towards the back and went into the bathroom his mother had been so proud of. Looking at himself in the mirror, he saw the ravages the illness and the general buffeting he had endured had carved into him. God I look rough, he thought. He lit the gas water heater and went through to the kitchen. The stove of course was out. The lady who came to "do" for him would not have been in, as he had said he would contact her when he was coming back. He sighed. He supposed he would be here for at least a night so he scribbled a note, went out into the street and hailed a small boy. He gave him the note and told him where to go, and gave him a penny for his trouble.

Back inside the house, he waited impatiently for the water to be hot enough for a bath and shave. In the end he decided he could not be bothered to wait any more, so had what would be described as, at best, a tepid bath. By the time he was finished he felt much better and the water was hot enough for a decent shave. As he carefully scraped his chin, he reflected that his time in France, despite the privations, had made him alive again, and eager to be a detective. And sod the senior officers!

He brushed his hair, then dressed and just as he was getting ready to leave again, his cleaning lady appeared through the door and fussed about him.

McGill explained he would be around for only a day or so, and that then he was off on police business again. He left the woman to start getting the range going.

He made his way to Liverpool Street Station and asked about trains to Fressingfield. He was told the closest railway station was Diss and he would be able to pick up a horse drawn gig there. There was a train leaving shortly for Norwich which stopped at Diss, so he bought a return ticket and made his way to the platform.

As he climbed into the carriage, he thought of the previous trains he had been in, all full of soldiers. This train certainly had some soldiers, but it was mostly civilians. McGill sat in a compartment with two elderly ladies who had been visiting a sister in London for a few days and were now returning to their home near Norwich.

The train rattled and bumped along the track firstly through the outskirts of London, then through the Essex and Suffolk countryside. Just under two hours later he was in Diss. He crossed the tracks and found several elderly men with heavy coats and drips on the ends of their noses, waiting for a fare off the train. McGill climbed aboard the first vehicle, told the driver where he wanted to go, that he would want to be brought back and that he would be leaving a handsome tip as well. The driver's rheumy eyes gleamed briefly. With a crack of his long thin whip, the horse set off at a goodly trot, and McGill wrapped the blankets around himself against the cold movement of air as the horse made its way through the country lanes.

In a little under an hour, the horse turned into a well-kept drive lined with trees. McGill could see the house at the end was quite large and well maintained. As they drew up outside it, an elderly butler opened the front door, and stood waiting for the new arrival.

McGill got down and spoke to the old retainer.

" I'm here to see Mr and Mrs Braintree." Without a word, the man turned, and, indicating McGill should follow, made his way back inside the house.

The hall was not overlarge, but a fine staircase to one side led upstairs. There was a long-case clock ticking regularly in a corner.

There were two double doors opposite the staircase, and the butler led McGill towards it.

" Who shall I say it is sir?"

" Detective Inspector McGill from Scotland Yard." The butler looked at McGill in astonishment, but opened the door and announced him to the occupants of the room.

McGill walked in to be met by the two middle aged people whose pictures he had already seen. The lady was dressed entirely in black. Her hungry look had not changed much but was now overlaid with sadness. The man stood, ramrod stiff, looking serious as befitted a pater familias. McGill suddenly realised he had no plausible reason for being there. His only thought was to give a version of the truth. After all, they could now get the body of their son back.

" Mr. Braintree, Mrs. Braintree. Thank you for seeing me at such a time."

The man inclined his head, the woman merely clasped her hands more tightly together.

" What is it you want?" McGill was surprised at the somewhat high-pitched noise that came from Braintree's mouth.

" I have some more news about your son." McGill saw a brief glow in the woman's eyes, but the man never moved. He hurried on." We have found your son's body." There was surprise on both faces.

" But – surely his body was found after the shelling at Albert! What do you mean?"

" I'm sorry, but I have to tell you that a mistake was made. The body at Albert was badly disfigured and in pieces. But I have to tell you we now quite definitely have your son's body in one piece. If you wish it can be sent back to you here or buried in France."

Braintree seemed to relax his pose, and tears filled the woman's eyes.

" I'm sorry to have to tell you this. I realise it must be a great shock."

Braintree inclined his head." Indeed, Inspector. I am at a loss to understand this situation."

" I am here at the specific instructions of Field Marshall Haig." Nothing like bending the truth to smooth the path, thought McGill.

The look of astonishment on both faces gratified McGill enormously.
" Your son died a hero, and the Field Marshal felt it correct that you should be informed as I have told you." Bent a bit too far thought McGill. He hurried on. " There are few enough heroes in this terrible war and he feels every single one should be celebrated and remembered properly." That was true enough.

" Thank you, Inspector, for telling us. I was sure he had done his duty. Was there anything else?"

McGill felt the sadness and anguish that emanated from the couple. They had given their only son, and, in a way, they had lost him twice.

" No sir. Except – would you like me to arrange for your son's body to be returned to England?"

Braintree's shoulders sagged. He glanced at his wife who was sitting staring at McGill, her knuckles white.

" Thank you, but no – I think we would prefer if he was buried with his comrades."

McGill nodded, bowed slightly, and turned to go.

As he did so, his eye fell on a collection of photographs on a side table.

He turned back to the Braintrees, indicating the pictures.

" May I?"

" Of course."

McGill crossed to the table and began to look through the collection. Mrs. Braintree rose and stood by McGill. She leaned forward and picked up a frame that held a picture of a young man with his arm around the shoulder of another. "My son."

" When was that taken?" asked McGill.

" The last summer before the war. That's his friend from school days."

McGill looked at the picture again, and noted the quite clear difference in ages.

"They were at school together?"

" Well, the General was teaching at the time my son was there."

McGill suddenly felt himself unable to breathe.

" The General?"

" Yes. They were best friends. We had such a kind letter from him."

McGill gazed at the picture of the man. Young Braintree had a look of supreme happiness, whilst the other looked smug.

Braintree crossed to a desk, opened it, and brought out a letter. Handing it to McGill, he said " We got this from his friend, the General." It was McGill's turn to be astonished, and he took the letter gingerly, then turned it over and looked at the signature. He gasped inwardly.

" General de Bonaventure? I had no idea your son was acquainted with him."

" Oh yes, they were great friends. My son was several years younger than the General, but they met at my son's school." McGill thought for a moment.

" Would they have been pupils together ?"

"Not at all. The General was standing in for a teacher for a term, I believe." McGill nodded. Oh no, he thought. I can't do this. And then he heard Crowie's voice in his head telling him to "ketch the bugger." He sighed.

" Did the General visit here sometimes?"

" Oh yes, Inspector. I was delighted that he took my son in hand. " He paused." Charles was always a bit of a mummy's boy, and I felt that de Bonaventure would be able to stiffen him up." My God, thought McGill, little do you know.

" Does the General live nearby?"

" No, he's from the West Country."

" But your son and he used to travel to stay with each other?"

"Oh yes. Whenever the General was on leave they would get together, either here or in Devon." McGill remembered he was holding the letter, and quickly read it.

De Bonaventure expressed his sorrow and commiserations, and mentioned Braintree had died in battle, bravely facing the enemy. He would be greatly missed. The last line jumped out at McGill.

" As you know I was immensely fond of him, and I will miss his companionship most keenly." And then he looked at the date and saw the letter had been written on the twenty sixth of October. Ralston/Braintree would certainly have been known to be dead on that date; but would the information have reached the General by then? And why would it anyway? And why was he saying he had died in battle?

Well, thought McGill, at least I'm now sure Braintree and de Bonaventure were both sodomites. But why is Haig pointing me at de Bonaventure? He handed the letter back.

" Mr. Braintree, Mrs. Braintree – I'm sorry I have had to put you through this". The couple glanced at each other. Braintree drew himself properly upright again.

" Thank you for coming, Inspector. Please give the Field Marshall our thanks as well."

McGill nodded and shook hands with both of them. Whilst saying his goodbyes, Braintree rang for the butler. He led McGill back out and through the hall.

She never said a word, he thought. But *she* knew.

In the gathering gloom, McGill made his way back to London, first by horse power and then by steam power. He was alone for most of the journey, which suited his sombre mood. He was practically sure de Bonaventure had something to do with Braintree's death, but he had no proof. His last chance was to speak to Trellawny and find out what he could, and thereafter to have some kind of conversation with de Bonaventure.

He still couldn't see a motive. Lover's tiff? Blackmail? If the pair really *were* lovers, why had de Bonaventure killed him? And why did Braintree have a contented look on his face? McGill shook his head time and again as he went over what he knew. There was no proof of any description. Nothing would stand up in court.

Once back in London he made his way to his house where his cleaning lady had prepared him some food. Gratefully he sat in the kitchen as it heated up on the stove, staring at the pot as it started to steam. There was a fresh loaf and butter for him, and he pulled off a chunk of the bread and spread it thickly with the butter. When the food was ready, he ladled some onto a plate and took a fork and knife from the cutlery drawer. What a mess he thought as he stolidly ate the stew.

The next morning when he awoke, McGill was unsure what to do. He lay in his bed with his hands behind his head. The only things he had learned at Fressingfield were that Braintree was definitely homosexual, and that he and de Bonaventure were friends. He would not necessarily have thought that strange apart from what Field Marshal Haig had written in the sealed letter.

He shook his head then got up, washed and dressed.

He awarded himself a hearty breakfast. He sat thinking for a while. He rose, went out of his front door and turned left. He knocked on his next door neighbour's door and when the man's wife answered, McGill explained about the loss of the bag and that he would either buy a new one or pay for the old one. The woman assured McGill grumpily that she would tell her husband, and then shut the door.

McGill made his way to where there was a small cluster of shops and bought himself a suitable bag. He would need to go back to Amiens and speak with Trellawny and de Bonaventure. He packed a few things and left a note for his cleaning lady. He would be as well to get back to France as soon as possible. There was nothing to be gained by delaying.

Toting his new bag, McGill made his way back to the Yard and went straight to Truman's office. The Sergeant from the day before stood as he opened the door. " The Superintendent said you were to go straight in ... sir."

" Very good – thank you." McGill dropped his bag on a chair, crossed to the inner door, and knocked.

Almost immediately it was yanked open and Truman stood there searching McGill's face.

" Come in", he said quietly, turning back to his desk. McGill shut the door and stood in front of Truman's desk. Truman shuffled some papers then looked at McGill again.

" Did you see them?"

" Yes sir, I did."

" And?"

" There is a family friend who would seem to have taken Lieutenant Braintree under his wing." Truman raised his eyebrows.

" A connection...."

" Indeed sir. This has nothing to do with politics or spying. I don't think there is much doubt both of them are homosexuals. And there's some circumstantial evidence this friend might have had keys to the house where Braintree was found. But I can't be certain he did and I still cannot think of any reason for the murder itself. And there's nothing to show that the friend was in the house at all."

Truman shook his head. " If you can't get any proof you can't even make an accusation. Accusing a General out there – well, it could be fatal for you. We are not the law in France – the Generals are"

" I know sir. I thought I would just have a private conversation and then hope for the best."

" Don't do it. Go and see Haig and tell him you can't find the murderer." McGill shook his head.

" No sir. I need to see it through. Even if it's only for my own peace of mind."

" I'm not joking, McGill. It could be fatal for you."

McGill grimaced. " I need to do it sir." Truman sighed.

" So be it. But the moment you're finished with him get out and get to Haig."

" I will sir."

Truman picked up some papers from his desk and thrust them at McGill." Good luck". McGill and Truman shook hands, and McGill passed through the outer office, picking up his bag.

He made his way back to Victoria. The jostling crowds were the same, but now McGill understood much more of what it all meant. He sat quietly waiting for the next train to Folkestone and proffered the travel warrant as he boarded. The guard looked carefully at the name. He glanced curiously at McGill. He punched the warrant and moved to take the next set of papers from a young Lieutenant. God thought McGill, will it never end? Do we have to kill all our young people?

The train jolted away and soon enough McGill was on the boat heaving across the channel. By the time it reached Boulogne he was starving, and as he disembarked he looked for a canteen or at least somewhere to have a drink. There were women handing out sandwiches and tea and he joined the queue. He felt in his pocket and took out his mug. A middle-aged lady handed him a thick coarse sandwich and a younger version took his mug and filled it with hot sweet tea. He moved aside and stood with his bag at his feet, chewing stolidly.

His paperwork said he was to go to Amiens and he decided to try to find the movements office. He wasn't sure if he would have to go via Etaples or if he could somehow by-pass it and get directly to Amiens. There was no Redcap looking for him this time, and, his sandwich and tea finished, he made his way to what looked like the centre of things in the vast sheds and quaysides that made up the port at Boulogne. His non-military garb drew curious glances from many of the men standing about, and even helped a bit to get him into the counter where a number of harassed military clerks were handing out papers and checking schedules.

When he finally got the attention of one of the men behind the counter he explained he wanted to go to Amiens – but not via Etaples. He was told his best chance was to take a train to Calais and try to wiggle his way across and down towards Amiens. It appeared that once he was away from Boulogne he would have a reasonable chance to make directly for Amiens.

Hefting his bag, he headed for the platform he was told would be getting a train headed for Calais shortly. He shook his head as he saw that, as elsewhere in France, there was no platform as such, just an area where people gathered and where a train turned up. There were already a few officers waiting for the train, and a steady stream of additional men joined him as he waited patiently in the gathering gloom. By the time the train finally pulled in, it was already dark, and he felt rather than saw the many curious glances he drew. Once or twice he felt eyes lingering on himself longer than strictly necessary. If he didn't know better he would have said he was being watched.

They reached Calais in reasonable time, but McGill knew that the next part would not be as easy. He had been told to change in Calais for St. Omer, and from there he could probably get a direct train to Amiens. The train was not as crowded as those going to Etaples or the front, and he was glad that he had had something to eat. His compartment housed several officers heading for different parts of the line, all of whom had a hip flask that made the rounds. By the time he made St. Omer it was nearly midnight, and he gratefully got off and stretched his legs along the platform. Some other officers got off, and McGill saw one or two hanging about some distance from him. He made enquiries and was told there was a train via Hesdin which was going to Amiens in about an hour, and he settled down in the waiting room along with dozens of others.

By the time the Amiens train arrived, McGill was heartily sick of the noise and crowding in the waiting room, and he gratefully made his way to the train. Quite a number of the others from the waiting room were clearly heading in the same direction. From the conversations around him, he gathered that Hesdin was a reserve holding area with many battalions and regiments scattered around it and flung forward towards the front as well.

By the time the train reached Amiens it was already starting to get light, and McGill was starving again. He sought out the ladies with their sandwiches and made good use of his mug. Once finished, he shook out the dregs of his tea, popped his mug into his coat pocket and picked up his bag. He sighed and squared his shoulders. All or nothing, he thought as he set off along the road towards Amiens headquarters.

Chapter 15

McGill felt slightly bereft now that Nobby was no longer with him. As he made his way to Amiens HQ, he thought it would have been good to have someone with whom to talk his thoughts through. He missed Nobby's company as well. He was worried that he had no authority to arrest anyone, let alone a General, and even if he did, he doubted he could get anyone to help. His only hope was to confirm his suspicions and then make for Haig's Headquarters.

It was with very mixed feelings that he arrived at the Headquarters building. He stood at the bottom of the steps and looked up to where he knew General Trellawney had his office. He sighed inwardly, and turned to one of the guards.

"Detective Inspector McGill, here to see General Trellawney."

The guard nodded, and motioned McGill up the steps. At the top stood the sergeant from days before. At the sight of McGill, he shook his head.

" Not you again! What is it this time?"

" I'm here to see General Trellawney."

" The General? Did he ask for you?"

" Not exactly, no, but I'm sure he'll see me." The sergeant snorted, but turned inside the doorway. A Major was sitting at a desk, scanning clipboards. The sergeant stamped to attention in front of the desk, and saluted.

" Detective Inspector McGill, here to see General Trellawney, sir."

The Major looked up, with a somewhat surprised look on his face. " Do you have an appointment?" he asked McGill

" No, but I'd be obliged if you would tell the General I am here and waiting to see him." The Major appeared to ponder for a moment. Then he sighed and stood up.

" Very well, you better follow me."

The sergeant saluted again then stepped back, allowing the Major space to lead McGill towards the internal stairs. They climbed swiftly. At the top, the Major pointed to a double door to the left. The door was opened by the two guards, and they entered the by-now familiar outer office of a senior rank. The room had desks and officers working away with another double door at the end.

A Colonel rose from his desk beside the door.

" Detective Inspector McGill to see the General." The Colonel reached behind himself, eyes fixed on McGill, and picked up a clipboard from his desk. He flicked papers back and forth, eyes following the lists of names, then glanced at McGill.

" Does he know you are coming? You're not on my list."

I'm wasting my time, thought McGill grimly. No one's going to let me in to see him.

" If you tell him I'm here, I'm sure he will make time to see me." The Colonel looked sceptical, sighed, and put his clipboard back on the desk.

" Wait here. Major, keep an eye on him."

" Sir."

McGill stood staring about him. This could be where he ended up shot or in a cell. Much to his surprise the Colonel reappeared and waved McGill through the door.

" The General says he can give you ten minutes." McGill sighed inwardly. That's all it would take to get himself taken out and shot.

The Colonel followed McGill into Trellawney's office. He left them and Trellawney looked curiously at McGill.

" So you're the chappy who found out who the murdered man was. Smart work. Sit down. What can I do for you?" McGill was permanently astonished at how much information seemed to percolate around. He sat in the chair Trellawney had indicated.

" Sir, I need to ask you some questions about the day you made an inspection at Amiens train station." Trellawney's bushy eyebrows shot up and he regarded McGill with astonishment.

" Really? How extraordinary! I don't pretend to understand why, but carry on!"

" Well sir, this case turns on a set of keys that went missing during your visit. I'd very much like to know if you or anyone else who was there that day knows anything about them."

Trellawney sat back in his chair and looked at McGill. There was no disguising his astonishment at the question.

" My dear Inspector, I'm afraid I know absolutely nothing about any keys. Are you sure this has something to do with the murder?"

Well at least he's telling the truth, thought McGill as he searched the General's face for any dissembling.

McGill nodded. " Oh, yes sir, the keys are the link to the murderer."

" Well I'm blowed! I suppose you want to know who else was with me."

" Yes sir."

" Well there was my ADC, Colonel Graham, my driver and a sergeant – can't remember who, but Graham will know. I was going on to see Field Marshall Haig."

" What about General de Bonaventure?"

Trellawney looked at McGill in amazement.

" De Bonaventure? He had nothing to do with the inspection! He was simply joining me in the car as he was going to see the Field Marshall as well. He didn't even come round with me."

He's forgotten, thought McGill. A little prompting would not go amiss.

" What about when you visited Colonel Bramlees in his office?"

" Oh, I see." Trellawney thought for a moment." Yes, yes he came in and introduced himself to Bramlees. Then we went to some Captain's office, I think, but de Bonaventure withdrew at that time."

Aha, thought McGill to himself.

" Do you think Colonel Graham might remember?" Trellawney shrugged.

"It's possible. But I can't see he'd have anything to do with something like that."

" Would you mind if I spoke with Colonel Graham and the sergeant?"

" Not at all – hang on. GRAHAM!"

The door opened and the Colonel who had ushered McGill into the room entered smartly.

" Graham, the Inspector would like to ask you a few questions."

The Colonel looked quizzically at McGill, who stood up and faced him.

" Colonel, I'm sorry to trouble you but could you cast your mind back to the inspection you made with the General at Amiens station some months ago."

" Yes, I remember it."

"Firstly, General Trellawney has said you were accompanied by a sergeant and a driver."

" That's correct."

" Can I speak to both of them?" Graham nodded.

" The sergeant was Cunningham who accompanied us on the inspection, but the General's driver was only in the car – he never entered the station." That's good, thought McGill, that's one less to worry about. He nodded.

" Do you remember being in an office belonging to a Captain Woodville?" Graham thought for a moment.

" Yes – yes I do. I think he was one of the movement officers."

" Indeed. And were you aware he had lost his keys?"

Graham looked at McGill goggle eyed.

" His *keys*? Is this some kind of joke?"

" I assure you it is not a joke Colonel. As I have told the General, this whole case revolves around Captain Woodville's keys." Graham shook his head.

" How extraordinary! But no, I don't think I knew anything about keys. It's not something that would be liable to crop up I don't suppose." McGill nodded. Graham was telling the truth as well. That only left Cunningham – and de Bonaventure.

" Could I speak to Sergeant Cunningham?"

" He's not here at the moment, he's off doing something for me, but he'll be back later in the day. Do you have something else to do or do you want to just sit around here and wait?"

" I'll wait if you don't mind sir. There's not much I can do until I speak to the Sergeant."

The Colonel indicated McGill should precede him from Trellawney's office, and the pair walked through to the upstairs hall.

" Where will you be?" asked Colonel Graham.

" I'll be in the mess, if that's all right sir." Graham nodded.

" Make for the Sergeant's mess – it's the handiest. I'll send for you there when Cunningham gets back – he should only be an hour or two." Graham turned on his heel and McGill walked slowly down the steps.

He made his way to the front guard post and asked where he could find the Sergeant's mess. A suspicious officer pointed him along a corridor and told him to listen for the noise. McGill walked a few yards down the corridor and immediately heard stentorian tones from a door to his right. He opened the door, and gazed on a room packed with Sergeants from several different regiments. The hubbub subsided as he entered, but the glances were not unfriendly and the noise soon rose again. McGill made his way to the serving table and fished his tin mug out once more.

The private behind the table grinned. " Don't need that in 'ere sir," and passed him a crockery mug which he proceeded to fill with tea from an urn. McGill took the proffered mug and looked for an empty seat. He sat himself down and started to sip the hot tea. After a short while one of the Sergeants came and sat beside him.

" You're that detective bloke, 'entcha?"

McGill put his mug down. " I am."

" I hears yer found out who the murdered bloke was. That were smart."

McGill nodded. " Yes – and thank you."

" Found the murderer yet?" McGill hesitated, but then said " No, not yet."

" Bet it were some Frenchie. Untrustworthy lot. Smelly and dirty too." McGill said nothing, but shrugged his shoulders. He picked up his tea again and the Sergeant moved away.

McGill took his notebook out of his pocket and glanced through all his notes. Just one more interview, he thought, and then I'll know for sure. He sat sipping his tea quietly, patiently awaiting the return of Cunningham.

After not much more than an hour, another Sergeant tapped him on the shoulder.

" You the detective? I'm Sergeant Cunningham." McGill rose and indicated they should leave the bustling room. Once outside, McGill suggested they might go somewhere quiet. Cunningham snorted.

"Nowhere quiet around 'ere. Wait a mo' – I'll see what I can find." He started opening other doors, and after the third one motioned McGill to join him.

" This'll do – so long as we 'ent too long."

" Well done Sergeant – thank you."

" So what can I tell ya?"

" You were with General Trellawney and Colonel Graham when they did the Amiens station inspection some time ago. You were accompanied by General de Bonaventure part of the time and you then all went off to Field Marshall Haig's Headquarters." Cunningham nodded.

" 'Sright."

" What can you tell me about the visit? Do you remember being in an office belonging to a Captain Woodville?" Cunningham thought, then nodded again.

" Yes. We visited that with Colonel Bramlees."

"What do you do on these inspections?"

" Well I'm there just in case there's anything needs doin'. The Colonel takes any notes on things." McGill nodded.

"And were you with the General all the time?"

" Yes, I was."

"When you were in Captain Woodville's office, do you remember anything about his keys?" Cunningham looked at McGill strangely.

"Not a thing." McGill sighed inwardly. It had to be de Bonaventure.

"Was there anything else out of the ordinary that day?" The Sergeant thought for a minute, then shook his head.

" No, can't say as there was. We were a bit delayed leaving as the driver wasn't at the car when we all got back there." McGill's senses prickled.

" Where was General de Bonaventure?"

" Oh he were sitting in the car, waiting like." McGill felt his stomach tighten and his breath catch.

" But no driver?"

" No, but it were only a moment or two."

" Please think very carefully Sergeant. Was anything said about that?"

Cunningham thought a moment." I think the Colonel said something like " Where's the bloody driver?," and the General said, Oh I'm sorry, he's just doing a little job for me." Got him, thought McGill. Shouldn't have dismissed the driver so quickly.

" Can I speak to the driver?"

" He'll be with the car out the back – I'll show you."

They left the room and headed towards the back of the building. Once outside, they headed for a cluster of smaller buildings where several cars and lorries were being looked after by several men.

Cunningham shouted. " Mitchell!"

A soldier with his jacket off and in his shirt sleeves and braces pulled his head out of one of the cars, and turned to face them.

"Yes sarge?"

" This is Detective Inspector McGill from Scotland Yard. He wants to ask you a few questions."

Mitchell looked uneasy and McGill guessed he may have been not quite as law abiding as an angel before the war.

" You've driven the General for some time?"

" Yes, more than six years." McGill was taken aback.

" From before the war?"

" Of course."

" And somehow he wangled you to come with him here?"

" Of course. I'm a bloody good driver." McGill shook his head in disbelief.

" So you would have been the driver the day the General visited Amiens railway station and then drove to Field Marshall Haig."

Mitchell nodded. " Yes I was."

" Can you tell me what happened that day?" Mitchell glanced at Cunningham, then back at McGill.

" How do you mean?"

" Sergeant Cunningham tells me you weren't at the car when the party got back from the inspection. You'd been doing a job for General de Bonaventure."

" 'Sright. He asked me to put some keys back in an office." McGill breathed out.

" And why was that?"

" General said as how he'd found the keys and they belonged to some Captain, and would I put them back in his office."
" You didn't think to ask how he knew who they belonged to?" Mitchell looked agog at McGill.
" He's a General. Soldiers don't ask general's questions." Of course, thought McGill. Anything a General wanted to do was fine by everyone else.
" So how did it come about?"
" Well, the General came out of the station and walked away. He came back about fifteen minutes later and asked me to drop the keys back." God he was lucky, thought McGill. So much could have gone wrong.
" So the General just asked you to take the keys to a particular office and drop them off. Can you remember the name of the Captain whose keys they were? And how did you get inside?"
"Can't rightly say as I remember the name now. Wood something I think. But there were no problem getting to the office, I just said I was the General's driver and I was doing something for him." McGill smiled grimly to himself. A General's powers extended to their underlings.
" And what did you do with the keys when you got into the Captain's office?"
" I just put them in a drawer."
Simple as that, thought McGill. De Bonaventure couldn't do it himself, everyone would notice a General walking about and would want to accompany him. Lucky *and* clever. " And by the time you got back to the car the rest of the party was waiting for you." Mitchell nodded.
" Yes, Colonel was none too pleased that 'tother General had me doing something for him, but there weren't anything he could say." McGill nodded.
" Well Private, thank you very much." McGill thought he saw a look of relief on Mitchell's face as he and the Sergeant made their way back towards the main building.
" Nothing else you need sir?"
" No – no nothing thank you. You've been very helpful."

" I'll cut along now then sir – Colonel Graham will be looking for me." So saying the Sergeant swung round and quickly made his way back into the building.

Chapter 16

McGill stood for a moment pondering the situation. He had some facts now, but still nothing to link de Bonaventure directly to the murder. His final throw would be to confront the General and see what came out. He might be dead by this time tomorrow. A General would have no compunction in disposing of an inconvenience like himself.

McGill went back into the building and made his way again to the front desk. The Major looked at him and dropped his papers on the desk.

" Yes?"

" I'd like to see General de Bonaventure now please." The Major sighed.

" This is all most irregular and most inconvenient. Can't you make an appointment with anyone?" McGill shrugged. "The General is in the right wing. I'll get someone to take you." The Major signed to a guard and told him to take McGill to General de Bonaventure's office.

They trailed through a couple of wide corridors then came to another magnificent staircase. At the top, the windows looked out onto the small park at the back of the Chateau, and McGill guessed this had been some kind of reception area for grand balls and the like.

The guard handed him over to another Major without a word and McGill introduced himself and explained he wanted to see the General.

" You're in luck. The General isn't busy today. I'll take you in." They went through the double doors into what McGill assumed was a ball room, traversed it, and the Major knocked on the doors at the end. Without waiting for an answer he entered with McGill following. A Colonel and two clerks sat at desks. The Major pointed at McGill. " Detective Inspector McGill of Scotland Yard for the General." The Colonel rose and knocked on the inner door, then went in. A few moments later he emerged and signalled that McGill should enter. McGill only had a moment to reflect that *this* General seemed much more open to seeing people.

The office was smaller than Trellawney's but rather more cluttered, with more maps and charts.

De Bonaventure was standing with his hands behind his back, looking out of one of the large windows.

" Detective Inspector McGill of Scotland Yard," announced the Colonel.

Without turning, de Bonaventure said " Please leave us." McGill heard the door shut behind him. De Bonaventure sighed, unclasped his hands and swung round to face McGill.

The face was that of an aesthete, overlaid with suffering and pain. McGill was quite shocked. It had nothing of the carefree happy face in the picture at the Braintrees. Although everything about the man was immaculate, from his carefully waxed short blond hair to the tips of his highly polished boots, there was an air of raggedness about him.

"So."

McGill didn't know what to say, confronted with what he was now sure was the murderer he had been chasing.

" What do you want to see me about?"

" You might care to tell me, sir," said McGill. De Bonaventure looked hard at McGill.

With a sigh de Bonaventure walked behind his desk then sat down, eyeing McGill who was standing in front of him. There was a whiff of scent in the air, a bit like after having a haircut, or shave. McGill smiled grimly to himself.

" Perhaps you would care to sit down, Inspector."

" Thank you sir." McGill moved one of the chairs so as to be directly in front of the General. De Bonaventure waved his hand. "Carry on."

" This is a story that doesn't have an ending as yet." McGill stood and paced, gathering his thoughts.

"There was once an army officer who went to teach at a boys' school. There, for whatever reason, he became enamoured of a young boy just starting his senior schooling. Whether they became lovers then or later is not relevant, but lovers they became. Over the years they met many times, and the army officer rose in the ranks, finally becoming a senior Colonel. People were somewhat surprised that he never married, but he was regarded as a thoroughly good chap by all and sundry, and of course squired some extremely handsome women to various events over a number of years." McGill glanced at de Bonaventure, who sat like stone.

"But all the time, the school boy and he were lovers. When war broke out, the Colonel was made a Brigadier and shortly thereafter a General.

Of course, as a General he was very much more under scrutiny than before. His lover had by now joined the Army, and the General longed to have him near. The boy could not come to the General, and the General could not go to the boy. So there was only one solution. A secret hideaway had to be found.

It could not be a hotel or somebody else's apartment. It had to be unknown by anyone apart from the two lovers.

That's when a bit of luck came the General's way. One day he was helping a fellow officer with an inspection when he spotted a set of keys lying on a desk. He popped them into his pocket and quickly got another set cut – probably said he needed a spare set for his batman or something. As soon as he had the new keys, he made his way back to where the keys had come from. He got hold of some lackey and told him to take the original keys back to where they had been found – said he had picked them up by mistake. That was a tricky bit. The lackey might have said the General had sent him, but the General was ready to say he had found them, had made enquiries, and had heard that a certain Captain had mislaid his keys, and were these they?

As a further bit of luck would have it, the keys got put back without anyone being any the wiser, except that they were put in a drawer rather than onto the desk top.

So now the General has access to a building that no one knows he has. He knows the name of the person whose keys he holds, and it would have been child's play to sort out when the house was empty." McGill looked at de Bonaventure again and thought he looked as if he had shrunk a bit.

" So that's when it began. The General got into the house and decided a room at the back would be the best for the lovers to use. Amazingly, the key to the room the General wanted was sitting on the hall table. The General took it, had it copied and put it back.

The only thing then was to make sure the lovers were both available when the house was empty. So the General organised that his lover's unit was always on leave at the relevant dates. They met in the house several times, and then something happened. Whatever it was, it led to the General strangling his lover. The only reason I've come up with is that the lover threatened to expose him — why at this juncture I don't know.

Somehow the General had to cover up what he had done and he took the lover's clothes, leaving him covered up in the bed they had been using. He could hardly carry a body through the streets, even pretending it was a drunken friend.

Much to the General's surprise, he was almost caught by an officer returning unexpectedly. Luckily — and I hope you have noticed how lucky the General has been all along — he was able to make good his escape." McGill paused. He had little else to say.

De Bonaventure unfolded his hands and sighed again.

"Is that it? Who is this story about?"

McGill sat silent for a moment, then quite deliberately looked at the General.

" It's about you — sir"

De Bonaventure stood up and walked to the window. He looked out, then turned back to McGill.

" I have absolutely nothing to say to you. I'd be obliged if you would leave now."

McGill sat for a moment, then slowly stood up. He'd played his cards and they lay in a heap on the floor, just so much dross.

As he reached the door, McGill turned slowly back to face him.

" Why did you kill him? He was your lover. What could make you hate him enough to do that?"

De Bonaventure stood as if carved in stone.

" Did he threaten you? Did he tell you he was a deserter? Was that it? Did that make you hate him enough to kill him?"

McGill stared hard at de Bonaventure.

"Or was it something to do with the fact of your mutual sodomy?" McGill thought he detected a slight wince in the General.

"That's it isn't it? He threatened to expose you." There was a definite reddening of the face that was looking at him.

"Of course, that's it. He was going to expose you, and you couldn't allow that, could you? So you killed him".

McGill's voice took on a bitter tone. "You killed him – just to preserve your precious reputation." McGill turned to the door again.

"Sit down. I have something to tell you." McGill turned, walked back to the chair and sat down.

"Yes I knew him. Of course I did. The thing you haven't mentioned is the love Rabbit and I had for each other. He was my Rabbit and I was his Buck." McGill grimaced inwardly. de Bonaventure must have seen something in his face and made a dismissive gesture. " There is no love between husband and wife after a while. There may be some between a man and his lover, but it is not like ours. We were two souls joined forever in love and joy. I would have done anything for him and he for me." There was a silence, and the General looked straight at McGill.

"Can you even begin to imagine what that felt like? To know one cherishes and loves and is loved in return is the only thing in life that matters. It is so sweet and full of contentment, you just can't understand." McGill nodded.

"I've never been as lucky as that." The General laughed, a harsh, bitter sound.

"Lucky? *Lucky?* It was like a noose around both our necks. You as a policeman know we could both have ended up in prison. I might have survived but Rabbit would certainly have been broken. I could never take that risk. I had to make sure he was always safe, even if I myself was in danger." The General paused again, and sighed once more.

"We had wonderful times. Just to hold each other and tell ourselves how much we loved one another was bliss. We both cried every time we parted.

Rabbit told me what the front was like. He went from a carefree joyous boy to an old fearful man. He cried in my arms piteously. He was sure he was going to die, or worse, end up mutilated. His greatest fear was that if that happened, he would lose my love. I had always told him how lovely his skin was as I stroked him, how soft his limbs, how I delighted in them as I kissed them. He was terrified that if he was scarred and disfigured I would leave him. Nothing I could say would persuade him otherwise. He would cling to me, endlessly saying " I love you" as I gentled him and kissed and stroked him, saying again and again I would never leave him if he was wounded."

McGill felt sad for Rabbit and Buck. He couldn't imagine what the secrecy and circumspection had done to them both. The fear of discovery, the fear of not being loved any more, the desperation to remain loved. If this had been man and woman, he thought, it would rank as one of the greatest love affairs ever. As it was, it couldn't be spoken about at all. De Bonaventure's face twisted and his eyes grew round and filled with pain.

"Rabbit had sent me a message that he had to meet me. God knows how he managed it. By luck I saw that the house would be empty in the afternoon and evening – not for as long as we usually had but long enough. I didn't know what he had done until we met.

Rabbit had got there first, and we always just went to the room so that no one could see us together. We both had keys. I wore an old coat over my uniform. I had an old hat from when I was a captain and used that.

When I got there, Rabbit was sitting on a chair with his head in his hands, sobbing. I went to him and raised his head so I could look in his eyes. What I saw there drove a stake through me.

There was fear and death and terror on such a scale as to almost un-man me.

Between sobs he told me about what he had done, how he had taken Ralston's movement order and pay-book to escape the front. How he knew he could not face it any more, especially after the bombardment. He begged me to move him out of his unit, to find him some kind of safe job.

I didn't know what to do. I had a deserter on my hands. There was no chance I could suddenly make him appear again where he was supposed to be and then have him transferred away. He'd almost certainly be court martialled and who knows what might have happened then.

Gently I talked to him, stroked him, kissed him and said we would find a way. Slowly the sobbing stopped as he clung to me. He started to kiss me back, to stroke me, to put his hand through my shirt to tweak my nipples. A watery smile came to his face as he took my hand and put it inside his trousers." De Bonaventure paused.

" We made love urgently, then lay together quietly. Rabbit clung to me, and started to talk, saying we would go away together, that he would be my slave that he wanted everyone to know we were in love. I told him that was impossible, but he wouldn't hear of it. He said he would escape and get back to England, that he would wait for me there. I knew it was all impossible and I tried to tell him, I tried to persuade him to turn himself in, to say he had lost his memory, had walked back to Amiens from Albert. In all the chaos there is, he might have got away with it. But the terror rose within him again, and then he said the thing that he should not have. He said he would make a complaint about me. Oh, he didn't want to do it, but do it he would if I didn't get him out of the whole mess.

I was stunned. Here was my love telling me I would be exposed. We had always been so careful, so, so careful, and here he was about to blurt everything out. I tried to reason with him but he just said if I did not keep him away from the front he would tell everyone about us. And he looked at me with such a cocksure expression on his face, and haughty too, that I knew he would." De Bonaventure paused again and lowered his head. When he looked up there were tears in his eyes.

" So you killed him," McGill said quietly.

De Bonaventure said nothing, but flinched, perhaps remembering thought McGill. He sobbed just once then went on in a lower voice.

" I think he might have killed himself rather than destroy me."

" I expect that's what you would like to think, General," said McGill quietly. " It doesn't alter the fact you are a murderer."

De Bonaventure said nothing, and walked behind the desk. He opened a drawer and when his hand came up it held a service revolver. McGill sat stock still as de Bonaventure moved from behind the desk so that he was standing just in front of McGill.

De Bonaventure grinned crookedly. " Get up and turn round." McGill rose slowly and turned. He felt something very hard and very heavy come crashing into his skull. He didn't even have time to tell himself what a fool he had been before he crumpled in a heap on the floor.

Chapter 17

When McGill came to he had no recollection of what had happened. Groggily he looked about and saw he was still in General de Bonaventure's office. His head hurt like hell and when he reached for it his hand came away bloody. He groaned. He put a hand out and gripped the desk, then pulled himself to his feet, swaying slightly. There, on the desk, sat the heavy brass paperweight covered in blood that had knocked him out. God what a fool, he thought. He staggered towards the closed door and yanked the handle. It was locked. Muzzily he shook his head then tried again.

A voice from outside penetrated.

" Is that you awake sir?" McGill groaned again.

" Of course it bloody is! Let me out."

" Sorry sir. Our orders are to keep you here until thirteen hundred hours." McGill groaned again, reached for his Hunter and saw it was just after ten thirty. He sat down heavily and shook his head, wincing in pain.

" Listen, I'm bleeding from a wound in my head and it needs medical attention. Do your orders allow me to receive it?"

There was a muttered conversation on the other side of the door.

" All right. I'll get a medical orderly."

A few minutes later, McGill heard the door being unlocked. A weasel faced man entered, complete with a small gunny sack. The door was locked behind him. Briskly he pushed McGill's head forward, and examined the cut. The blood was beginning to congeal, but the gash was a couple of inches long.

" I'll need to put some stitches in that." The orderly opened his sack extracting needle, some cat gut and a bottle of iodine. Placing these on the desk, he took out a swab. Opening the bottle and holding the swab over the aperture, he up-ended it and allowed the iodine to soak through. Righting the bottle, he put it back on the desk then turned to McGill.

"This is going to hurt". McGill winced as the orderly started to dab and swipe the iodine-soaked gauze over his wound. After the first three or four dabs the pain receded, and the orderly worked away cleaning up the mess. He threaded the needle and quickly put three stitches across the gap in McGill's head. Taking another swab from his bag, he held it on the now-sewn gash, and with his other hand reached for a bandage in the sack. Holding down the end with the thumb of the hand holding the swab, he carefully unwound the bandage around McGill's head, securing the gauze. When he finished he tucked the end of the bandage under the edge and stood back.

He surveyed his handiwork. " That'll do. Get it changed each day for a week and you should be fine." He gathered up his bits, and McGill mumbled thanks as he made for the door. He rapped on it and McGill heard the lock being undone. He made to follow, but stood up too quickly, and promptly had to sit down again. The orderly turned back to McGill.

" I wouldn't try that sir. I wouldn't try anything until after thirteen hundred hours," and he nipped through the door. McGill heard the lock clicking into place again.

He dozed a bit and two hours or so later he heard the door lock being opened.

A smartly dressed Colonel entered.

" Good afternoon, Inspector. I've been sent from GHQ to take you to Montreuil."

" Montreuil? Isn't that where Field Marshall Haig has his HQ?"

" Correct. I am to take you to him." McGill slowly rose to his feet, slightly dizzy.

" I'm sorry, I don't understand. How did he know where I was?"

" The Field Marshall received a dispatch from General de Bonaventure saying you were here and that he should meet with you."

" Really? Where is the General?"

" I'm afraid I don't know sir. My instructions are simply to take you to Montreuil. But I was here already when I got a message from the Field Marshall." McGill looked at the Colonel.

" Have we met before?" The Colonel grinned and shook his head.

"I'm sure I've seen you before."

" You may have seen me but we have never met."

" Before we leave, can I have something to eat and a drink?" The Colonel nodded.

" A medicinal tot? I just might join you!"

The Colonel stood back and allowed McGill to exit the room ahead of him. McGill glanced sideways to see two soldiers with fixed bayonets and the sergeant from the steps from so long before. They were all watching him curiously. McGill turned to the sergeant.

" I suppose the General came out locked the door and told you to make sure I didn't leave until one o'clock?"

" Yes sir."

"And he sent a dispatch to the Field Marshall before he disappeared?"

" Yes sir. He telephoned through. He didn't disappear though sir. His driver took him to the station."

McGill nodded. He turned to the Colonel.

" Colonel, it's imperative I go to the station. I must find out where the General has gone."

The Colonel looked doubtful.

"It won't take long and it's almost on our way. Please Colonel. I won't be able to give Sir Douglas a full report unless I do this." The Colonel thought briefly.

"All right. I suppose it won't delay us very much. This way."

They walked through the ante-room and out onto the landing, then down the stairs, followed by the sergeant and the two guards. It's almost as if I'm being escorted from the premises, thought McGill.

The Colonel led the way to a room at the back of the building which served as the officer's mess. Officers were eating, but paused and looked at the strange vision of a colonel and a bandaged civilian apparently being escorted by a sergeant and two guards. The Colonel signalled to one of the mess servants who hurried over. " Two whiskies and two plates." The Colonel gestured at some of the seated dinners and two of them rose, taking their plates with them. He sat down at one of the vacated places and gestured to McGill to do the same.

The whiskies appeared almost instantly followed by two plates of food. The Colonel raised his glass to McGill.

" Cheers." McGill doffed his own glass to the Colonel and downed it in one. He wasn't sure if he felt better or worse. The drink finished, they took up knives and forks and ate silently.

Chapter 18

McGill didn't know if the Colonel knew anything at all. He wondered whether this was the same Colonel who had visited Truman. He wasn't sure how to handle the information he had. He knew it was dangerous knowledge, and he knew he had little factual proof. Even what the General had told him wasn't a confession of murder. It was a confession of sodomy, nothing more. If it came to a court of law it would be his word against that of the General. But it wouldn't be a court of law. It would be a Court Martial and he knew that facts were less important than the rank of the witness. What chance would he, a civilian, have against a General? He decided to test the waters.

" Colonel, do you know anything about this case?" The Colonel raised his hand.

" My orders are you are not to discuss it with anyone, even me or your superiors at Scotland Yard before you report to the Field Marshall."

McGill nodded. " And are your orders to shoot me if I do?"

" My orders are to deliver you safely to the Field Marshall. But I will certainly prevent you talking to anyone before then." McGill sighed.

" It'll be a long silent journey then."

The meal was finished, and they rose. As they crossed the room, the eyes followed them again, and their escort fell in behind them.

When they reached the top of the steps that led from the building to the street, the sergeant and guards peeled off. McGill turned and watched them go.

" Would they have shot me if I'd tried to get out?"

" I don't know what their orders were. But if they were ordered to do that, then I have no doubt they would." My God, thought McGill. Orders! What a wonderful excuse for everything!

As they reached the bottom of the steps, the two guards there snapped to attention and saluted. One was Nobby. McGill made to speak to him but a slight shake of the head stopped him. A very small smile was all that passed between them.

There was a car and driver waiting, and the Colonel motioned McGill to get in first. He was surprised to find Major Watkins already on the back seat. Sitting beside him, he suddenly found himself sandwiched between Watkins and the Colonel.

McGill laughed grimly. " Not taking any chances are you?"

" No sir," said the Colonel." Our orders are to get you to the Field Marshall safe and sound." The car started off and the three men jerked back in their seats.

Streams of soldiers were marching along the roads as they headed towards the station. McGill looked out of the window and saw either the despair of those on their way to the front or the relief on those back on leave.

Although the driver was good at dodging the columns, it still took some time to get to the station. It was after two by the station clock.

The unlikely trio got out and made their way to the movements office, McGill closely kept company by Watkins and the Colonel.

It was still the heaving, shouting mass that McGill had seen before, but luckily Grimes spotted him and quickly raised the flap to let he and his escorts through.

" Hello Grimes. Is Colonel Bramlees here?"

" Yes sir. I'll take you to him." They exited at the back of the room and Grimes shut the door, deadening the noise.

" Bit of a knock sir?" McGill laughed.

" You could say that!"

Grimes led the way along the corridor to Bramlees' office. He knocked and almost immediately McGill heard Bramlees telling them to enter.

He was sitting behind his desk, but when he saw McGill he started and rose.

" Inspector! I hardly expected to see you here again!"

" Needs must, Colonel. I need some information. I believe General de Bonaventure came here today."

Bramlees looked puzzled but nodded.

" Can you tell me what he wanted and where he went?"

Bramlees considered for a moment, glanced at the Colonel and Watkins, then looked at McGill.

" It was all very strange. He just walked onto a platform and took the first train. He was alone, which was strange too."

" So what happened? Didn't he need a movement order?"

" He's a General. No one's going to question what he does."

McGill smiled grimly. Of course, he thought. Whatever he did would be fine with everyone.

" Where was the train going ?"

" Albert." McGill groaned inwardly. He suddenly knew what de Bonaventure intended. "Woodville was on duty in relation to that train. He sent me a message to say he was going to accompany the General. He didn't think it right that he was travelling without an ADC." McGill groaned again. Bloody stuck up fool! Woodville had managed to stay alive so far but now, for a piece of etiquette, he was going to die.

"When did the train leave?"

Bramlees picked up a clipboard from his desk.

" Oh nine sixteen"

Plenty of time to get to the front. McGill sighed.

"Can we get a message through to Albert?"

"We can, as long as the lines haven't been blown up," and Bramlees reached for the phone on his desk. He asked to be put through to HQ at Albert, and was informed it might take some time as there was a heavy attack taking place to the front of Albert.

McGill suddenly felt impotent and very tired. He groped for a chair and sat down. Watkins and both Colonels were looking at him strangely.

" What's this all about?" asked Bramlees.

McGill was about to speak when the Colonel laid his hand on McGill's arm.

" No" he said simply. McGill nodded. There was nothing he could do anyway.

He stood up and reached across to Bramlees. They shook hands.

" Thank you for all your help. I don't expect we'll meet again."

" Glad I was of assistance," said Bramlees gravely. " And take care of yourself." He pointed vaguely at McGill's bandaged head.

McGill turned and made his way back the way they had come. The car was still sitting waiting for them at the station entrance. Wearily he climbed in, followed by Watkins. The Colonel went round the other side and got in.

McGill sighed and turned to the Colonel.

" You do know what he's going to do don't you?"

The Colonel nodded. " No one has ever doubted the General's personal courage. In his shoes, I'd do the same."

God what a mess thought McGill. I'll look a complete idiot in my report.

As the car headed towards Montreuil, McGill dozed. Not a word was spoken as the car threaded its way along the sixty odd miles towards its destination. The day turned to night. At last they were in the outskirts of the town, and the Colonel nudged McGill.

" We are to stay the night and see the Field Marshall in the morning." McGill nodded.

" It's too late anyway. It's been too late since nine o'clock this morning."

The car drew up outside a small hotel. The Colonel waved towards it.

" This is where we will be staying. I'm sorry, but I will have to lock you in when you go to bed. And there will be a guard on your door and outside as well."

McGill smiled. " Taking no chances."

" I have my orders." Bloody orders again, thought McGill.

They ate in silence but well, McGill suddenly ravenous. Half way through, a mud-spattered dispatch rider came into the dining hall, looked about, then headed for their table. He saluted and handed the Colonel a note.

He opened it and scanned the contents. He sat back with a sigh and looked at McGill. He tossed the paper to him. " You were right," he said.

McGill put down his knife and fork and read the note. It was from Haig.

" Tell McGill General de Bonaventure led a critical counterattack personally today and drove back the enemy. He was killed in the action. Without his valour and fortitude, our position could have been compromised. He died a hero's death. Captain Woodville who was with him also perished"

McGill tossed the paper away, swore, and stared into the distance for a moment.

" The whole thing's a bloody disaster," said McGill.

The Colonel shook his head. " I don't believe the Field Marshall will necessarily see it quite that way."

They finished the meal in silence, and McGill made his way to his room.

" I'm just here beside you," said the Colonel." I'm sorry but I *will* have to lock you in. I'm at your service if there's anything you need. You need only call on the guard and he will waken me. I'll send a medical orderly in the morning to change your dressing."

" Thank you," said McGill, shutting the door behind him. Immediately he reopened it. " Colonel, did you by any chance deliver a file and letter to Superintendent Truman at Scotland Yard?" The Colonel smiled but said nothing. McGill turned back into the room. He stopped and whirled round again.

" You were on the train! You've been following me all along. But you weren't a Colonel. You were a bloody Captain!" The Colonel said nothing, smiled again and shut the door. Almost before he had released the door handle, McGill heard the noise of the key in the lock. He went over to the window and looked out. There were two guards marching back and forth in front of the hotel. Had the Colonel been watching his back all along? But as a Captain? McGill shook his head.

I hadn't really intended escaping, he thought, as he drifted off to sleep.

The following day, with a new bandage on his head, McGill was taken out of Montreuil to Sir Douglas Haig's Headquarters at the Chateau de Beaurepaire . As they drove, McGill reflected that they had well and truly left the mud and filth behind and he was happy to see fields and trees again after the blasted landscapes and crashing noise of the guns and mortars. Here all was polish and snappy salutes. Messengers running in and out of the Chateau, guards at attention and senior officers conferring.

The car took them to the grand steps leading to the main entrance of the Chateau. The three men clambered out and made their way up the steps, saluted all the way by guards at attention.

Once inside, they climbed another magnificent marble stairway. As they reached the first floor, the Colonel asked McGill to wait. The Colonel passed through a set of double doors, and McGill walked over to the full length windows. Haig's office overlooked the front of the Chateau and out towards the gate. In the ante-room as he waited, McGill could see the scurrying officers below. He doubted any of them had actually been under fire in the trenches.

The door, where the Colonel had disappeared, opened, and a gesture told McGill he was to enter. He smiled wryly to himself. The set-up was always the same. An outer office with officers at desks, then another set of doors to the great man's presence.

The Colonel knocked and the door was opened. McGill walked through and was greeted by Haig with a handshake, before he turned and resumed his seat behind his desk. My God, thought McGill, this man commands nearly two million men.

" Sit down, Inspector. Colonel, please clear the room outside and post a guard on the outer door. I'll call when they can come back." The Colonel nodded, and withdrew as two secretaries rose and left, and the door was shut behind them. McGill could hear chairs scraping in the other room as Haig sat quietly, then a door shutting. Haig looked up. "Now, Inspector, please let me have your report." The voice was quite soft but carried immense authority. The eyes seemed to drill into McGill, and he started to relate all that had happened.

When he finished, Haig steepled his fingers and rested his mouth on the tips. Then he glanced up and looked directly at McGill.

" Thank you very much. I'm sorry in one way that this has turned out the way it has, but in another I am quite glad. I'm sure you appreciate we can't have a senior officer implicated in sodomy."

McGill shrugged. " It's what happened sir. We can't take it back, or bring Braintree back to life."

"Yes that poor boy. And yet he died without a struggle and almost with a smile on his face, I understand. All to get away from the front.

I'm sure de Bonaventure could have arranged something, even after he ran away. The problem of course was de Bonaventure himself."

" You knew?"

" Oh yes. There's very little that goes on I don't know about. If word had got out it would have been a disaster." McGill thought for a moment.

" Did you know it was Braintree who had been murdered? And by the General? Is that why you called us in after the Redcaps couldn't find anything?"

" No I didn't know who the murdered man was. It was pure chance the Colonel was in Amiens when it happened. I'd sent him there to find out what was going on with de Bonaventure – there had been rumours. Of course when no one could work out who had been strangled, and when the Colonel told me de Bonaventure was unaccounted for at the time of death, I'm afraid I jumped straight to a conclusion. That's why I insisted on the Yard being involved. And why I asked for *you* to be sent." McGill nearly fell off his chair.

"Me? But why me? You know nothing about me!"

" On the contrary. I spoke with the Commissioner and told him I needed someone who was intelligent and able to see round corners – even someone with a lack of respect for senior people. Sir Giles assured me you were the man."

" But that's incredible! Inspector Brown took most of the credit for all the cases I've been involved in. I didn't even know the Commissioner knew who I was."

" Oh, I think you'll find he knows the weaknesses and strengthens of all his men. A bit like me really. One has to in our positions." McGill sat stunned and silent. " You were actually made up to Detective Sergeant the day you left England with Brown, so you can hardly have been overlooked."

" Brown told me it was because he had to take a sergeant with him and he wasn't allowed any of the existing men." The bugger thought McGill.

Haig snorted.

" Bit restrained in his praise then, eh? I may say you've done a superb job here. Thankfully de Bonaventure was polite enough to knock you out and then get himself killed. And in what I could only describe as a most useful way."

" I can hardly take this all in sir. It's as if you used me to flush out the game."

Haig smiled bleakly. " I wouldn't put it that way. There was no guarantee you would get anywhere. What would I have done then? Somehow I had to find the truth without a scandal and without questions being asked about it. Your own native wit has made all this possible." McGill shook his head.

" And you had the Colonel following me."

Haig spread his hands, saying nothing for a moment. " What did the Braintrees want done with the body?" McGill had stopped being astonished at what Haig knew.

" They wanted it buried beside his comrades who died at the same time."

Haig grimaced. " I suppose we better ship him out to Albert then. That's where he is supposed to be." They were silent for a moment.

" The General told me he loved Braintree very much. I think he would have done anything to help him. In the end, the only thing he could do was strangle him"

A look of distaste and chagrin passed across Haig's features.

" Did he tell you he did it?"

" No sir, but I'm sure he did."

" Love is a terrible thing," Haig said sadly. He sighed and went on." It remains to be seen what we do about all this. I take it you have kept to the instructions I sent Superintendent Truman – that you have not yet written your report to the Yard?"

"No sir, my instructions were to report to you first. And your Colonel made sure of it."

Haig smiled." Quite right." He paused." Would you care for a drink? I usually have one about this time of day." McGill nodded, wondering if it was a good idea to start quite so early. Haig rose and went to a sideboard. There, a decanter and several glasses stood, along with a water jug. He poured two stiff measures and passed one to McGill.

" I assume you don't take water. Dreadful stuff. Ruins the taste my family have spent years putting into the whisky." Of course, thought McGill. Haig's whisky.

Haig raised his glass in a mock toast to McGill, who did likewise. The taste in his mouth was exquisite. In a reflex action, he looked into the glass, then took another sip.

" Good isn't it? " said Haig " It's something special I get sent over."

" Yes sir, very good." Haig walked over to the windows and looked out, sipping gently at the glass. After a minute or two, he turned back to McGill.

" I'm going to ask you to do something for me and for the country."

" I have to say I thought there would be something," said McGill quietly. " By the way, I assume you *have* had the Colonel following me about the place?"

Haig smiled slightly." I can see all I've been told about you by young Francis is correct." Who is Francis, thought McGill. Haig saw the blank look and smiled. "Nobby to you". McGill spluttered into his drink and nearly dropped it. " Oh didn't he mention it? Nobby is my cousin's son. And General Lee speaks very highly of your father." McGill was astonished at Haig's knowledge. There had clearly been more going on in the background all the time that he had been investigating. Haig took another sip, then drained the glass and put it down on his desk. He leaned forwards towards McGill.

" I have to ask you not to mention anything in your report about homosexuality or about the General. I simply can't have it."

"And if I refuse?"

" I will have you placed under arrest and shot as a spy"

McGill started." On what grounds? I'm just a policeman!"

" Oh, I think you'll find I can do anything I want out here. We are in an area under martial law, and here, I AM the law." Truman was right then, thought McGill.

" And how will you know I won't agree today and change my mind next week?"

" I don't. But from all I know about you, you are an honourable man. If you agree not to put these things in your report, and you give me your word, that is more than good enough for me. I'm sure you see nothing will be served by blackening a hero's name, nor by announcing to Braintree's family that their son was a sodomite. But I need your word."

McGill thought for a moment. " I think his mother knows. I will still have to make a report. What am I to put in it? And who else knows about all this?"

" You and I are the only people in possession of all the facts. Nobby of course has much of your thinking, but I know he can be relied on. Oh, I daresay a few others have bits of the puzzle, but they won't dig any deeper. What's to be served by it? Your report? Ah yes. We need to do that don't we? I think it will show what a superb job you did finding out who the dead man was, how you meticulously followed up all the leads, and how you could not find a perpetrator. Your best guess might be that it was some Frenchman intent on robbery."

McGill snorted. " Ever since I got here, everyone has suggested that's the likeliest solution."

Haig nodded, and murmured " The wisdom of crowds . You do see I simply can't have a hero smeared. God knows there are few enough about, and the country needs some inspiration. He'll probably get a VC."

" I can see that sir. But it doesn't sit well with me."

" If it did I would think much the less of you. You've done a superb job and found the truth. Unfortunately, sometimes the truth is just too much. Will you help me?"

" I don't have much choice do I? I'll just need to swallow a few principles – and another of your whiskys." Haig laughed and nodded. He poured McGill another tot, and another for himself.

" This war has led to many of us doing the same. You know, I'm quite certain that after this is all over, I'll be applauded for a while as the winner, but I'm equally certain I'll eventually be excoriated for being a butcher."

" Are you sure you *will* win?"

" Oh yes, I have no doubts. I'm quite certain God is on our side."

" Do you even know what the front is really like?"

Haig was quiet for a moment. " Yes. Yes I do. I've been in the trenches incognito. What my men put up with is indescribably awful – but they cling on relentlessly. A few break but nearly all remain doggedly fixed of purpose. The Hun can't last for ever. They can only lose as the Americans get fully trained. We've already used them a couple of times to good effect. My belief is that come the spring the Germans will make one last gargantuan effort to win which will be held and defeated. It'll be a damned close run thing, but they will finally be exhausted. Thereafter it will only be a relatively short time until it's all over."

" I wish I could believe you."

Haig nodded." We all need faith. You're the only person I've told this to. You must keep it to yourself. But I *will* win." There was a silence, then " So are we agreed?" and he extended his hand to McGill.

McGill only hesitated for a moment, then rose and stretched his hand to Haig. " As long as Woodville gets a medal as well. He died pointlessly because he insisted on being with the General."

Haig nodded." We are agreed." They shook solemnly, and Haig moved back behind his desk.

" I've been drafting a letter to your superior. Would you like to hear it?"

" Go on."

Haig raised a single sheet. " I won't bother you with the preamble. The bit that matters is this paragraph: Inspector McGill has proved an outstanding investigative officer. When no one had been able to ascertain the name of the murdered man, his deductive powers and dogged determination found his name. Through no fault of his, the murderer has remained uncovered even although Inspector McGill followed every clue, at some substantial risk to his own life, and however seemingly irrelevant, to the end. He was able to rule them all out. I understand he received what in my parlance would be a field promotion. From my own dealings with him, I judge him to be an exceptional man. It is my express wish that his acting rank of Inspector be made permanent, and that he be given duties of a substantial and elevated nature commensurate with his talents."

Haig put the paper down. McGill had been growing more bewildered as Haig read, but by the time he had finished, his mouth had set into a grim line.

" A bribe."

" No, not at all" said Haig, shaking his head." I believe every word I have written. You do have talent and you do have honesty and goodness. These are the very qualities we will need to rebuild our shattered nation once we finish with the Hun. I can't make things better but I can at least try to bring the right people to the right place. In my view you've shown your place as that of being a senior detective."

McGill looked at Haig, who throughout had appeared calm and, as befitted his rank, completely in charge.

" Thank you sir. I appreciate the vote of confidence. I'm not sure how it's going to go down at the Yard, and I'm not sure the other inspectors will look kindly on me."

Haig smiled. " Your reputation will be made. The whole army couldn't find one name and you did? Amazing! But after the war things will never be the same. We will need to rebuild our institutions and our nation. It will be a back-breaking and long winded operation. People such as yourself will be at the forefront of the new battle. I have every confidence in you." He rose, came round the desk and stuck his hand out to McGill again. " Goodbye, Inspector. It's been a pleasure meeting you. Bon voyage."

McGill rose and shook the Field Marshall's hand.

" Goodbye sir. And thank you." Haig smiled bleakly.

" You may be the only man who ever will."

Epilogue

Isabelle de Bonnefoix reached desperately into her bedside table and pulled out an old chamber pot. She retched and heaved into it then lay back exhausted.

She was sure now. She had noticed her missed period but had not paid it much attention – she had always been a bit irregular. But the last two mornings she had been sick. The first time she put it down to something she had eaten. Today she had no such excuse.

As she recovered, she could not help the smile starting to spread over her face. It would create a terrible scandal of course, but she would go away for a trip when she started to show, and come back with "an orphan" - there would be many after the war.

She hoped it would be a boy and a boy like Alan – strong and gentle and good –and beautiful.

She thought back to the night she had conceived and her smile spread. She rose, pulled on her dressing gown, and made her way downstairs to her study.

She opened her desk and took out a piece of paper, then sat down and picked up her pen.

She hesitated, and stared at the paper for a moment blankly. Then her eyes cleared and she seemed to resolve a dilemma. She smiled, and started to write.

" My darling Alan…"

Printed in Great Britain
by Amazon